ALSO BY

Minx

Brutal Birthright
Brutal Prince
Stolen Heir
Savage Lover
Bloody Heart
Broken Vow
Heavy Crown

Sinners Duet
There Are No Saints
There Is No Devil

Grimstone
Grimstone
Monarch

Kingmakers
Kingmakers: Year One
Kingmakers: Year Two
Kingmakers: Year Three
Kingmakers: Year Four
Kingmakers: Graduation

KING MAKERS

YEAR THREE

SOPHIE LARK

Bloom books

Published by Bloom Books, an imprint of Sourcebooks
P.O. Box 4410, Naperville, Illinois 60567-4410
(630) 961-3900
sourcebooks.com

Originally self-published as *The Bully* in 2021 by Sophie Lark.

Cataloging-in-Publication data is on file with the Library of Congress.

Printed and bound in the United States of America.
KP 10 9 8 7 6 5 4 3 2 1

This one is for my Dramione lovers ♥
XOXO

Sophie Lark

SOUNDTRACK

"Killer"—Valerie Broussard

"I'll Make You Love Me"—Kat Leon

"Bound"—Indiana

"Play with Fire"—Sam Tinnesz

"Do It for Me"—Rosenfeld

"Black Sheep"—Metric

"Crimson and Clover"—Joan Jett & the Blackhearts

"Come as You Are"—Imaginary Future

"Hypnotic"—Zella Day

"Heaven"—Julia Michaels

CONTENT WARNING

The Kingmakers series is dark Mafia romance in a university setting. Expect all the violence and plotting a bunch of conniving young adults from crime families will commit. Due to violence and sexual content, these books are intended for mature readers.

This book may contain, but is not limited to, the following potential triggers:

- Sexual blackmail
- Dubious consent
- Bullying and degradation
- Dominant/submissive power play
- Corporal punishment

Previously On Kingmakers:
Cat's desperate act to save her sister is successful,
but at terrible cost...
Dean Yenin has learned her secret and
struck a devil's bargain.

This Year:
Dean takes advantage of Cat from the moment
she steps foot on the ship to school.
It's not long before she's doing things
she never thought she'd do... 🐈‍⬛

There's a spy at Kingmakers 👀
Can you discover their identity before Year Four?

KINGMAKERS

YEAR THREE

DEAN

CAT

THE SPY

SASHA

ARES

ANNA

LEO

SNOW

MISS ROBIN

LUTHER

HEDEON

KINGMAKERS

YEAR THREE

JASPER

CARA

RAKEL

SILAS

MILES

ZOE

LOLA

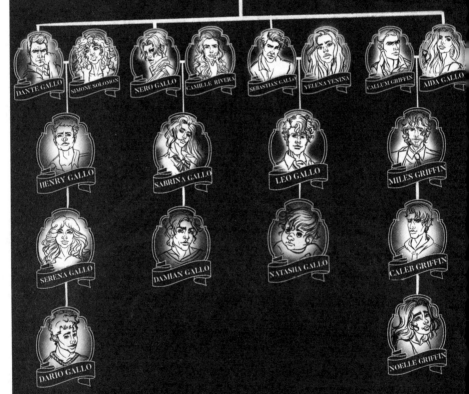

GALLO
Family Tree

FERGUS GRIFFIN

IMOGEN FITZGERALD

CALLUM GRIFFIN · AIDA GALLO · RAYLAN BOONE · RIONA GRIFFIN · NESSA GRIFFIN · MIKOLAJ WILK

MILES GRIFFIN · MARSHALL BOONE · COLE BOONE · CREED BOONE · TEDDY BOONE · ANNA WILK

CALEB GRIFFIN · CARA WILK

NOELLE GRIFFIN · WHELAN WILK

GRIFFIN
Family Tree

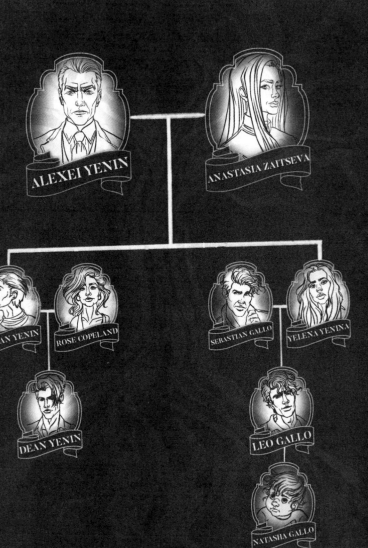

CHAPTER 1
DEAN

MOSCOW

The Bratva high table meets tonight in a private room on the top floor of the Bolshoi Theatre. This is a meeting my father cannot skip. He'll have to leave our house on Noble Row for the first time in months.

As accustomed as I've become to the chaos inside our mansion, I was still shocked when I came home from school in the spring. From the exterior, the sandstone facade looked as expensive and well maintained as ever. But the moment I opened the front door, I was hit with a wave of fetid, rotting air.

No clear path into the house remained. My father's burgeoning collection of trash overflowed into the entryway: stacks of books, newspapers, magazines, boxes, bags, and packages piled to the ceiling in labyrinthine channels that forced me to weave my way down the hallway and up the stairs.

Where the house used to smell of dust and mold, now I had to pull my shirt up over the lower half of my face to filter out the stench of something that had died beneath the mounds of garbage. Rats certainly, and perhaps even a pigeon or a cat.

He banned the maids from the house years ago. I doubt you could offer them a king's ransom to return.

My father hadn't met me at the airport—I had no expectation that he would. I scaled the stairs in anger and resentment at how far he had allowed our house to continue to decay. It's like he wants it to collapse on top of him so he can suffocate in the rubble.

I went straight to his office.

That space, at least, he had always kept clean. And he had always maintained his personal appearance, even as the rest of our home fell into ruin.

But I found him sitting behind his desk in a filthy robe, his hair down to his shoulders and his fingernails two inches long. He looked up at me, confused, with his one good eye bleary, the other milky and blind.

"What are you doing back here?" he muttered.

"School is done for the year. It's summer holiday."

He stared at me like he had no idea of the year, let alone the month. Then, slowly, he seemed to understand.

"They sent me your grades." He nodded toward a heavy gray envelope with a handwritten report.

"I finished second in my class."

"Who was first?"

My jaw twitched. "Anna Wilk."

"A *girl?*" My father sneered.

"She's heir to the Chicago Braterstwo. You know her father."

Then it was his turn to flinch. We never mention Chicago. And we certainly never mention the people who live there still—not even our closest living relatives.

"Next year, I expect you to place first," he snapped.

"I intend to."

Anna and I scored within a percent of each other on our final exams. We didn't know who had triumphed until the results were posted in the commons.

She congratulated me as if she hadn't beaten me.

It was the first time we'd spoken since…a very long time ago.

I still felt a tightness in my chest at the sound of her voice. My skin burned where her long, silvery hair brushed my arm as she turned away. I crushed those sensations like insects beneath my heel.

I learned my lesson from that infatuation. I will *never* allow love to make me weak again.

I feared that my father had been neglecting his work as much as his hygiene, but the stack of ledgers strewn across his desk seemed to indicate that he at least had not forgotten how to do his job. He's the head bookkeeper for our territory in Moscow, with a team of accountants beneath him. Luckily for him, it's one of the few jobs in the Bratva that can be done from home.

He hates to be seen.

My father was handsome once. Athletic, charming, beloved by women of all ages. He couldn't smile in the direction of a woman without her blushing red and slipping him her phone number.

Of all the pretty girls in the world, none adored him more than his twin sister, Yelena.

Then she betrayed him.

She married his mortal enemy, Sebastian Gallo.

Sebastian tied my father to a chair on the top floor of his mansion. When my grandfather threw a Molotov cocktail through the window, Sebastian left my father to die, burning alive in the collapsing house.

But he didn't die. His lungs bubbled, his flesh peeled off, his hair burned away, yet he survived. He was carried to the hospital, where they stuffed him full of tubes and shoved an air hose down his throat. A pretty blond nurse named Rose Copeland attended him.

Dozens of surgeries followed: surgeries to cut away the charred flesh and scrub the ash and dirt out of what remained. Surgeries to slice healthy skin off the uninjured half of his body and graft it over the open wounds.

They gave him drugs. Cocktails and pills and mainlines dripped directly into the vein. None of them could dull the agony of the exposed nerves. He screamed alone in the hospital because there was no one left to visit him. He refused to see his treacherous twin, and his father was dead, murdered by Sebastian Gallo.

His only solace was the blond nurse who stayed long after her shifts ended to hold his hand—the good hand, the one that wasn't burned.

He suffered in that hospital for months.

Then he returned home to his father's empty house. The nurse came with him, to inject him with morphine at night and change the dressings on his healing wounds.

She read to him. It was the only thing that could distract him from the pain. He had never been much of a scholar before. The nurse introduced him to Hemingway and Hawthorne, Tolstoy and Tolkien. She gave him dozens of the books that lined our shelves when I was young, when our house was bright and clean.

Now you could never find those shelves through the stacks of books leaned up against every wall of this house. He has no discernment for literature anymore. He'll buy any book and never even read it: thrillers and mysteries, romance and science fiction. Textbooks, biographies, memoirs. The desire to read has been subsumed in the desire to hoard.

I don't think he leaves the house at all except to bring in the groceries delivered to the front step.

But he has to visit the Bolshoi Theatre tonight, and he's demanded that I accompany him.

For the second time today, I shower the scent of this filthy house off my skin. Then I dress carefully in my nicest suit. It's a little too tight in the chest and shoulders. I put on muscle this year at school.

The suit is black, as is my father's. He looks like a priest with his simple cleric collar and his monochromatic shirt.

I'm glad to see that he remembers how to dress at least. He's washed and combed his hair on the side where it still grows. Shaved that half of his face too. Trimmed his nails and scented his wrists with cologne.

When I stand on his left, I see a man who looks keen, intelligent, austere.

When he turns to the right, I see madness. Crackled, bubbled flesh. A withered arm and clawlike hand. And one blind, staring eye with no lid.

"Are you ready?" the left side of his mouth says.

I nod.

I've called a car to take us to the theater. As my father descends our front steps, he pauses on the sidewalk, wincing in the glare of the streetlamps. I don't think he could have tolerated full sunlight. The unblemished side of his body is pale as talcum powder.

He stoops to enter the car, leaning on his walking stick.

I follow after him, taking a deep lungful of the town car's leather interior and the pleasant scent of scotch from the open bar. So much better than the musk of the house.

I want to clean our house, but I think my father might kill me if I try. He goes into a rage if I touch anything, even the food in the fridge. Everything has to stay exactly where he put it. Only he can see the order in his jumbled system.

I don't have to tell the driver the address of the theater. Everyone knows the Bolshoi—it's featured on the hundred-ruble note. The neoclassical pillars are as familiar to Russians as the Lincoln Memorial is to Americans from their penny.

The Bolshoi is our phoenix. Four times destroyed by fire and once by a bomb, we've rebuilt it every time. Its last renovation symbolizes something rather less inspiring—classic Russian graft. The billion-dollar taxpayer bill was sixteen times the estimated price, and the lead contractor was paid three times over for the same work.

State construction projects are how the oligarchs funnel public money into their pockets. Politicians, businessmen, and Bratva are one and the same in Russia.

Ballet tickets are sold in bulk to Mafia dealers, who provide them to the public at double the face value. We have our hand in every pocket. No commerce can be done without the Bratva taking their cut.

I've been to the Bolshoi many times before. I know the rehearsal rooms, the backstage, and the secret passageways just as well as the front lobby.

My father and I easily make our way through the bustle of dancers in their ripped tights and battered shoes, the air redolent with the scent of hair spray, nylon, and sweat.

"Adrian and Dmitry, it's been too long," Danyl Kuznetsov greets us, dapper in his navy suit, with his dark hair and beard freshly trimmed.

Danyl is the one who helped secure my admission to Kingmakers. For that, I owe him two years' service after I graduate.

"I hear you're doing very well at school," Danyl says, clapping me on the back.

"I enjoy the classes," I say, which is mostly true.

"Now you get a little break. Even God rested for a day." He chuckles, then pulls me close against his side, nodding toward the pretty little ballerina scurrying by. "You want to fuck one of those? I can bring one upstairs for you. Or two if you like! They'll do anything for a part in the next show. Or a handful of rubles. They make no money here, not until they become principals."

"No, thank you," I say stiffly.

"What's wrong? You don't like to fuck?"

"I don't like dancers. Too skinny."

I don't want to fuck a ballerina. Just standing in this theater is reminding me of things I don't want to remember.

"Suit yourself." Danyl shrugs.

He doesn't bother asking my father. All the Bratva know that Adrian Yenin won't disrobe for anything. And they probably prefer it that way. Even the most hardened soldiers don't enjoy looking at my father's face.

"Come have a drink at least," Danyl says, leading us up the back staircase to the private elevator, where we ascend to the topmost floor.

The penthouse suite is as lush and gleaming as the rest of the theater, every inch of space covered in red velvet, gilding, and sparkling chandeliers. I recognize most of the men already gathered, including the three Moscow bosses.

Moscow is divided into three territories, each with its own *pakhan*. My father's territory is run by Abram Balakin. Danyl is his lieutenant, and my father is third in line in terms of authority, though he could never be boss himself, not with his particular proclivities.

Since neither Abram nor Danyl has any children, it's possible that I could become *pakhan* someday. That's the reason I was accepted to the Heirs division at Kingmakers. But my position is not assured. I'll have to prove myself at school and then in the ranks of the Bratva after graduation.

Abram greets me warmly. He's always liked me and my father too, because of all the money my father has saved the Bratva through his meticulous recordkeeping and careful investment.

"You look strong, Dmitry," he says approvingly. "They feed you well at school."

Abram has been fed a little too well himself. His tailors must charge him twice the usual price for a suit, with the vast amount of fine Italian fabric required to cover that belly. His cheeks are florid from alcohol, and you could fit a weekend's worth of luggage in the bags under his eyes.

Success has defeated Abram when no enemy could do it. He's become lazy and complacent, a shadow of the warrior who once slaughtered thirty rivals in a single night.

He must cede his place sometime in the next five or ten years, before it's taken from him forcibly. I'm sure he knows this. He's transferring assets out of the country and promoting the men beneath him.

I can almost taste Danyl's ambition as he stands shoulder to shoulder with his boss. He wants to be *pakhan*, badly.

And who will be lieutenant then?

"Abram," Egor Antonov says. "I brought you one of those Don Arturo cigars you love so well. Smoke with me. My son is home for the summer."

Egor holds out the cigar to Abram, subtly shouldering aside my father so that he and his son stand in a better position. My father takes a step back, leaning on his walking stick. I clench my fists inside the pockets of my trousers.

I know Vanya Antonov from Kingmakers. He's an Enforcer in my year, friends with Bodashka Kushnir and Silas Gray. He's tall and well-built, square-jawed, with a bold Roman nose and dark features. He has an arrogant tilt to his chin and a smile that's more of a smirk.

"Now there's another well-built lad." Abram slaps Vanya on the back. "I wish all my soldiers came from Kingmakers."

"Vanya is strong as an ox. And fights like a bear! He's knocked a few heads together at school."

"Oh really?" I say coolly. "I didn't see you fighting in the tournament last year, Vanya. You weren't chosen, were you?"

Vanya turns his head to look at me, cocking one well-groomed eyebrow. I bet he plucks them, the prissy bitch.

"No, I wasn't," he chuckles. "Probably because it was your cousin doing the choosing."

"We all know how that goes," Egor snorts.

Nepotism is an art in Russia.

"I was chosen based on talent," I remind Vanya. "Leo Gallo and I despise each other."

"So even your own family doesn't like you," Vanya replies, smirking all the more.

The other men laugh, and I take a swift step forward, pulling my fists out of my pockets. The only thing preventing me from propelling one of those fists directly into the center of Vanya's arrogant face is my father's good hand pressed flat across my chest.

"Control yourself," he hisses.

"I placed first in the tournament and second in marks," I tell Vanya. "Whereas I've barely heard your name spoken at school. I almost forgot you attended until this moment."

Abram gives a little snort. Vanya hears it. Now it's his turn to color, because he has no good response for his complete failure to distinguish himself at Kingmakers.

"I'd be glad to give you a lesson in my skills right now," he barks, the veneer of civility between us completely rubbed away.

"No need for that, boys," Abram says in a bored tone. "We have other entertainment planned for the evening."

He claps his hands. The double doors at the end of the private suite swing open. Twenty elegant women swarm through, dressed in sparkling gowns and diamond jewelry. Every one is tall and slim, their shining hair piled high on their heads. These are no chorus dancers but the prima ballerinas, expected to drink and dance and socialize with the Bratva. Like geishas, they offer the highest levels of cultured feminine charm. When the Bratva want to fuck, they visit their own brothels. When they want to be entertained, they bring in the ballerinas.

The next hour is spent drinking and socializing. A table along the wall groans under the weight of a mountain of crab legs, caviar, boiled quail eggs, fern salad, sizzling sprats, and suckling pig.

I make my way over to the food, intending to eat, until I see fresh strawberry pie with a shortbread crust. My mother used to make that. She tried to learn all the traditional Russian dishes because it made my father happy to come home to her cooking, even when it was awful, even when her borscht was shit.

My father would laugh and try to gulp down her terrible food, and she would smack him with the dish towel and say there was no need, we could visit the restaurant on the corner. He would grab her and kiss her and say that he'd prefer to order in, and they would send me to bed early so they could be alone. My mother would bring me up a piece of strawberry pie, which was the one thing she could actually make reasonably well.

I look at the pie.

I know it will taste like sawdust in my mouth.

I grab a glass of chilled vodka instead and swallow it down, liking the way it burns.

When everyone has had their fill of food and women, the ballerinas are dismissed. Isay Zolin calls the meeting to order. He controls the second-largest territory in Moscow. While his holdings are secondary to Nikolai Markov's, Isay is the president's cousin, and thus has been given chairmanship of the Bratva for the time being.

Isay checks that all the *pakhans* are in attendance, including those from St. Petersburg. When he calls the name of Ivan Petrov, a tall, fair-haired man with a scar down his left cheek says, "I'm here in my brother's place."

That must be Dominik Petrov, flanked by his two black-haired sons. I've never met them, but the eldest son, Adrik, is a legend at Kingmakers.

"This meeting is for all the *pakhans*," Isay says severely. "I expected Ivan."

"He sends his regrets," Dominik says. "As you know, his business in America has been highly lucrative for all of us, but it demands no small attention. An emergency delayed him."

"Has he authorized you to vote on his behalf?" Isay demands.

"He has," Dominik says with a curt nod.

"Then we will proceed," Isay says.

Now comes the tedious portion of the evening when the bosses vote on the minutia of shared Bratva business, including what percentage of the vast fund held in common should be given in disbursements and where the remaining portion should be invested.

Each Bratva boss runs his own operation, but a percentage of profits is pooled, some used to secure our mutual goals in government and business and some allotted for administrative expenses, bribes, legal defense, and so forth.

If the bosses don't agree, then the lieutenants and *derzhatel obschaka* like my father are called on to likewise cast their votes. It's all very democratic, as far as democracy prevails when you know that the man above you might cut your throat if he doesn't like your opinion.

I check the gold watch on my wrist—a gift from my father on my eighteenth birthday. A traditional gift. Usually it would be engraved. Mine was not.

It's well past midnight.

Once the votes conclude, my father takes me around the room, introducing me to anyone of importance that I haven't already met. He doesn't care to climb the ladder of the Bratva himself—he wants no additional leadership or responsibilities. But he understands the importance of alliances.

The ballerinas have been permitted to return. Plenty of the bosses have pulled the girls onto their laps, preferring flirtation over further networking.

Not Dominik Petrov. He stands stiffly against the wall with his arms folded over his broad chest, rebuffing the advances of the stunning women who would prefer to drape themselves against his muscular frame instead of the fat and sweating bodies of the older Bratva who have let themselves go to seed.

Dominik is clearly uninterested, though his eldest son, Adrik, looks like he might have accepted the attention of one particularly lovely redhead had his father not shooed her away with a hiss.

"Dominik." My father holds out his good hand to shake. "Ever faithful to Lara, I see."

"A man does not drink from a toilet when he has fine wine at home," Dominik replies dismissively.

"Don't let Isay hear you liken the feminine flowers of Moscow to a toilet," my father chuckles.

"I wouldn't share a fork with Isay, let alone a woman," Dominik says.

I can't help but admire his nerve in insulting Isay Zolin within earshot of a dozen Bratva bosses. There's something likable in his insouciance and his complete disregard for any woman who isn't his wife. It shows respect for his sons.

"This is your son Dmitry?" Dominik holds out one large, calloused hand to shake.

"I go by Dean at school."

My father shoots me a warning look. Russians look down on westernized names. He instructed me not to use Dean around Bratva. But that's the name he agreed on with my mother, and I resent the fact that he wants me to erase it.

"I miss Kingmakers." Adrik tosses back his mane of black hair. "Life was simpler at school."

Adrik doesn't strike me as someone prone to nostalgia. He has a wild, ferocious look about him, like an animal chafing at the restrictions of his suit and tie.

His younger brother is slimmer built, with an intelligent, watchful expression.

"Kade will be attending in the fall." Dominik places his hand on his younger son's shoulder.

"Dmitry can keep an eye on him," my father offers.

"That would be kind," Dominik says with an approving nod.

"What division will you be in?" I ask Kade.

"Enforcer. Like Adrik."

"I'm an Heir. But I'm sure our paths will cross regardless."

"Has Danyl named you his successor?" Adrik asks in a tone of confusion.

"No," I admit.

"Interesting."

I don't think Adrik means to mock me, but I can feel my face coloring all the same. It's true—I don't really deserve my position in the Heirs division without a formal acknowledgment from Abram and Danyl. The chancellor may have misunderstood the terms of Danyl's letter of recommendation, or it may be that Danyl and Abram intended to formalize the arrangement, then hesitated. Perhaps because the Antonovs got in their ear.

All it means is that I have to continue to perform to the highest standards at Kingmakers. I intend to place first in grades in my final two years. Nothing and nobody will stand in my way. Not Anna Wilk, and certainly not Vanya Antonov.

CHAPTER 2
CAT

After a long and achingly sweet summer in Chicago, I'm boarding the ship to Kingmakers once more.

The reality of my situation is crashing down on my shoulders.

It was easy to forget how much trouble I'm in when I was whiling away the hours sightseeing with Zoe and Miles and Miles's little brother, Caleb.

I never imagined I could be treated so well as a guest. The Griffins embraced me like one of their own, even though it's Zoe who will marry into their family, not me.

They took care of my every need, ferrying me around the city, buying me delicacies and souvenirs, making sure I was never bored, lonely, or lacking for the smallest thing.

I shut out the memory of what I had done at Kingmakers.

I pretended to belong among the Griffins, like Chicago had always been my home.

But now it's all over.

I returned to my father's house in Barcelona for one dull week before packing my bags again.

My father was in the best mood I've ever seen him. The deal he struck with Miles Griffin has surpassed all his wildest dreams in the sheer volume of money pouring into his account. That was the bargain: Miles's dark web drug pipeline in exchange for Zoe. Miles has made my father and his associates into very rich men.

As a small sweetener, Miles stipulated that my father refrain from coercing me into any unwanted marriage contracts. My father has upheld his end of the bargain: he left me alone my entire week in Spain, not even demanding that I accompany him and my stepmother, Daniela, to any of their tedious parties.

Still, it was a long, lonely week after the warmth and bustle of the Griffin household.

I miss Zoe already.

I miss her horribly.

She asked me again if I wanted to come to Los Angeles with her and Miles. I wanted to accept so badly. I feel safe with those two. Zoe is the only person on the planet who truly loves me, who would do anything to protect me.

But I knew I'd only be a third wheel, an anchor dragging them down while they try to build a life together.

I have to return to my own life at Kingmakers. Even if there's something horrible waiting there for me.

It's ironic. My father is forbidden from forcing me into a marriage contract against my will, but I've already trapped myself in something far, far worse.

The moment I step foot aboard the ship to Kingmakers, I'm looking around for Dean Yenin.

I remember the last words we spoke to each other as though it were three minutes ago instead of three months.

"I know what you did...

"I saw you...

"I won't tell. But understand this...I own you now. When we come back to school, you're mine. My servant. My slave. For as long as I want you."

I almost spilled my secret to Zoe a hundred times. I almost told her what I did.

But in the end, I stuffed the words down again, into the ball of frozen fear that's been lodged deep in my guts all this time.

This is my burden to bear, not hers.

If I told Zoe the truth, she'd never feel free to go to LA with Miles. She'd be compelled to stay with me, to try to protect me from something she simply can't prevent.

Dean knows what I did. He could tell the chancellor at any time. Nothing can stop him from doing that. My only chance is to stay on his good side. To trust in his mercy.

The only problem is that I don't think he has any goddamned mercy.

I'm trying to please a man who can't be pleased.

Dean is spiteful. Vengeful. Full of rage.

He could destroy me with a single word just because I looked at him sideways.

The train of his hatred is long and complicated.

He hates Leo Gallo because of the feud between their families.

He hates Miles and Zoe because Miles is Leo's cousin.

And he hates me because I'm Zoe's sister.

But that barely scratches the surface of his fury.

I've thought about this long and hard over the summer, wondering how I truly attracted his ire.

The *real* reason he hates me is that I saw him in a private, unguarded moment.

I saw him sobbing after Ozzy's mother was executed by the chancellor. I saw him hunched over, tears streaming down his face, as he gave in to the storm of pain inside him.

And he will never, never, never forgive me for that.

I saw Dean weak and vulnerable. He'll have me killed before he'll chance me telling anybody else.

Like a fool, I handed him the perfect leverage over me.

I murdered Rocco Prince, my sister's intended fiancé.

And Dean knows it.

The rule of recompense is the most ironclad law of Kingmakers: an eye for an eye, a tooth for a tooth, a life for a life.

If Dean tells anyone what I did, I'll be executed, just like Ozzy's mother. I'll be forced to kneel before the school so the chancellor can slit my throat.

This is the situation in which I find myself as I stand on the sunbaked deck of the ship. One wrong move, and Dean will throw me to the wolves. My only chance of survival is to hope and pray that somewhere, deep inside Dean, there lives a spark of humanity.

Or maybe he'll just get bored of fucking with me and move on to something else.

I can't see any other way out.

"Cat!" Perry Saunders cries, throwing her arms around me in a hug. "How was your summer?"

Perry is blond and bubbly, curly-haired and apple-cheeked. She dresses like an American Girl doll, already wearing the plaid skirt and jaunty academy jacket that forms our school uniform.

My roommate, Rakel, was likewise crossing the deck to greet me, but as soon as she sees Perry, she does an abrupt about-face to head in the opposite direction. I grab her by the arm and haul her back, deciding that this year, Rakel is going to be social whether she likes it or not.

"Perry, have you met my roommate?" I say, slinging my arm around Rakel's slim shoulders so she can't get away.

"No!" Perry chirps. She holds out her hand to shake. "Periwinkle Madeline Saunders. Nice to meet you."

Rakel forces a smile that looks more like a snarl and shakes Perry's hand with two fingers in a pincher grip. "Just…Rakel," she says.

"I wish the Accountants roomed down in the undercroft!" Perry says enviously. "All the other divisions have such cool dorms, and ours is dull as dishwater. It might as well be cubicles in our tower. We don't even have a view off the cliffs."

"We don't have windows at all," Rakel reminds her in a monotone.

"I know, but at least that's spooky!" Perry says.

Rakel flashes her dark eyes at me in a way that clearly intimates that she will seek revenge on me later for involving her in this conversation. I smile back at her, knowing that nobody else wants to room with Rakel, so she's stuck with me.

"Who does your nails?" Perry examines Rakel's silver-ringed hands. "They look like claws!"

"They grow that way naturally," Rakel deadpans while Perry's eyes go big and round in total belief.

Anna Wilk and Leo Gallo climb the gangplank hand in hand. Anna is one of Zoe's best friends. She was exceptionally kind to me during my first year at school when I was drowning in terror at the arcane demands of Kingmakers.

"Cat!" she cries, hugging me.

I saw Anna in Chicago over the summer, but she squeezes me like we've spent months apart.

"It makes me so sad to see you here without Zoe. Are you gonna come hang out with me and Chay all the time anyway? You have to fill your sister's spot, or we'll be miserable."

"I would love that," I promise gratefully. I wasn't sure if Anna and Chay would want me hanging around now that Zoe decided not to return to school.

"I miss Miles too," Leo says glumly. "Trust him to take off right when he was finally turning into a reasonable human."

Dean Yenin is next to board the ship, flanked by his best friends Bram Van Der Berg and Valon Hoxha. Instinctively, I shrink back behind Leo's substantial bulk, but it's pointless. Dean's sharp eyes alight on me at once. For the first time in memory, I see his face break out into a smile.

His smile is far worse than his scowl. The even white teeth don't fool me for a second. That's a grin of pure malice.

Oh my god, I can't fucking do this.

"What's he so happy about?" Leo says suspiciously.

"Who knows!" Anna shrugs, careless and unconcerned. "Let's go find somewhere to sit before the whole ship fills up."

We make our way toward the bow, where the air is fresher and the sea breeze blows directly into our faces. We're departing from the port in Dubrovnik, sailing toward the isolated island of Visine Dvorca where Kingmakers' castle fortress resides.

Once the ship sets out, we won't return to civilization until the spring.

I'll be trapped on that island with my tormenter.

Perry peels off from our group to join her Accountant friends. To my pleasure, Rakel actually sticks around. Despite despising me at the beginning of last year, she and I are slowly becoming something like actual friends.

With Zoe gone, I need all the friends I can get.

Perhaps noting a kindred spirit in Anna's heavy black makeup and torn-up tights, Rakel strikes up a conversation about the concerts she attended over the summer. Anna enthusiastically responds with her own tales of outdoor venues, raging mosh pits, and outrageous prices for shit beer.

"How are you doing?" Leo asks me kindly.

"I'm fine!" I lie.

Has anyone in the history of the world actually been "fine" when they responded that way?

I'm a people pleaser. Like Zoe, I've never felt free to share my burdens with others. Especially not someone as handsome and intimidating as Leo Gallo.

I sink down on a pile of coiled rope, joined by Ares Cirillo, who sits by me in companionable silence, watching the sailors work. I know he owns a little skiff that he sails around his tiny Greek island. He looks quite at home on the ocean, with his turquoise eyes and streaks of sun in his hair.

As the ship pulls out of the harbor, the breeze picks up, and a pleasant salt spray blows in our faces. However, the sun beats down on our heads, and soon students are shedding every possible article of clothing, including academy jackets, stockings, and even shirts.

Dean Yenin leans against the ship's railing, stripping off his white dress shirt. The skin beneath is barely darker than the shirt, rippled with muscle hard-won through countless hours in our school gym. As he turns to lay his shirt over the railing, I see the Siberian tiger crawling up his back. Dean reminds me of a white tiger himself—pale and vicious, composed of lean, hard muscle and the desire to rip flesh from bone.

Bram Van Der Berg is rubbing tanning oil on his swarthy skin, apparently determined to darken himself another shade before reaching the island.

"Give me that," Dean mutters, swiping the oil from Bram's hand.

He strides over to me, a smirk already spreading across his face.

"Cat!" he barks, making me jump. "Rub this on my back."

Anna laughs derisively.

"Get Bram to do it," she says. "Cat's busy."

Dean ignores her, his pale purplish eyes fixed on my face.

"Now," he says quietly.

I feel myself jumping up from my position on the pile of ropes, snapping to attention before I've even formulated a thought.

"Okay," I murmur, my face flaming.

Anna frowns. "You don't have to listen to him," she says to me.

Anna and Dean dated briefly in their first year of school, but I know that's not why she's defending me. Anna is the sort of feminist who always protects her sisters, whether she knows the man in question or not.

Dean is watching me, his face darkening as I fail to obey his order.

"I really don't mind," I stammer, stumbling over my own feet as I hurry across the pitching deck.

Anna, Leo, Ares, and Rakel watch me with identical expressions of confusion while I take the oil from Dean and squirt it into my hands.

"Rub it on my back," he says. "Slowly. And don't spill one fucking drop."

My hands shake and my face burns as more students watch the bizarre performance of me, a shy little nobody, oiling up the back of one of the most vicious boys at school.

Dean's skin is smooth and sun-warmed, the muscle beneath the flesh iron-hard.

"Rub out those knots," he orders.

I try to obey, but my small hands are no match for the tough muscle. I can't sink my fingers in at all.

Dean makes me rub his back and shoulders, then all the way down his arms.

"Now the chest," he says, smirking.

He turns to face me, looking down into my face while I spread oil across his pectoral muscles. I can't meet his eyes. I feel utterly humiliated, forced to do this in front of hundreds of watching students. Dean is so much taller than me that I have to stretch up on tiptoe just to reach the tops of his shoulders.

Standing in such close proximity to him makes my whole body shake. I feel like a mouse forced to dance around within the confines of a tiger's claws. I'm trembling, my brain telling me that this is much too close, that I need to flee immediately.

I can smell Dean's skin beneath the coconut oil. He smells clean and freshly showered, but as the sun beats down on us both, I get a hint of his actual scent, an intense and titillating aroma like the green-tinged fumes of absinthe. It makes me weak and wobbly.

"You can stop," he says, abruptly dismissing me.

He turns away from me and strides back to his friends like I don't even exist.

I feel oddly disappointed. Almost angry.

I rubbed him for twenty minutes. He could have at least said "thank you" or "good job."

Then that spurt of idiocy fades away, and I'm simply relieved that he let me off so easily.

I return to Anna and the others.

"You don't have to do what he says!" Anna says indignantly. "I know he's scary, but he's not going to do anything to you with us around."

I know Anna's intentions are good, but in this particular instance, she's very wrong.

I *do* have to do what Dean says.

And the consequences are dire if I refuse.

CHAPTER 3
DEAN

SETTLING INTO KINGMAKERS IS OLD HAT AT THIS POINT. WE'RE IN the same dorm as before, though I've moved up to the third floor of the Octagon Tower along with the rest of the junior male Heirs.

I feel at home as I pass through the vast stone gates into the sprawling medieval campus. My first year at school was bitter, due to my disastrous infatuation with Anna Wilk. Since then, I've become master of my emotions and master of my domain at this school. The Dutch Penose, the Armenians, and half the Moscow Bratva answer to me. I'm already proving my leadership skills, my ability to make soldiers follow my orders.

Not to mention I'm the undisputed champion when it comes to fighting. No one can beat me in the boxing ring. No one ever has.

My father's house is chaotic and filthy. Kingmakers suits me better. It's full of power and history. A true meritocracy, where an Enforcer like Adrik Petrov or a would-be Heir like me can rise to dominance purely by proving our skill and intelligence.

Most of the third-year students keep the same roommates they've had all along. I stick with Bram because we're used to each other at this point. Irritating as he can be, he's still better than Valon or any of the others. Bram at least knows better than to make a mess, and I prefer his surly silences to Valon's inane chatter.

As we each unpack our single suitcase, my mind is drawn back irresistibly to the specter of Cat Romero obeying my orders on the deck of the ship. Though Cat is weak and timid and hardly worth bossing around, the sheer weight of my leverage over her fills me with a blissful sense of power. She has to do whatever I say; she has no other choice. The extent of that control is intoxicating.

Forcing her to obey me in front of Anna, Leo, and Ares was particularly enjoyable. They have no idea why she answers to me. Their bewilderment adds spice to the proceedings.

Instead of looking forward to the commencement of my classes, I'm planning what I'll make her do next. I'm remembering her flushed pink cheeks and how she squirmed under my gaze. I'm thinking about how I can humiliate her further. The more I push her, the more I prove my power over her. It might be fun to see how far I can stretch her before she finally snaps.

I wish we were in the same year so we had classes together. Unfortunately, she's only a sophomore.

That's fine. I can stalk her easily enough between classes and in the dining hall.

"What was the deal with the little chickadee on the ship?" Bram inquires, running a hand through his shaggy dark hair.

"What about her?" I say, hiding my smile.

"Why are you fucking with her?"

"Why not?"

Bram looks at me, narrowing his wolfish eyes. He knows I'm up to something, but he couldn't guess the truth in a hundred years. He has no vision.

He could have watched Cat climb back in that infirmary window and never guessed a thing. Only I'm smart enough to put the pieces together. Nobody else on this campus would ever guess that shy, awkward little Cat is a full-blown murderer.

I'll admit, I don't know how she had the balls to tangle with Rocco Prince.

It intrigues me. There must be more to that timid little kitten than I guessed. I want to peel back her layers one by one and see what's inside.

"She's not your usual type," Bram says, smirking. He wants to rub it in my face that I chased after tall, glamorous, gorgeous Anna Wilk in our freshman year. The Gothic ballerina and fellow Heir, lethal and brilliant—opposite in every way to Cat Romero.

But for once, the mention of Anna doesn't sting me.

I'm not thinking about Anna. I'm fixated on my new plaything.

Cat Romero is a useful distraction in more ways than one.

Bram is looking over his handwritten schedule. Everything at Kingmakers is handwritten by the administrative staff in ornate, old-fashioned script, which makes it damned hard to decipher, especially if you're only semiliterate to begin with, like Bram. He squints at the page until the scar across his left eye forms one continuous line.

"How come I've got boxing *and* combat now?" he demands.

"Let me see," I say, snatching the schedule out of his hands.

Sure enough, I see a boxing class scheduled three times a week in addition to his regular combat classes.

I check my own schedule, finding the same thing.

"Who's Professor Snow?" Bram says.

"You don't think..."

"What?"

"Filip Rybakov fought under the name Snow."

Bram stares at me, uncomprehending.

"He was the heavyweight champion. He held all four titles at once."

"When?" Bram says.

"Twenty years ago."

"You think he's here? To teach us?"

I shrug. "Could be. He got his start in St. Petersburg in the underground matches. He could be Bratva."

"We'll find out soon enough," Bram says. "First class is tomorrow morning."

The next morning, Bram and I cross the commons to the armory with a pleasant sense of anticipation. Rumors have been flying around the school that we are indeed to be receiving instruction from one of the most famous boxers of the modern era.

The other students are jealous as fuck because only a select group of us have been enrolled in boxing. Everybody else has to be content with their normal combat classes with the decidedly less glamorous Professor Howell.

It's a mark of honor to have been placed in Snow's class. I'm not surprised to see Silas Gray, Bodashka Kushnir, Kenzo Tanaka, Leo Gallo, Ares Cirillo, and Hedeon Gray already waiting inside the gymnasium. I'm less pleased to note Vanya Antonov in attendance, straining the bounds of a white T-shirt deliberately bought two sizes too small.

Bodashka Kushnir is trying to chat up Ilsa Markov, one of the only female Enforcers at our school. Her father, Nikolai, was at the meeting I attended in Moscow. Ilsa is tall and well-built, with her long, dark hair pulled back in a ponytail, and her Wonder Woman thighs filling out her gray gym shorts. I can only imagine the continual harassment she must get from idiots like Bodashka in the male-stuffed gatehouse. But Ilsa has no problem taking care of herself.

Bodashka seems to be bragging about his summer exploits, which apparently involves him flexing his substantial biceps for Ilsa. Pretending to be impressed, Ilsa challenges him to try to hold his arm at a ninety-degree angle while she pulls down on his elbow. Bodashka agrees, planting his sturdy legs while Ilsa pulls on his arm with all her might, even hanging off it so that Bodashka is holding up her entire weight with one arm.

Bodashka grins, sure that he's impressing her. Until Ilsa abruptly lets go of his elbow, making Bodashka punch himself in the face.

Bodashka stumbles and almost falls while Ilsa throws her head back and roars with laughter. Vanya, Leo, Ares, and Hedeon all join in. Even Silas Gray chuckles, and he wouldn't know a joke if it danced naked in front of him.

Bodashka shakes his head, stupefied by the force of his own ham fist. He knows he's a fucking fool, but Ilsa's laughter is so infectious that even he has to shrug and admit that the prank was well played.

Usually our classes only include students from our same year, but the senior Spy Jasper Webb is leaning up against a heavy bag, methodically cracking the flexible knuckles of his skeleton-tattooed hands. His dark red hair hangs over his face, and he looks moody and standoffish. Still, he gives me a nod as I pass, which I suppose means that he doesn't hold a grudge over the fact that I beat him in the final round of the tournament last year.

I see Kasper Markaj, likewise a senior, and August Prieto, a sophomore, which must mean the boxing class will be attended by anybody good enough to fight.

With only one minute left before class time, Kade Petrov comes sprinting through the door, along with a baby-faced blond boy who must be a freshman, though he's as big as any of the seniors. His face looks familiar to me. When he says to Kade, in a French accent, "We barely made it!" I realize he must be one of the Paris Bratva.

The blond boy is right. The moment the clock hits 10:00, Snow comes striding across the mats.

There's no fighter like an old fighter, with shoulders and traps harder than petrified oak and fists of pure calcified bone. His face bears the marks of a thousand punches, delivered by men who train on heavy bags, tires, and even fence posts.

His nose is broad and broken, his brows scowling, his mouth sternly set above a jaw as hard as steel. His graying hair lies closely buzzed against the skull, and his ice-blue eyes pierce each one of us in turn as he surveys the students lined up before him.

"My name is Snow," he says in a deep, booming voice that instantly silences even the slight shifting of feet on the mats, until you could hear a butterfly's wings beating in the still air. "Boxing is the fight for perfection. We can never be perfect because we are human and flawed. But every single day in this gym, we will strive for perfection. We will believe in perfection. And we will inch toward it, with infinitesimal steps, until we are the closest to god that man has ever been."

He walks up and down the line of students, those sharp eyes examining us as if he's already tallying up the weaknesses in every one of us. He sees Bodashka's swollen face and Ares's dingy, torn sneakers. His gaze fixes on me, and I hold his eyes, refusing to flinch beneath that frosty stare. He won't find a hair out of place on my person. My body is already a shrine to the gods. I sculpt and shape it every fucking day.

"The fight is not won in the ring, in the brilliance of shining lights and the cheering of the crowd. The fight is won here, in this gym. It's won in countless hours of training and conditioning, in the punishment you'll take and the honing of your skills, for months and years before you ever face your opponent."

I can feel the fierce energy swelling in my fellow students. Snow has the powerful presence possessed by all great teachers and leaders. He sets a standard before us. He's painting a picture of what we could become: tempered, hardened, perfected. Already we strain against the bounds of inaction, wanting to show him that we can do as he says, wanting to impress him.

I feel something else: a desire to prove to him that I'm already superior to the rest of these fools. I want to distinguish myself above them all.

"This is not a fundamentals class," Snow says. "All of you have been selected because you already know how to fight. We will focus on higher-level skills, which are more complicated and precise. You will follow my instructions exactly. Particularly when sparring with your fellow students. Remember, if you fuck up in golf, you get a mulligan. If you fuck up in the ring, you'll wake up eating through a straw."

We wrap our hands and don our padded training gloves.

Snow breaks us into sets of two, assigning the pairs himself. Though he doesn't know any of us yet, he's able to judge our size and skill level with fair accuracy so that most of us are evenly matched: Leo with Ares, Silas with Bodashka, Kade with August.

However, he matches me with the blond freshman, which I can't help but take as an insult. While the kid is tall, he's obviously young and inexperienced.

He introduces himself in his gentle, accented voice. "Tristan Turgenev."

"Dean," I say curtly back to him, facing off across our mat.

He must be related to Claire or Jules Turgenev. I don't really give a shit which it is. I'm annoyed that I'm babysitting instead of getting proper practice with someone like Jasper or Leo.

I love fighting. I love falling into my stance, easy and natural, knees bent and fists raised. I love the energy that flows through my frame and the knowledge that I can strike and hit as hard as I want. When my opponent answers back, I'll slip his punches like I can see them coming from a mile away.

"I'm going to assume you all know the basic strikes and footwork," Snow says, standing in the center of the gym. "Today we're going to work on the left jab counter. A jab from a right-handed opponent is the most common punch you'll encounter. To turn a left jab into an attack, you want to slip the punch, sending their glove over your left shoulder. Then you counter with a jab of your own right to their chin."

He demonstrates the movements against an invisible opponent. Though he slows down his speed for instructional purposes, I can tell how tight and precise he remains, even after a decade out of the ring.

"Begin," Snow barks.

Tristan and I circle each other. Tristan has a decent stance, but he's slow and hesitant.

I snap out a lightning-fast jab to his face. He fails to slip the punch. My glove connects with his nose, and his head snaps back. He stumbles back a step, shaking his head. A fine thread of blood dribbles down over his upper lip. He ignores it, continuing to circle.

Now it's his turn to jab. He punches out, straight and true, and I slip it easily, responding with an even harder jab to his lip. Tristan grunts, the lip splitting and beginning to bleed as well.

This happens six or seven more times.

I become infuriated that he's failing to block my punches, and I jab him harder and harder. I'm annoyed that we're paired together because it's ludicrously easy to avoid his blows, not a challenge at all. I up the speed of the exercise until he's dizzy and stumbling from a dozen direct hits to the head, while he's failed to strike me even once.

Finally he can't even keep his hands up, and I hit him with a hard right cross that knocks him on his ass.

"Stop!" Snow shouts.

He stomps across the mats, jaw set and eyes blazing.

"What do you think you're doing?" he demands.

"A left jab counter," I reply. "Exactly as you said."

"That was a right cross."

"He's not keeping his hands up. He needed a reminder."

"Do you think you're in charge of discipline in my class?" Snow says, standing only an inch away from me. We're almost exactly the same height—though he's ten or twenty pounds heavier—so we're eye to eye and nose to nose.

"You said everyone here should be experienced. He's not even in my league."

"You think you're better than him?"

"I know I am," I say, barely holding back a laugh. "I'm better than everyone here."

"Everyone?" Snow asks, his voice low and dangerous.

I realize too late what I implied. But I won't take it back now. Maybe I am better than this washed-up has-been. He's got to be in his midforties at least, maybe even fifty. I'm twenty-one years old and a physical specimen. I think I can take him.

"Maybe so." I fold my arms across my chest.

"Let's find out," Snow says softly.

Instinctively, the rest of the students form a circle around us, giving us plenty of space.

I face the old boxer without fear, only keen interest.

I've always believed I could beat anyone in a fight. Perhaps it's time to prove it.

Everyone is watching: Leo, Ares, Ilsa Markov, Vanya Antonov with ill-disguised malice. He wants me to lose. Fuck him, and fuck this teacher.

"Begin," Snow says.

I attack hard and fast, ferocious and unafraid. I'll show the old man what I'm made of. I'll remind him what youth looks like.

I throw a flurry of punches directly at his face, the fastest combinations to ever leave my gloves.

Every single one misses.

It's like Snow has turned to rubber. His hulking frame dips and glides with eerie speed, slipping away from me like oil on water. His feet are a blur of motion, his body tight and precise as he rolls his shoulders. My blows glance off, even ricochet. I can't land a clean punch, not anywhere on his person.

It's a nightmare. All my strength and speed evaporate in the face of his skill.

He's not even trying to hit me back.

With a grunt of rage, I attack him even harder, sure that if I redouble my efforts, something has to hit. I'm panting and sweating because this is the secret of boxing: the most exhausting thing you can do in a fight is throw a punch and miss. Impact rejuvenates; punching air will suck the life out of you.

I'm trying to speed up, but instead I'm getting slower and clumsier. Despite countless hours of running and jumping rope and bag work, I'm tiring, I'm actually tiring. This has never happened to me before.

And still Snow hasn't thrown a single punch.

He waits until I realize the awful truth: I'm about to lose.

Then he goes to work on my body.

He hits me with tight, hard punches that feel like rocks propelled into my sides. I know he's holding back, using only a fraction of his strength. Yet the air grunts out of me, forced from my lungs by the relentless impact.

He begins to taunt me.

"You think because you have abs, you're ready to box?"

Thud. Thud.

He hits me in the ribs, the kidney, right in the gut.

My eyes water, and my breath wheezes out. I'm dizzy and light-headed because I can't draw a full breath. A punch to the jaw can shut off your brain, but bodywork takes the heart out of you.

"You think because you can beat up a boy, you're ready to face a man?"

Thud. Thud. Thud.

I try to block the blows as Snow did, but my arms are burning and aching. I can't even hold my gloves up anymore. I've become as dazed and weak as Tristan.

I won't give up. I won't be beaten—not by this old man, not in front of everyone.

Roaring, I attack him again with a combination that never loses, my own creation that uses an unexpected overhand right, sandwiched by a jab, a hook, and a cross.

Sure enough, as he shifts to block the overhand right, I'm able to hit him with the cross. The punch is straight and true, direct into his jaw. A punishing blow that should knock him on his ass.

It does…nothing. Absolutely nothing. It's like he can't even feel it.

It evokes no anger in him, no pain. I may as well not even exist.

Snow responds by hitting me in the face two, three, four times in quick succession. The last punch feels like an explosion in my head, like he shoved a stick of dynamite in my mouth and lit the fuse. I fall straight backward.

I sink all the way through the mats, down, down, into the blackness of the earth.

Faintly, a low voice murmurs, "Class dismissed."

I hear shuffling feet.

No jeers, no exclamations, not even from Vanya.

They're all as shocked as I am.

Or as shocked as I was when I still had conscious thought.

I drift in darkness until I feel something cold pressed against my face.

Snow has hauled me to my feet and sat me on a stack of mats. He presses a bag of ice against the swollen left side of my face.

His broad face swims into view. Unmarked by any punch from me, bearing only the scars of better men.

His blue eyes stare into mine. Still clear and hard as ice but not cold. Instead, I see something far worse in them, something more painful.

I see pity.

"I'm not your enemy," Snow says.

"Then I'd hate to see what you do to people you don't like," I mumble through bruised lips.

Snow chuckles.

"You show promise, Dean. You're bold. Your technique is reasonably good."

I bristle. Even after that humiliating defeat, I deserve better praise.

"But you will never learn to conquer your opponent if you can't conquer yourself."

"There's no one more disciplined than me," I retort. "I never miss a day of training. Never eat one fucking thing I shouldn't. I hone the mind and the body."

"And what about this?" Snow says, laying one heavy, calloused hand on my chest.

I shake it off, irritated by his presumption.

He doesn't know me. He doesn't know anything about me. What the fuck is he even talking about? A lot of spiritualistic nonsense.

"I *will* be the best fighter at this school!" I inform him. "And that includes you. By graduation day—"

"I'm only staying a year." Snow stands up. "I came here as a favor to the chancellor."

"To teach us to box?"

"Actually, he needed a new medic," Snow chuckles. "Herman Cross retired. My wife, Sasha, is a doctor. She agreed to fill in for a year until they could find someone permanent. I'm just tagging along."

"Oh," I say, not sure how to respond. I hadn't imagined Snow having a wife and possibly children. He hardly seemed human before this moment.

"Keep ice on that face," Snow says, standing up. "I'll see you on Wednesday."

CHAPTER 4
CAT

I DON'T KNOW HOW IN THE FUCK I'M GOING TO SURVIVE TWO MORE years at Kingmakers with Dean if he couldn't wait until we got to the island to start harassing me.

I don't understand why he even wants to.

I mean, I know I embarrassed him, catching him in an unguarded moment. But at the end of the day, he's one of the most skilled and feared students at the school, while I'm a fucking nobody. If he weren't keeping an eye out for me, he probably never would have noticed me again for the rest of our lives.

I've never done anything dramatic or surprising in my whole damn life. Except the one thing Dean happened to see.

God, what a comedy of errors. The fucking luck I have...

Why, why, why did it have to be Dean who saw me? If it were anybody else, they wouldn't have thought two things about it.

Only Dean already had a grudge against me.

Only Dean is conniving enough to put the pieces together.

This man has been living in my head rent-free all summer long when I should have been enjoying my first trip to America—two uninterrupted, blissful months in which the Griffins were overwhelmingly kind to me, including Caleb Griffin, Miles's little brother, who was so friendly and attentive that Zoe thought he had a puppy-love crush.

I don't think that was the case. Like Miles, Caleb just likes to prove himself. In this case, he wanted to prove what a good host he could be.

Still, we're friends now, and I'm glad Caleb will be coming to Kingmakers next year.

I shouldn't have been fretting over Dean the whole summer, yet I could hardly think of anything else. He popped into my head a hundred times a day. He haunted my nightmares.

But my worst dreams featured Rocco Prince.

I'll never forget the look of pure hatred on his face as the noose tightened around his wrist, jerking him forward. I'll never forget the way his knife sliced down at me, missing my face by millimeters, before he was jerked over the parapet.

And then the long, strangled howl as he tumbled down…

And the birds. The fucking birds.

As we returned from the Quartum Bellum, I saw that flock of gulls wheeling and circling over where Rocco had fallen, screeching like they were screaming my guilt to everyone around. Tattling on me.

They dove down to the rocks, squabbling and fighting as they tore his body apart. Then they rose up in the air again, their beaks stained with blood.

I can hardly hear the sound of a gull without vomiting all over again. Their cry is a constant reminder of what I did. An accusation and a threat. Proof that what I thought could be hidden was instead immediately discovered in a way I never would have guessed.

I rip a comb through my damp curls, trying to clear my head.

I'm in the shared bathroom of the undercroft, the air full of steam from the students taking their early morning showers.

I found Dean crying in a bathroom very much like this.

Why was he so upset that day?

Why did the death of Ozzy's mother strike him so hard?

I don't understand Dean Yenin. I don't understand why he's so full of rage and bitterness.

God, my head is a jumble of thoughts, none of them pleasant.

Rakel comes to stand at the mirror next to mine, her short, choppy hair already drying and a towel wrapped around her body. Her face looks blank without her makeup, as if she hasn't put on her personality for the day.

"What's wrong?" she asks me.

"Nothing," I say.

"You look stressed."

"I'm fine."

There it is again. Nobody is ever actually fine.

I watch Rakel arrange her collection of brushes and pots, then begin the delicate process of painting her face.

Anna Wilk tends toward classic goth makeup, but Rakel's oeuvre is much more varied. Some days, she looks vampiric with dark red lipstick and chalk-white cheeks. Others, she looks consumptive with pink all around her eyes and dark shadows under her cheekbones. And some days, like today, she resembles a wicked fairy with thick black eyeliner, two-inch lashes, and shades of sparkly purple all over her eyelids, cheeks, and even the tip of her nose.

She finishes her look with three different nose rings, a spiked eyebrow stud, and a serpentine cuff that winds up her ear.

"You're an artist," I tell her.

Rakel smiles. "Thank you," she says. "That actually means something, coming from you."

"I filled half my sketchbook this summer," I say, with a glimmer of happiness. "The Bean, the Willis Tower, the Ferris wheel... Now I'll never forget what I saw in Chicago."

"You should show me after class."

I look at my own decidedly less-interesting reflection in the mirror.

I've never dressed with much panache. I'm so petite that my clothes swim on me. Half the time, I look like a kid playing dress-up. My hair is a mess of black curls. My face...cute, I suppose, but nowhere near as stunning as Zoe's. She's the beautiful one. I've always just been the kid sister.

"Could I borrow a little makeup?" I ask Rakel.

"Sure." She shrugs.

I stare at the rainbow array of products, having no actual idea what I'm doing.

Rakel laughs. "You want some help?"

"Yes, please," I say gratefully. "I mean…I'm not trying to dazzle anybody. I just want to spice my face up a little."

Rakel surveys my features with a professional objectivity.

"Your eyes are your best feature," she pronounces. "And we'll keep your freckles."

She starts painting my face.

I watch in the mirror to see what she does.

It really is like painting, in the sense that she outlines and shades the contours of my face just as you would paint a portrait to show depth and perspective.

I'm mildly frightened to have those pointed nails so close to my eyeballs, but Rakel works with surprising gentleness. The brushes and powders and creams feel quite lovely against my skin.

Rakel uses shades of plum, peach, and golden brown that match my Mediterranean coloring nicely. When she's finished, I look older. Confident and glamorous. But still myself, not a wicked fairy.

"That's really good!" I say, thoroughly impressed.

Rakel is pleased. "I watch a lot of tutorials."

The fresh look cheers me up a little. I'd rather be glamorous Cat. She'd know how to keep out of trouble and how to stand up to Dean without him torpedoing her entire life.

With new energy, Rakel and I return to our room to change into our uniforms.

I kept all the same clothes from last year, yet as I pull on my skirt, I notice one tiny inch of bare flesh between the top of my knee socks and the bottom of the pleats.

"Look at that!" I say to Rakel. "I must have grown. A bit at least."

"Wow," she says mockingly. "Keep it up, and you might hit five two."

"You're not tall either!"

"Compared to you, I'm Shaquille O'Neal."

I scowl at her. "Now I don't know if I should give you your present. But you did do my makeup pretty nice…"

"What present? What is it?" Rakel demands, eyes bright with curiosity.

I dig through my half-unpacked suitcase, finding the painting I made for her, carefully backed with cardboard and wrapped with paper so it wouldn't crumple or flake on the journey over.

Rakel rips off the brown paper wrapping, eager but careful.

"Oh!" she gasps, face alight. She turns the painting so I can see it, as if I don't already know what's on the canvas. "I'll hang it up on the wall."

"That's why I made it for you," I say. "So we'll have a little life down here."

Rakel snorts. The album cover I painted for her is the furthest thing from "life" in the sense that it depicts a Daliesque sphere of melting skulls, but it's from Rakel's favorite band, so I knew it would make her happy.

"This is a good gift," she says in her honest and unsentimental way.

I'm sure she would have told me it was shit if she didn't like it. Which is nice, because now I know for certain that I did a good job.

"Come on," I say. "We better hurry, or we won't have time for breakfast before class."

Rakel and I hustle up the stairs to the ground level, dazzled as always by the brilliant burst of morning sunshine after the soft golden lamplight of the undercroft.

We only have a few minutes to stuff ourselves with bacon and coffee before we have to run across campus to the keep.

Kingmakers is so large and sprawling that I could stay fit just by sprinting from class to class. Unfortunately for me, that's not nearly the only exercise I get. My schedule includes grueling conditioning sessions, combat classes, and classes that aren't meant to be particularly taxing, like Marksmanship and Environmental Adaptation, but that strain my limits all the same because I'm so damn small.

At least I know what to expect this year. I packed plenty of Band-Aids for all the blisters that will blossom on my palms and feet, and I'm already well acquainted with the location of the infirmary and the ice dispensers in the dining hall.

Rakel and I find our Interrogation class on the second floor of the keep easily enough. I spread my notebooks and pens out across my desk, determined to take notes on every single word that comes out of Professor Penmark's mouth. I want to score well on my exams. In my freshman year, I was simply trying to survive. This year, I'd like to find out if I might just have what it takes to run with the rest of the mafiosi.

Professor Penmark slouches into the classroom in his creepy, silent way. He looks even thinner than last year, his pallid skin stretched tight over his bones, his many tattoos a jumble of colorless shapes. He has a long, unsmiling face and dark eyes without any glimmer of life, like a dead thing dug up from the ground.

I always found him off-putting. Now I despise him.

I'll never forget how he dragged the chained-up Ozzy across the floor of the grand hall without a hint of sympathy in those black eyes. I almost think he enjoyed it.

I *know* he enjoys teaching the Torture Techniques class. He forces us to practice nonlethal torments on our fellow students, including electrocution, stress positions, pressure points, and dryboarding. If we don't comply with enough enthusiasm—a.k.a. sadism—then he "demonstrates" the procedures himself.

Luckily, today's Interrogation class involves only psychological techniques.

We've already covered ego fragmentation and learned helplessness. Now Professor Penmark lectures us on deception.

"Information is useless if you cannot tell if it is true or false," he says in his thin tenor. "How do you know if your subject is lying?"

His dark eyes crawl over us as we sit captive behind our desks.

"Lack of eye contact," Joss Burmingham guesses. His room is across the hall from mine, but we've never spoken because I've never seen him outside class not wearing headphones with the volume turned all the way up. He and Rakel must be in a competition to see who can go deaf first.

"No, too *much* eye contact," Lola Fischer contradicts him.

Dixie Davis gives Lola an approving nod. The two girls share the room next to mine. They're both from Biloxi, Mississippi, and were already best friends before they came to Kingmakers.

"Correct," Professor Penmark says. "And also incorrect."

Lola's smirk of satisfaction fades away as quickly as it arose. She scowls at the professor, as confused as everyone else in the room.

"Try again," the professor says, enjoying our discomfort.

"Vague details?" Charlotte King ventures.

"Stuttering?" Jacob Weiss says.

Professor Penmark's flat stare gives nothing away. I would never know if he were lying or being truthful. The only thing I can tell about this man is that he enjoys inflicting pain. Which is why I'm sure he was a very effective debt collector for the Las Vegas mob. You can't get money from a dead man. But you can make a man wish he were dead…

"Subjects can display a lack or an excess of any particular behavior when lying," the professor informs us. "They may sit still to avoid physical tells. Or they may squirm under your gaze. They may babble and include far too many details in their fictional narrative. Or they might speak in sentence fragments and fail to provide details when pressed. You cannot determine whether a subject is truthful or deceptive unless you first establish a baseline. Which is why you must ask questions to which you already know the answer, then observe the subject's responses when they answer correctly as well as when they obfuscate."

I scribble away in my notebook, trying to capture every tip. I understood what the professor said, but it's much easier said than done. Especially in real life, without time to think or plan.

"I need two volunteers," Professor Penmark says.

No one raises their hand. When Professor Penmark asks for a volunteer, nothing pleasant ever follows.

"Lola." The professor smiles, baring his crowded teeth. "Why don't you come to the front of the class."

Lola rises from her chair, wary but determined not to show a hint of nerves. She marches to the front of the room, her plaid skirt swishing around her long, shapely legs. Carter Ross gives a wolf whistle, and Lola smiles as she spins to face us, making the skirt flare out almost high enough to show her underwear before it settles in place once more.

"Who else…?" Professor Penmark muses, looking over each of us in turn, enjoying the way most of the students refuse to meet his eyes. I can't tell whether I'd be better served to avoid him or boldly stare back. I go for the latter.

"Cat!" the professor barks. "Front of the class."

Wrong choice.

I slip out of my seat, stumbling over my own feet before hurrying up to join Lola. Nobody whistles for me. A couple of students snicker until Rakel turns around and glares them into silence.

Lola faces me, knowing we'll probably have to compete in some way. She's smiling, pleased that she'll only have to beat me and not somebody intimidating.

Lola is intimidating. Her big blue eyes and soft southern accent don't fool me for a second. She's a killer.

Professor Penmark hands us each a plain envelope.

"Read your objective. Don't show your opponent," he says.

I crack my envelope, then scan the card within. The single sentence reads: *Find out if their father has ever been in prison.*

How in the hell am I supposed to figure that out in a subtle way?

"Each of you has a piece of information you must extract from your subject," Professor Penmark says. "You must answer your opponent's questions, but you are allowed to lie if you wish. When you think you've captured the intelligence, raise your hand."

Lola purses her full pink lips as she reads her own card. She looks up at me, smiling with anticipation.

I'm sweating.

From what I've learned so far in our Interrogation classes, the usual methods to get someone to disclose information are threats, appeals to conscience, and incentives. It will be hard for me to apply any of those techniques against Lola.

Despite rooming right next to each other, I don't know much about her. Only that she's beautiful and she knows it. She takes great care with her appearance, waves of caramel-colored hair lying over her shoulders, subtle gold jewelry, and the wardrobe of a Manhattan socialite. Even on the island, she's somehow managed to procure a professional-level manicure.

It's curious too that she embraces this look of doll-like femininity when the rest of the Dixie Mafia are a rough, countrified bunch, partial to filthy, ripped jeans, cowboy boots, and necklaces of gator teeth. This includes Lola's right-hand woman Dixie Davis, who, with her wild mane of ginger-colored hair, freckles like paint spatters, and harsh voice, is as crass and unkempt as Lola is refined.

What I infer from this is that Lola cares very much about controlling how other people perceive her. She's prideful and vain. Justifiably so, perhaps. But that may be her weak spot.

Is Lola's objective the same as mine? Is she going to ask about my father? Maybe her question is completely different.

God, this is brain-bending. I can't be sneaky in five different ways at once.

Should I start asking about her family? Is that too obvious? What if she lies? Will I be able to tell?

"Don't be nervous, Cat," Lola says, giving me a smile that shows all her gleaming white teeth. "We're just having a friendly conversation."

"Right," I murmur. "It should be fun."

"You're from Spain, aren't you?" she says, resting a hand casually on her hip and cocking her head at me.

I'm already tensing up, thinking I shouldn't answer any questions honestly. But Lola already knows the answer to that, and it wouldn't be the objective on her card because it's common knowledge.

"Yes," I say carefully. "I'm from Barcelona. And you're from Biloxi."

"That's right," Lola says lightly.

I suppose we both have a baseline for honest answers now.

"Any siblings?" I ask her, hoping to ease around to the topic of parents.

"Just me," Lola says, still smiling.

Now that one's a little trickier. Lola certainly has the pampered look and confidence of an only child, but she's not in the Heirs division. So either her father isn't a boss, which would be strange considering her standing among the rest of the Dixie Mafia, or he has a different successor in mind—an uncle or older sibling of Lola's.

Fuck, I don't know which it is. I don't think I'm very good at this.

"I know you have a sister," Lola says softly. "Zoe... She's gorgeous, isn't she? It's hard to be the ugly sister."

Carter Ross snickers from the front row of desks.

I can feel the dozens of eyes watching us, none more than Professor Penmark, who feeds off my discomfort and Lola's malice like a psychic vampire.

The gloves are coming off—Lola took that shot at me to stoke my emotions. She wants me upset and incautious.

"I always thought Zoe was the prettiest girl at our school," I reply calmly.

It's a subtler jab than Lola's and more effective. I'm used to being second to Zoe. Lola doesn't want to be second to anyone. I see the slight narrowing of her eyes—she didn't like that at all.

"Zoe ran off with Miles Griffin, didn't she?" Lola persists. "That's quite the upgrade from Rocco."

My hands twitch involuntarily. I really don't want Lola to pursue that line of questioning. Her card can't possibly have something on it about Rocco Prince, can it?

Lola sees me flinch. She pounces like a cat on a mouse. "You aren't jealous, are you? Zoe's living the dream in LA, and you don't even have a boyfriend yet?"

There it is.

I think I know her objective.

"I've had plenty of boyfriends," I lie.

Lola giggles, not believing me for a second.

"Plenty of boyfriends?" She scoffs. "Come on, Cat. You're going to have to do better than that."

I'm going to have to switch tactics, because if Lola's objective is to suss out my sexual history, she's going to figure out that I'm a virgin in two seconds flat.

It's time to go on the offensive.

"Carter Ross might think you're dressing up for him," I say to Lola, "but your aesthetic has daddy's girl all over it. That's who it's really for, isn't it? The pink blush, the strawberry lip gloss… I bet if I checked that gold locket you're wearing, it's a gift from dear old Dad."

Lola's big blue eyes narrow into slits. I've already learned that particular tell—it means I hit her in a sensitive spot.

No time to fuck around. I have to press the advantage.

"You don't have any siblings, yet you're not an Heir. Which means no matter how hard you've tried to please Daddy, he hasn't named you as his successor."

The color rises in Lola's cheeks. She hasn't answered back.

I'm making wild assumptions, one after another, but I think I'm right.

"Is it plain old sexism? Did you fuck up somehow? Or maybe he just doesn't know you well enough after his time away? He still sees you as his little baby. Maybe if you try really, really hard, you can prove you're all grown-up now…"

"You have no fucking idea what you're talking about," Lola snarls at me.

That's not a denial.

In fact, that's what people say when the facts are correct but they don't like your interpretation.

I raise my hand.

"You think you have the intel?" Professor Penmark inquires.

"Yes," I say. "Lola's father was in prison."

Lola's mouth drops open. Her whole face is now the color of Dixie's hair.

"You filthy little cunt!" she shrieks.

Before she can slap my head off my shoulders, Professor Penmark steps smoothly between us, plucking Lola's card out of her hands. I can just make out the single typed sentence:

Find out what age they had their first kiss.

I'm deeply relieved that Lola failed to reach her objective. I'd rather jump out the second-story window than have the entire class find out that I've never been kissed, not once in my life.

My satisfaction ebbs away when I catch sight of Lola's shaking hands and livid face. I just embarrassed her in front of the whole class. And she's not exactly the forgiving type.

"Not bad," Professor Penmark tells me. "You didn't get verbal confirmation from the subject, but implied affirmation can be useful."

It's the first time I've ever received a compliment from Professor Penmark. I can't say I enjoy it—it's quite unpleasant having him stand this close to me, looking into my face with those dead black eyes.

"Thanks," I mutter, hurrying back to my seat.

I can practically hear Lola fuming behind me. Waves of loathing radiate in my direction.

Oblivious or just not giving a shit, Rakel says, "Nice job! I thought you were fucked for sure."

"Thanks for the vote of confidence."

"I was betting on you," Joss Burmingham says, leaning across his desk to give me a little fist bump.

Joss has never spoken to me before. I've got to admit, it feels good to earn some admiration outside our programming classes.

Until Lola hisses at me, "You think that was clever?"

"It's just an exercise," I say. "No hard feelings."

"Get fucked!" Lola barks, only quieting down when Professor Penmark shoots her a look telling her to pipe it so he can continue with his lecture.

I pass the rest of class wondering if I should have just answered Lola's questions. I could have let her win. It would have been easier.

The other half of me rebels against that idea.

Why does Lola get to be aggressive and cruel and I just have to roll over and take it?

I saw my opening, and I went for it.

Was it a little mean?

Maybe. But that's why we're here—to learn how to get what we want.

And in that moment, I wanted to win.

Class ends, and Rakel and I gather up our bags.

Dixie Davis slams into me as she passes, almost dislocating my shoulder.

"Watch it," she says.

Lola tosses her hair over her shoulder, still fuming.

"Gonna hold on to that one, isn't she?" Rakel says, watching them stalk off down the hall.

"Apparently," I sigh.

"Well, good thing we only have pretty much every single class with them," Rakel laughs, giving me a friendly punch on the very same shoulder Dixie just tried to destroy.

I follow Rakel down the stairs, already losing any sense of pleasure earned by my win.

Fuck me. I've gone and made another enemy.

Why can I not go five goddamned minutes without getting myself in trouble?

I'm so consumed by my own thoughts that I run right into Dean Yenin waiting for me outside the keep.

I know he's waiting for me by the way he grabs the front of my shirt and lifts me up off my feet, totally unsurprised by my appearance.

"Watch where you're going, *Cat*," he hisses into my face.

"Let go of her," Rakel says.

"Fuck off, Black Death," Dean snarls at her.

"Eat shit, Zack Morris," Rakel sneers back at him.

"Rakel!" I gasp, half choked by Dean's grip on my collar. "Just... go on without me."

She stares at me like I'm speaking Swahili.

"Please!" I wheeze. "Just go."

She looks between Dean and me for several seconds. Then she narrows her eyes and says, "Fine. If that's what you want." She heads off to the dining hall without me.

Dean releases his grip on my shirt so I can breathe again.

"That's better," he says softly.

Actually, I'm sure it's about to get worse.

Dean looks anything but cheerful. His face is heavily bruised on the left side. He's got a cut on that cheek and a nasty black eye, the purplish marks especially dire against his fair skin. He looks like an angel stripped of his wings and fallen all the way to earth.

"What happened?" I say without thinking.

Wrong question. Dean's top lip pulls up in the snarl that I've quickly come to recognize as the harbinger of his most intense aggression.

"Never mind that," he growls. "Where the *fuck* have you been all day?"

"Breakfast. And class," I stammer.

"Why weren't you waiting for me outside the Octagon Tower this morning?"

"I... Why would I be?"

"Because you're my slave, Cat," Dean says in a tone of stating the obvious. "What good are you to me in the dining hall and at class?"

"But...I have to go to class," I squeak.

"Yes, you do. And you'll walk from class to class with me. Carrying my books. Every single day."

"*What?*"

"You heard me."

Dean's eyes are fixed on mine, steady and unblinking. His pupils are so large that the irises comprise barely more than a thin halo of violet.

"Why do you... I mean, okay," I say, knowing better than to argue.

"You mean, 'Yes, sir,'" Dean corrects me.

My cheeks flame, and I feel an intense impulse to tell him to fuck off. But that would be suicidal.

"Yes, *sir*," I hiss through gritted teeth.

"Good girl," Dean says softly.

His low purr sends a thrill through my body.

Am I completely fucked in the head that I feel a flush of warmth at his approval? Maybe it's just relief that he might not have me murdered in the immediate future.

His smile of satisfaction quickly turns to a scowl.

He seizes my chin in a steel grip.

"What the fuck is on your face?" he demands.

"Makeup," I say, trying to twist my chin out of his grasp.

He pinches it all the harder.

"I hate it," he hisses. "Wash it off."

"What? No, I just—"

"Clean that shit off your face," he barks. "Do it now, then get your ass over to the dining hall."

He lets go of me so abruptly that I stumble back.

I want to scream with frustration at this fucking maniac and his ridiculous demands. But I can't do it. I can't say one damn word to him, and he knows it. All I can do is spin on my heel and march off toward the bathrooms in the keep, where I wash all Rakel's expertly applied makeup off my face.

What the fuck is his problem?

Since when does he hate makeup?

Anna Wilk wears a shit ton of product on her face, and it never seemed to bother him any.

I don't think he hates makeup at all. He just relishes my misery.

With my face freshly pink and shiny, I walk back to the dining hall, dragging my feet the whole way.

I don't want to go in there.

I don't want to experience whatever new humiliation Dean has been dreaming up.

But I'm hungry. So I join the line of students waiting for their portion of pesto chicken pasta, then I carry my tray toward the tables.

I see Leo, Anna, Chay, and Ares already eating, laughing together at some joke. They look so lighthearted and comfortable. God, I wish I could join them.

I can feel Dean's cold stare fixed on me. When I turn to meet his eyes, he jerks his head toward the empty seat he's saved right next to his own.

Please, God, let the ground swallow me whole.

I feel like the entire hall of students is staring at me as I turn toward Dean's table.

Anna has spotted me. She calls out, "Cat!" thinking I didn't see her. I have to give her an awkward shrug before resuming my hateful journey over to Dean.

Bram Van Der Berg, Valon Hoxha, Pasha Tsaplin, and Motya Chornovil watch me approach, silent and unsmiling. I dislike every one of them. They're a bunch of spiteful bullies who delight in tormenting weaker students. I feel like I'm voluntarily lowering myself into a den of vipers as I drop down into the only empty seat at their table.

If they're vipers, then Dean is the king cobra. He strikes with lightning speed the moment my ass touches the seat.

"Where's my milk?" he demands.

"I didn't know you wanted milk," I mutter.

"Go get it. Now."

Biting back the retort I'd like to give him, I stand once more.

Valon sniggers.

"Get me a milk too," he says.

"You don't give the orders," Dean rebukes him, his tone as sharp as a slap. It smacks the smile right off Valon's face, and he sulks instead.

"She's getting up anyway," he grouses.

Dean ignores him. He wants to enjoy watching me cross the dining hall once more so I can retrieve his fucking milk.

I walk as quickly as I can to get this over with, grabbing the first frosty glass bottle of milk I see and carrying it back to him, slamming it down just a little too hard in front of him.

"There you go, Your Majesty," I say.

My face is flaming as I sit down once more.

"I want grapes too," Dean says.

I turn to stare at him, thoroughly incensed.

"Why didn't you tell me when I—"

It only takes one look in those crazed eyes to shut my mouth. Dean is fully invested in this game, and that means he's only too happy to deal out consequences if I disobey. Silently, I stand once more to walk back over to the food.

Dean's friends watch this parade with avid interest. I'm quite sure that none of them know how Dean acquired his own personal servant, and their curiosity is mixed with envy. For a bunch of power-hungry douchebags, nothing could be more appealing than a girl forced to jump to attention every time they snap their fingers.

I seize a bundle of purple grapes, grown in the vineyards outside the castle grounds, and I ferry them back to Dean like an obedient little waitress. I plop them down next to the milk and resume my seat, praying he doesn't have any other cravings.

"Feed them to me," Dean orders.

I stare at him in disbelief. "You want me to feed you grapes?"

"That's right," he smirks.

I hope he chokes on these fucking grapes. I'd like to ram them right down his throat.

Instead, I pluck off one dusky purple orb and hold it out to him. Dean's full lips part as he opens his mouth.

I place the grape on his tongue. As I pull my hand back, my fingers graze his lower lip. A shiver runs down my spine.

I'm certain Dean sees me twitch. He doesn't miss a thing.

He bites down hard on the grape, crushing it in his mouth.

"Very good," he says in that deathly low voice.

Every boy at the table is staring like they're watching a peep show.

"What else can you make her do?" Pasha whispers.

I'm sure Dean's friends aren't the only ones watching this mortifying display. I don't dare look over at Anna's table. She must think I've morphed into a masochist in the few short weeks since Chicago.

The problem is that if I can't look at Anna and I can't look at Dean's leering friends, the only place left to fix my eyes is on Dean himself.

Strangely, his injuries, the marks of his mortality, only make Dean seem all the more inhuman because he refuses to acknowledge them. Refuses to be cowed or humbled.

I watched Dean win that boxing tournament almost unscathed. I'd hate to meet the man who actually landed a blow on him.

"Another," he says, his eyes drilling into mine.

I pluck another grape off the stem, lifting it to his lips.

This time, his tongue slides against the ball of my thumb as he takes it from my fingers. That instant of wet, hot friction sends a flushing warmth through my whole body. I know my face is bright red. I know I'm squirming in my seat. I don't understand how my body can betray me like this when *I fucking hate Dean!*

How can I loathe someone so much yet I can't take my eyes off him? I've never been so present. I see the tiny golden hairs on Dean's skin, the minute lines on his perfectly shaped lips, the edges of his strong, white teeth. I feel his breath on my fingertips, warm from his lungs and faintly scented grape.

"That's enough," Dean says softly. "Clear my dishes away."

I'm happy to clear his dishes, just to get away from him and the encircling mass of the other four boys, who have leaned over the table so they can watch our every movement. Bram Van Der Berg frowns suspiciously, his vertical scar and narrowed eye forming a shape like the crosshairs of a trigger pointed directly at me.

Why does Dean have to be so public about this? People are going to ask questions.

He doesn't give a fuck. It's the brazenness that excites him.

I drop the dishes off with the kitchen staff, not having eaten a single bite of food. Dammit, now I really am starving.

Too late. Dean appears at my side, already carrying my book bag. He thrusts it into my hands, and then as soon as I sling it over my shoulder, he dumps his own armful of books on me.

"Carry those," he orders, tossing back his shock of white-blond hair.

"Fine," I mutter, staggering under the weight of the books.

I'm seething with fury, and it's only the first day of this treatment.

I'm not going to make it through the school year. I'm just not.

I'm going to snap and strangle Dean, and then he's going to rat me out to the chancellor, and they'll reopen the investigation into Rocco's death, and they'll find evidence that it was me because I wasn't that fucking sneaky. I know there's some mistake, some piece of evidence I missed that will tie me to his death as soon as Luther Hugo knows where to look.

I stalk alongside Dean, arms burning under the combined weight of his books and mine.

Once again, I'm a little shadow, stuck to the side of a smarter, stronger person.

Only this time, it's not my lovely sister I'm trailing.

I'm bound to the devil instead.

CHAPTER 5
DEAN

MY CONTROL OVER CAT ROMERO IS AN APHRODISIAC TO WHICH I am quickly becoming addicted. Every morning, my heart rate quickens as I descend the stairs of the Octagon Tower, knowing she'll be waiting there for me, her big dark eyes taking up half the space of her face, and her arms wrapped tight around her petite frame.

I've spent all night long imagining how I'm going to order her around. Picturing that indignant pink flush that suffuses her cheeks, drowning out her freckles, and the way her body trembles with barely contained fury as she's forced to stuff down the retorts she'd so sorely love to return in favor of simply obeying.

She hates it, yet she has to do it.

And that is indescribably delicious to me.

All my life, I've been fucked over. My father bitter and maimed, spiraling into claustrophobic rages until he drove my mother away. My mother fleeing when I was only ten years old, abandoning me to my father's madness. The remnants of our once-proud family sidelined by the Bratva, while those who betrayed us flourished in Chicago.

Then I came to Kingmakers, only to watch the one girl I'd ever desired reject me for my worst enemy, my own fucking golden-boy cousin who lives the life I should have had.

Nothing has ever gone right for me.

Until now.

Cat is a gift that fell into my lap.

And nothing and no one can take her from me—because I know her secret. I hold her life in my hands. As long as she and I are the only two people who know what she did to Rocco Prince, I'm free to torment her to my heart's content.

God, how I love it.

I love the way she serves me, resentful but submissive. I love the way Bram and the others are racking their brains, dying to know why this girl follows after me like an obedient puppy. And most of all, I love the way it's driving Anna Wilk and Leo Gallo crazy because they can't comprehend why Cat leaves the shelter of their protection to return to me again and again.

Miles Griffin would have figured it out. But he's six thousand miles away in Los Angeles, along with Cat's sister. Cat is all alone, completely at my mercy.

I'm slowly expanding my control over her.

Testing her.

I tell her what to wear each day and how to wear it. I like her green skirts the best, and her thick black knee socks that highlight her innocence. Her hair has grown longer since last year, the wild curls down below her shoulders. I tell her when to put it up in a ponytail and when to hold it back from her face with a band.

She's my own personal doll that I can dress to my tastes.

I know it infuriates her. My demands are arbitrary and capricious. And that's exactly what I enjoy—never letting her get comfortable. Never letting her know what's coming next.

I spend a lot of time watching my little pet. I've come to know every freckle on those delicate cheeks. Every thick, black lash on those wide-set eyes.

Cat Romero is pretty.

Her beauty isn't as obvious as her sister's.

But the more I see of Cat, the more I begin to fixate on the details of her person. Her smooth, tan skin and her perfectly shaped hands, like a suit of armor made in miniature to show the craftsmanship. Her pale pink lips, as heart-shaped as her face. Her sharp white teeth that flash into view when she dares to snarl at me.

I wondered if I would get tired of this game, but the more I play with her, the more I want.

My classes seem interminable because I'd much rather be greeting her outside the door, her face flushed and sweating because she had to run across campus from her class to mine.

It amuses me to see her struggle to carry my books. She's so small that she can hardly bear a burden that I could lift with two fingers. I could hoist up all of Cat with one hand. My arm itches to do it. I remember the times I've picked her up right off her feet, the sense of complete control it gave me to lift her and hold her like she really were just a tiny kitten dangling from my jaws.

I've been making her write my papers for me. I could easily do it myself, but it's tedious to write out the paragraphs by hand. I get a perverse pleasure watching her pause between sentences, shaking out her cramped fingers. I've spent hours watching her work, tilted back in my chair while she sits on the other side of the library table, her delicate neck bent over the page, her dark curls covering her angry expression.

I want to push her further. I'm craving it.

I'm consumed with dark fantasies of what I could make Cat do...

Meanwhile, I've returned to Snow's boxing class.

That Wednesday after I tried to fight him with humiliating results, I entered the armory gym with shoulders back, head held high. I was daring the other students to say one fucking word about that fight. I planned to put them in their place before the sentence left their lips.

But Snow was already standing in place on the mats, silencing even Vanya Antonov with his formidable bulk.

He gave us a lesson on footwork, then split us up once more to practice.

This time, he paired me with Kade Petrov.

I had to swallow my irritation, knowing that he was testing me to see if I would use excessive force against a freshman again.

I certainly was tempted. Kade was only a little better than Tristan Turgenev—quick and eager but sloppy, undisciplined. He'd keep his head for a couple of rounds, then get overconfident, leaving himself wide open.

I popped him a few times as a reminder, but under the watchful eye of Snow, I was careful not to exceed the bounds of the exercise.

"*Zaebis*, you're good," Kade said admiringly.

"You could be too if you kept your focus," I muttered.

"How long have you been boxing?" he asked me.

I shrugged. "All my life."

I learned how to fight as soon as the boys at school got a look at my father. They already mocked me for my accent—I spoke English too much at home with my mother. They called my father a monster and my mother an American whore. I fought three, four, five of them at once, coming home every day with bloody noses and blackened eyes, until I learned to do enough damage to shut their fucking mouths. Some of those boys became my friends. Some fought me in the underground matches years later.

One is at Kingmakers with me now—Pasha Tsaplin. He's Bratva too, though his father is a drunken disgrace. He only got into school on the strength of Danyl's recommendation, same as me. He owes Danyl four years' service for that favor. I suppose I got off lucky with only two.

"My brother taught me to box," Kade said.

"Adrik is famous at Kingmakers," I said.

"I know," Kade sighed.

I supposed it was a lot to live up to. But that's the nature of our world—you must surpass the achievements of your father, your grandfather, and your great-grandfather. That is empire building.

After class, Snow clapped me on the shoulder.

"You did well today," he told me.

"You mean I was a better babysitter," I snorted.

"If you can't teach something, then you don't know it very well yourself," Snow said.

I nodded, struggling against my residual resentment over how easily he'd beaten me.

As he was about to tidy up the gym, I burst out, "What was it like fighting Rueben Hagler?"

Snow turned back, cocking one graying eyebrow.

"It was one of the hardest fights of my life," he said, his gravelly voice heavy with exhaustion just from the memory of it. "Hagler was known as an intelligent and adaptable boxer. No matter how you tried to change your strategy in the fight, he would match it. I was past my peak at that point. Defending my belt against the up-and-comer—"

"I know!" I interrupted, unable to help myself. "I watched the fight live on TV. My father let me stay up. We were in Moscow, so it was late, almost two o'clock in the morning before it even began."

Snow shook his head. "You must have been a baby…"

"I was four. I did fall asleep, but my father woke me up when you walked out to the ring. Hagler had played his fight song, like boxers always do, but when you entered, the lights went down until there was only this pale white beam on the ring, and no music, only a soft, whispering noise like snowflakes falling down…"

Snow chuckled. "He hated that sound. All the boxers did. They were trying to amp themselves up before the fight. The quiet took the heart right out of them."

"It was mesmerizing," I said, fully immersed in the memory of sitting on my father's lap, heavy with sleep but glued to the television screen where the powerful boxer stepped into the ring, pale and blond just like me, with eyes of glittering ice. I'd never seen anyone more terrifying.

"The fight started out rough. I tried to keep my distance. I had a good reach, and Hagler was known for using lateral movements, working the body. But it was no good. He kept the pressure on me, finding the perfect moment to throw his power blows right to my fuckin' liver. I had never taken hits like that. They bent me over."

Snow winced as if he could still feel the phantom blows.

"God, he was quick too. He frustrated me. He would hit me with a punch, I'd try to return one, and I couldn't fucking find him. It was like he'd turned to smoke. He was damaging me. I couldn't feel all the hits, but I felt myself getting slow and stiff."

I remembered all this. How the older champion had been attacked again and again by the vicious young phenom who had doubled the odds at the bookies. Everyone said Hagler would be the man to take Snow down.

"Did you think he would win?" I asked Snow, watching his face closely to see the truth, whatever he might reply.

"No," Snow said, firm and decisive.

"Not even for a minute?"

"No." Snow shook his head.

"But…how? How did you know you'd come back and win?"

Snow smiled to himself.

"I knew I would win because I promised Sasha I would," he said. "And I've never failed her yet."

I looked at him narrowly, thinking he was joking.

It was a ridiculous answer. No boxer could win a fight just to please his wife.

Snow could see my incredulity.

"A fight isn't won by belief. But once you've done all you can in the gym…" He tapped my chest once more, reminding me of our previous conversation. "The last bit is in here. You'll know that it's true. Once you've found it yourself."

I found it infuriating that Snow kept talking about boxing as if it had anything to do with emotion. Yet I kept thinking over what he said as I ran to my next class.

I'd already missed Cat, who must have gone on without me when I failed to appear. I also missed International Banking, Professor Graves having already shut and locked the door.

I ended up walking through the greenhouses, wondering if there was any truth to Snow's ideology. I had always thought of him as the ultimate machine, fighting with what looked like cold logic and unfailing brilliance. I thought it was his wit and nerves that sustained him.

He was trying to tell me it was…what? Love?

The idea was laughable.

Still, I lingered after class to talk with Snow several more times. And I began to enjoy his sessions more and more as the intricacy and difficulty of the instruction increased.

Now it's become my favorite class.

I think that sentiment is shared among all of us who attend. It's impossible not to respect Snow's methods or his skills, which hardly seem to have dulled since his days as a champion.

Every one of the students is improving in leaps and bounds. None more than me, in my not-so-humble opinion.

I keep working with Kade, who shows flashes of brilliance when he can control his impulsiveness. Sometimes I pair with Jasper Webb, one of the better fighters in the class. He's definitely the quickest, which is useful for honing my reflexes.

Even Vanya Antonov is developing, though he's still sloppy and arrogant. I despise him, and the feeling is clearly mutual. He needles me every chance he gets, trying to goad me into losing my temper in front of Snow. I haven't obliged just yet, but I'm aching to wipe that smug grin off his face.

I know a conflict is coming.

Vanya can't beat me in grades or performance.

So I know he'll be looking for another way to bring me down.

CHAPTER 6
CAT

As I suspected, Lola has been increasingly aggressive since I embarrassed her in that Interrogation class. It was just a stupid exercise, it didn't even count for grades, yet she seems to have taken it as a grave insult. I suppose the insult is that I dared to show her up, when I'm supposed to be a pathetic nobody.

Well, I'm not that pathetic anymore. I'm actually doing pretty damn well in most of my classes.

And I'm not really a nobody anymore either. Of course, I'd prefer to do without the kind of fame that comes from following Dean all over campus like his own personal butler, but it's definitely made me stand out.

Anna and Chay have asked me twenty times if I'm okay and if I want them to tell Dean to fuck off for me. I beg them to leave it alone.

"He's not bothering me," I say, unable to meet the combined weight of the girls' concerned gaze. "We're just…friends."

"Friends?" Chay says in disbelief.

"If he's threatening you…" Anna says.

"No!" I lie. "He's not. We just…uh…like studying together."

It's ridiculously weak, but what can they do? There's no law against making somebody carry your books around.

Lola is less easily appeased. She and Dixie Davis have taken to harassing Rakel and me every chance they get. Which is pretty damn often, considering we sleep within twenty feet of each other.

"What happened to southern hospitality?" Rakel grumbles after Dixie shoulder-checks her so hard that her textbooks and papers scatter halfway across the undercroft.

"I thought you said you were gonna pop her eyeballs out like cherry tomatoes the next time she did that," I tease Rakel.

"Well, they're both so damn tall!" She scowls, furious at the injustice of genetics. "If we had one single bicep between the two of us, that might be helpful."

"I don't know which one's meaner," I say.

"Definitely Lola," Rakel says. "She's the boss of those two, which means that however nasty Dixie can get, Lola must be worse. She's just a touch more subtle."

"Not very subtle," I say, remembering how Lola tore up my paper on banking regulations five minutes after I completed it. "Between the papers she ruins and the ones Dean makes me write, I'm gonna need a double hand transplant before the semester is over."

"Care to tell me *why* you're writing all those papers for the albino asshole?" Rakel inquires for the hundredth time.

"No," I say flatly, "so you can quit asking."

"Well, I wish your master would let you eat lunch with me once in a while. I actually sat with Perry Saunders yesterday. That's how desperate I was."

"Perry's nice!"

"She asked me if witches are real."

"Well?" I say, trying not to laugh. "Are they?"

"I can't believe her father works for the Malina. If he's anything like Perry, I'd expect Marko Moroz to barbecue his kidneys out of pure annoyance."

"He isn't like Perry," I assure Rakel. "I met him once in Monaco. He's more like *my* father. And Perry's mom was a famous equestrienne."

"That explains a lot." Rakel nods. "Perry has major horse-girl energy."

Since Rakel is descended from Vikings, I'm sure pursuits short of pillaging seem rather tame to her.

Rakel's parents run an underground gambling ring in Reykjavík. Once Rakel graduates, she hopes to expand their operations to include online poker and sports betting.

"We'll need the money," she tells me. "My older brother Gunnar thinks he's the emperor of Iceland, and he spends like it too. He's crashed three cars this year."

"Maybe the next one will kill him," I joke, already knowing how much Rakel loathes him.

"We can only hope," she sighs.

I have to part ways with her to hurry up to the dining hall so Dean doesn't give me shit. I just know he's getting bored with the relatively minor torments of making me his Sherpa and busboy. He'll be looking for a reason to punish me.

Indeed, his eyes lock on mine the second I step through the doorway. He snaps his fingers and points at the empty chair he's saved at his side.

I haven't even had a chance to get my food yet.

I stomp over to him, sitting down but immediately saying, "I have to get my lunch."

"No," Dean says coldly. "You have to get here on time if you want to eat."

"I'm *starving*," I hiss.

"Not as hungry as you're going to be if you keep whining."

"What the fuck does that mean?"

"It means I'll tie you up in the ice house and leave you there for a week if you annoy me."

I want to scream with frustration. I am so fucking sick of Dean's petty tyranny.

Not to mention his chicken and peas smell delicious. Almost all the food we eat at Kingmakers comes from the greenhouses or the farms on the island. It's always fresh and expertly prepared by the kitchen staff.

Dean has two rolls on his plate. I reach out to take one. He slaps the back of my hand, quicker than I can blink.

"I'm hungry!" I complain even louder.

"I've got something you can swallow," Valon sneers.

I start to retort, but Dean is too quick.

"Shut your fucking mouth," he barks at Valon.

"What the hell?" Valon says, glowering. "I was just joking."

"Your jokes are stupid."

Dean stares Valon down, daring him to respond.

Valon shifts in his seat but keeps quiet.

"It's tedious bringing your little pet over here if you're not going to share," Bram drawls, leaning back in his chair. He lets his wolfish eyes roam over me, not caring that Dean's face is getting darker by the moment.

"She belongs to me, not you," Dean says. His voice is all the more deadly for how soft it's become.

I sit silent and mutinous next to Dean, feeling like a pressure cooker reaching its boiling point. I know what he's trying to do. He's seeing how far he can push me—escalating from telling me when and what I can eat to not letting me eat at all.

You would think I'd get used to Dean, with all this time spent glued to his side, but you don't get used to him—not at all. He doesn't become less intimidating or less striking. In fact, every day, I notice more of his strange beauty—the soft curve of his lips above the broad, rigid lines of his jaw. The carved muscle of his forearms and his fists like white marble. The swoop of pale blond hair that hangs over his left eyebrow and then the soft, velvety texture at the nape of his neck where the glittering silver hair is shaved short.

And then, most insidious of all, his scent…

Every time Dean shifts in his chair, I smell the subtle amalgam of his signature. Dean's scent is clean and warm like rain-washed earth, with a mild sweetness like vanilla, and then something sharp and enticing, an intense thread of testosterone and aggression that stings in my throat.

It takes me over every time I'm within his sphere of personal space. It makes my head swim. And sometimes later, when I'm down in my room in the undercroft, I'll catch the scent of Dean lingering on my clothes, and my heart begins to race.

I might be noticing it more today because of my hunger.

Jasper Webb has finished loading his tray with food. He's walking toward his usual table that once held Rocco Prince, Wade Dyer, and a dozen other friends.

Now only Dax Volker sits there, sullen and surly.

Rocco and Wade are dead, and the rest of their clique dispersed around the dining hall, welcomed into other groups.

I know it shouldn't bother me, but the sight of all those empty seats at Dax's table makes my guts churn. I look at the blank chair where Rocco used to hold court. It's my fault he's not there anymore. My fault he'll never be there again.

Rocco was a sadist, a monster.

Yet the finality of forever eats at me.

I killed him. I'm a murderer. And I can't seem to feel okay about that, no matter how much he deserved it.

Dean nods to Jasper, inviting him to sit at our table.

"No!" I squeak. "I hate him!"

Too late. Jasper's already sliding into place across from me, fixing me with his pale green stare.

"Hello, Cat," he says.

I shiver. I didn't know that Jasper knew my name. I suppose it makes sense—he must have been on the receiving end of all Rocco's sadistic plans for my sister.

Jasper held my sister down while Rocco threatened to cut out her eye. He was part of the fight that resulted in Wade's death and the execution of Ozzy's mother. I hate him more than anyone at this table. Maybe even more than Dean.

"Don't talk to me, you fucking animal," I hiss at him across the table.

"Oooh," Valon chortles, mocking me. "Watch out, Jasper. Kitty's got claws."

"I don't hold a grudge against you," Jasper informs me with cold insouciance.

"Oh, you don't have a grudge against *me*?" I scoff. "How benevolent. Unfortunately, *I* have a bit of a grudge against *you* for torturing my sister for that lunatic Rocco!"

"Quiet," Dean says to me, placing a warning hand on my thigh. His touch makes me shiver, even through the thick material of my skirt.

It won't stop me. Dean may have decided that Jasper is his friend and welcome at this table, but I disagree.

"You disgust me," I hiss at Jasper.

Jasper takes a bite of his peas, chewing calmly.

"I saved your sister's life," he says after he swallows.

"You don't get credit for that!" I cry. "When you chase someone up on a wall and scare them into jumping off, you're not a hero for grabbing their ankle!"

"Well." Jasper shrugs. "She'd be pretty dead if I hadn't."

I leap to my feet, incandescent with rage.

"You're a fucking psychopath just like Rocco! All of you are psychopaths! A bunch of vicious, conniving, bullying assholes!"

"Sit down!" Dean snaps, grabbing my arm to jerk me back into my seat.

This time, I'm too quick for him. I twist my wrist free and snatch up his tray of food instead. Then I dump it right in his lap.

Dean bolts up. The rage in his eyes hits me like a bucket of cold water to the face. My burning anger is doused in an instant. All that's left is terror.

Dean's going to fucking kill me for that.

He seizes my wrist in a manacle grip and drags me out of the dining hall.

Nobody tries to stop him.

Dean drags me from the dining hall all the way to the Octagon Tower. He pulls me up the steps like a child, yanking my arm so hard that my feet barely touch the ground as I try to keep pace with his much longer strides.

I twist and pull my hand, trying to free it from his grip. My wrist might as well be welded to his fingers.

Not until this moment have I truly felt Dean's immense strength. He's half carried me across campus and up three flights of stairs, and he isn't even breathing hard. He overpowers me without effort. We aren't even the same species.

As he hauls me down the hallway, we pass Erik Edman, another junior Heir. He raises a blond eyebrow at the sight of us but says nothing as Dean wrenches open his bedroom door. It's clear that Erik is too intimidated by Dean to speak a word, let alone report us.

I'm not sure which outcome I'd prefer at this point. I don't want to get in trouble for going into Dean's room. Even less do I want to be trapped in that small space alone with him when he looks angry enough to rip my head off my shoulders.

Dean slams the door behind us and starts tearing off his dirty clothes, his trousers stained from the chicken and peas I dropped in his lap. He rips off his pants, not caring if the material tears, balling them up and flinging them in the corner like they're diseased.

I stand awkwardly by the door, wanting to run but pinned in place by Dean's bizarre atavistic reaction. Though his shirt is only marred by one or two tiny spatters, he rips that off too, a button pinging against the window as he flings the shirt into the corner.

Only once he's stripped to his boxer shorts does he turn to face me, chest heaving with anger, every muscle standing out on his frame.

He looks like a furious god, like Zeus in all his anger, pale and shaking with eyes like churning storm clouds.

"*How fucking dare you*," he seethes.

"That was your fault!" I squeal. "You pushed me and pushed me!"

He crosses the room in three strides, seizing me by the throat right under my jaw so his thumb forces my chin up to look at him.

"And I'll keep pushing you," he hisses. "I'll twist you and stretch you and bend you till you break. And you'll do as I fucking say, or you'll suffer the consequences."

"I don't care!" I cry, my voice compressed by his hand on my throat. "I won't sit at a table with Jasper! I hate him! And I hate *you*!"

"You'll sit on his lap if I order it," Dean says, his face close to mine.

He has to bend down to my level. His eyes are terrifying at this proximity, long and narrow with pinpoint pupils, like a beast. Heat radiates off his bare chest.

"I own you, Cat. Don't you ever fucking forget it."

I shove Dean with all my strength. It barely moves him a millimeter.

"I'll throw you off that same fucking wall if you keep pushing me!" I shout.

Dean lets out a long, slow breath.

"Now we're coming to the truth of it, aren't we, Cat?" He releases my neck, but he doesn't step back. He stands very close, looking down at me. "Are you planning to kill me too, little kitten?"

"N-no," I stammer, guiltily digging my fingernails into my opposite arm. "I didn't mean that."

"I think you did."

"No! I just… You're so fucking unreasonable!"

"And that's what you meant, isn't it, kitten? You spoke in anger, and it's supposed to sound like a joke. But the implicit threat is there underneath. You're reminding me that you did in fact kill Rocco Prince, and you'll do it again if I make you mad enough. If I make things hard on you. If I scare you, if you think I'd spill your secret… I'll become a threat that has to be eliminated, just like Rocco."

There's a difference between someone insulting you with lies and someone peeling back the cover from an ugly truth. One is much more unpleasant than the other.

Dean has found my deepest, most painful place, and he's driving a spike into the aching flesh.

My sister thinks I'm a good person. Anna and Chay do too.

Dean knows the truth.

"No," I say numbly. "That isn't true."

"We both know it is," Dean says softly, his eyes fixed on mine.

"No!" I shake my head until my curls are a dark whirl in front of my eyes. "I wouldn't do that. I *had* to kill Rocco. I had no choice!"

"You don't have to defend it to me," Dean says. "I agree with you. Zoe never would have done it. Miles might have, but he hesitated. He wanted to find the more humane way. Only you saw what had to be done. You murdered Rocco. I would have done the same."

Dean believes we have something in common. He thinks I did something admirable.

It makes me want to vomit.

"No!" I cry, backing away from him. "I'm not like you."

Dean laughs quietly.

"You think there's a difference between you and me because you did it for Zoe? There's no fucking difference. All Mafia crime is committed on that premise. We're all doing what we think needs to be done for the good of the family. It's the core ideology of our world. You can justify each individual action any way you like, but the difference between civilians and mafiosi is that we put the good of our family above the law."

Dean is advancing toward me again. I keep trying to retreat until my back hits the wall.

My stomach is churning.

I hate what he's saying.

I'm not like my father or Dean's father or Dean himself. I'm not like the chancellor or Professor Penmark. I may have come to enjoy Kingmakers some of the time, but that doesn't mean I belong here! It doesn't mean I'm one of them.

Dean reaches out one of those deadly, pale hands. This time, he draws the back of his fingers softly down my cheek, each point of contact an electric spark.

"What you did to Rocco proves that you're as Mafia as the rest of us. Maybe even more."

"I'm not!" I cry, slapping his hand away. And then, when he won't back up, when he keeps me trapped against the wall, I shove him again, raging against his immovable body.

"You want to hit me, Cat?" he growls, pinning me to the wall with his hands on either side of my face. "Go ahead and do it, then."

I don't understand this game.

I don't understand any of his games.

All I know is that I'm trapped, and I've never liked small spaces. Never liked confinement.

"Hit me," he hisses. "You think you have the balls to throw me off the wall? You can't even raise one little paw to touch me."

"Fuck you!" I shout back at him.

"Do it," he says, getting right in my face. "Fucking do it, you little coward."

I slap him hard across the face, my hand whipping out before I can stop myself.

The sharp *crack!* echoes in the room. A livid pink mark jumps into being on his pale cheek.

"Hit me again," Dean says, his eyes glittering bright.

I hesitate.

"Hit me!"

I slap him again, even harder. So hard that my hand stings.

A bright bead of blood rises on his lower lip.

Dean seizes me by the back of the neck and kisses me hard. I taste the blood on his lip, like salt and iron.

I bite that lower lip, seizing it between my teeth and gnawing and sucking on it until my whole mouth fills with the taste of metal.

Dean lifts me up and slams me against the wall, holding me up at a height where he can kiss me without bending. His tongue plunges in and out of my mouth, and those full lips swallow me whole.

Without meaning to, I've wrapped my legs around his tight waist and my arms around his shoulders. My hands twist in his hair so I can hold his head against mine, so I can kiss him back just as rabidly.

And I am kissing him back. I'm not fighting him, not trying to push him away.

I've wrapped my whole body around him, and I'm dropping myself down into this kiss, giving in to it, letting it take me over completely.

I don't want to think about Rocco and what I did to him. I don't want to consider if I'm good or bad or justified.

I want to lose myself in this moment of ferocity, where letting go feels right and where Dean's aggression has transformed into something pleasurable through an alchemy I don't understand.

His hands on my body are just as strong as ever, just as violent, but as he grasps my breasts through my shirt, that rough friction makes the blood thunder through my flesh. It makes my nipples stiff and hard and aching, so rigid that the only thing that can satisfy is his rough grip.

I'm grinding my body against his, my skirt rucked up around my waist, only thin cotton panties between me and Dean's bare torso. I can feel the heat of his flesh and my own wetness soaking my underwear.

Dean feels it too.

He shoves his hand down the waistband of my skirt, down into my panties, and he starts rubbing my pussy against his palm.

I've never been touched there by anyone but myself.

The difference between my own hand and Dean's is like the difference between a firecracker and a nuclear bomb. His hand is warmer than mine, stronger than mine, just a little bit rougher than mine. It feels incredible against my throbbing flesh.

He shoves two fingers into me. I bounce and grind against his hand, his fingers thrusting in and out of me, his palm rubbing hard against my clit.

All the while, our mouths are locked together in a kiss that only grows more violent, more deep, more desperate.

I moan into his mouth, I bounce up and down on his fingers, and I feel something coming, something as massive and hectic as a tornado ripping through me.

Dean pulls his hand away. He stops kissing me and he grabs my face instead, pinching the soft flesh of my cheeks. I can feel my own wetness on his fingers.

He looks into my eyes.

"You don't get to come," he growls.

I let out a pathetic gasp of disappointment and desperation.

I need to come. I have to. I might die if I don't.

Dean is already carrying me over to his bed.

I have one wild moment of hope that we're going to lie down so he can keep kissing and touching me, but instead he sits on the edge of the bed, yanking me down across his knees.

I don't understand what he's doing.

I try to stand up, but he shoves my head down with his left hand. With his right, he pulls my skirt up around my waist and rips my panties down around my knees.

"I *hate* getting dirty," he growls. "You embarrassed me, Cat. You made me angry."

He brings one large, hard hand crashing down on my bare ass cheek.

Smack!

I shriek.

"Ow, fuck! What the hell!"

Smack!

He spanks me again on the other cheek.

"Ow, Dean, don't you fucking dare!"

Smack!

"I told you not to call me that."

Smack!

"Ow!" I howl, trying to squirm away.

Smack!

Smack!

"You need to learn to behave," Dean says.

For a moment, his hand rests on my throbbing ass cheek. His palm is warm. As he squeezes my buttocks, the gentle pressure soothes my stinging flesh.

He massages my ass, then lets his hand slide down between my legs so he can stroke his fingers against my pussy again.

"We don't have to fight, little kitten," he says. His voice is smoother than melted butter. "If you're an obedient pet, I could be a very kind master..."

His words fill me with rage. I'm not a kitten, and I'm sure as fuck not his pet.

But his fingers against my clit are a shot of dopamine direct to the brain. They make my whole body flop limply across his lap, like I really am a little kitten being scratched behind the ears. His touch makes me weak. It makes me squirm against him, begging for more pressure, more penetration...

"Please," I murmur.

"Is this what you want?" Dean slips one finger inside me.

"Yes," I groan.

"Then promise. Promise to do whatever I say."

I bite my lip, outraged at his demands. Outraged at how he's treating me.

At the same time, I'm rolling my hips against his hand, wanting him to use two fingers again, wanting him to give me what I need.

When I fail to answer, Dean pulls his hand away.

Smack!

He slaps me on the ass again, even harder. The flesh is already red and throbbing from before. This second spanking makes my ass burn like his hand is coated in hot pepper.

"Ow!" I cry.

Smack!

Smack!

Smack!

"Say it," Dean hisses.

I shake my head, pinned down by Dean's arm on my back, my nails digging into his calf.

Smack!

Smack!

Smack!

"Say it!" he barks.

"Alright!" I cry.

"Say, 'Yes, sir.'"

"Yes, sir!"

That punishing hand returns to my pussy once more, and this time he rubs me like he did before, with steady, firm pressure and two fingers pushed inside me.

The relief of getting what I want is immense. My eyes are closed, my face turned in toward his thigh. I'm humping his hand with no thought for how stupid I might look, how degrading it is to be this desperate.

His ring and pinky fingers slide in and out of me, and his index and middle finger rub my clit. I press my face against his thigh and take a deep breath, inhaling the scent off his skin.

The tornado hits. I'm caught up in the whirlwind, the whole room spinning around me as I come harder than I ever have in my life, all over the hand of my enemy.

When it's over, I lie limp and shaking across Dean's lap.

The position is humiliating. My throbbing ass is humiliating.

But I feel a deep and intense pleasure as Dean growls, "Good girl."

CHAPTER 7
DEAN

CAT STANDS UP SHAKILY, HER FACE AS RED AS HER ASS.

She can't look me in the eye.

She pulls her panties up from around her knees and smooths down her skirt.

Her hair is a wild halo of black curls. Her skin has never looked more clear and glowing. Her dark lashes lie like twin fans against her freckled cheeks.

Cat has changed since she came to Kingmakers. She used to look weak and childish. But when I felt her body, there was a new firmness to the flesh, a flexible and pliant strength like a gymnast. When I picked her up, she easily wrapped her legs around my waist and held up her own weight while she bounced up and down on my hand. I doubt she could have done that a year ago.

Her hair is longer than it was. Wilder. I've enjoyed telling her how to wear it each day. Enjoyed seeing the slim stalk of her neck when her hair is pulled up in a ponytail or bun. Enjoyed even more the days when it's loose and wind-blown.

My heart beats like a war drum.

I want to pick her up and throw her down on that bed again.

But I have to pull back for a moment. I have to give her space.

Because I just discovered something very interesting about my timid little kitten.

She has a hunger inside her.

And when she's hungry, she'll do anything to eat.

I just gave her a little snack.

If I wait, she's sure to want more.

Cat is fidgeting in place, unable to speak and embarrassed by the silence. I know she wants to leave, but I'm not done looking at her yet.

I'm fascinated by the dichotomy between her diminutive frame and the ferocity with which she kissed me. Fascinated by her innocent face hiding the depravity that lives inside her.

Who the fuck is this girl? Who is she really?

"I don't know what that was," Cat says awkwardly.

Her tone is half apology, half resentment.

"Yes, you do," I reply.

Now those dark eyes flit up for just an instant before dropping again. Cat flushes redder than ever, biting hard on the corner of her lip. Her lips are swollen from kissing, a streak of my blood at the corner of her mouth.

"Cat," I summon her.

Her eyes rise again without her control, fixed on mine as if mesmerized.

"Go to class on your own tomorrow," I say.

She looks confused and almost disappointed. She doesn't know if that's a punishment or a reward.

I don't clarify. I just stride over to the door and hold it open so she can leave.

Cat hurries out without a word of farewell.

I close the door and lock it before returning to my bed. I lie back against the pillows, staring up at the bare wooden beams of the ceiling.

I slip my hand inside my boxer shorts, gripping the shaft of my rock-hard cock.

I picture Cat's ass, round and firm, glowing red from spanking, with a distinct handprint from the hardest slap.

I remember the way she squirmed against my thighs and the

little shrieks and moans she let out, helpless against the pleasure and the pain.

My hand slides up and down the shaft of my cock, the flesh rigid and hot, the head throbbing as my palm glides over it.

Never in my life have I enjoyed a sexual encounter more, and I didn't even come.

I've fucked pretty girls. Dozens of them.

But fucking hell, there's something different about Cat's tight, petite little frame. The way I can lift and manipulate her so easily, the way I can hold her down with one hand.

I love my control over her.

Even more…I love the way she responded.

I wasn't forcing her. I wasn't making her do it.

She wanted it. She wanted it just as badly as I did. Maybe even more.

From the first instant that I kissed her, she responded like a little wildcat, feral and starving. She clawed me and bit me, clinging to me like she needed me for life.

And when I touched that wet little pussy, she was putty in my hands.

I lift my hand to my face, inhaling that sweet, musky scent off my fingers. My mouth waters, and I lick my fingertips to taste her.

All the while, I'm pumping my cock with my other hand, imagining that Cat is touching it, imagining that I'm thrusting the head between those soft pink lips…

The orgasm explodes out of me without warning. Thick, hot come pours over the back of my hand.

I picture her on her knees before me, begging to lick my fingers clean.

For the next week, I leave Cat alone.

It's extraordinarily difficult because my craving to take control of her again is almost irresistible.

But I know the same impulse is working on her. If I give her time for the shock and shame of our encounter to fade away, then all that will remain is the nagging desire to be touched again.

Meanwhile, I'm consumed by two things at once: my fixation on Cat and my growing obsession with my boxing classes.

I've always loved to fight, but I've never been trained by a professional on Snow's level. He sees *everything*. It can be frustrating because he detects even the tiniest flaws in my form. But it's also incredibly rewarding because whenever I follow his instruction, I improve tremendously.

Our training sessions are long and grueling. I've never put my body through so much. Yet I'm becoming faster and stronger by the day, and that's a fire that fuels itself. I'm greedy. I want more.

Everyone in the class seems motivated by the same desire to take advantage of Snow's coaching for the single year he'll be at the school. Leo and Ares work with feverish focus. Ares surprised me last year when I fought him in combat class. He almost seemed to be holding back deliberately. Then when he finally lost his temper, he was a far more imposing opponent than I'd guessed.

I hate to admit it, but Leo is likewise talented. It infuriates me that his skill comes without discipline. Still, I'd be lying to myself if I tried to deny his athleticism.

Leo Gallo has been the thorn in my side for as long as I can remember. The tormenting vision of what my life should have been. He has everything I should have had. Parents who love him. A safe and happy childhood in Chicago. A network of uncles, aunts, and cousins and now a baby sister too. And Anna, the only girl I ever admired, wildly in love with him.

I've hated him for so long.

Our fathers tried to kill each other. How different things would have been if mine had triumphed.

It's not the sins of the father that are visited on the head of the son. It's his failures.

My son will never feel that shame.

I'll secure an empire for my son, or I'll have no son at all.

Snow is late to class today, unusual for him. He's strictly punctual as a rule.

Ilsa Markov is warming up on the speed bag, muscles standing out on her arms and shoulders. Corbin Castro jumps rope, while Jasper rewraps his tattooed hands.

Kade Petrov and Tristan Turgenev shadowbox against the far wall where all the medieval weapons hang—swords and axes, maces and crossbows, notched and dented on their edges from the battles of centuries past.

"We've got weapons like this in the monastery," Kade says, nodding toward an ornate broadsword. "All sorts of antiques, furniture and rugs, chandeliers and wine barrels... It's a lot like Kingmakers, actually."

"That's in St. Petersburg?" Tristan says, puffing as he jabs toward his own shadow on the wall.

"Yup," Kade says. "I've lived there all my life. It's a huge old place. My brother lives with us, and my father's men, in their quarters..."

"You mean your uncle's men," Vanya Antonov says.

He's sitting cross-legged on a stack of mats with Bodashka and Silas, not warming up, just watching Kade and Tristan.

Kade frowns, tossing back his dark hair.

"It's the same thing," he says.

"No, it isn't," Vanya says, sliding off the mats and standing up. His hands are tucked in the pockets of his gray gym shorts, but the set of his shoulders and the tilt of his jaw are anything but casual. "Ivan Petrov is *pakhan*, not your father. Ivan owns that monastery and all those soldiers. Your father's just a lieutenant."

"I never said otherwise," Kade retorts, patches of color coming into his cheeks. "They're brothers."

"But Ivan's the eldest," Vanya says, taking another step toward Kade and dropping his hands to his sides.

"What's your point?" Tristan says quietly, no longer shadowboxing.

"My point is that Dominik Petrov came to the meeting in Moscow as if he were boss. He's been doing a lot of things as if he were boss. Giving orders. Making changes."

"What the fuck do you know about it?" Kade demands.

"I know your father has been taking money out of the Gazprombank," Bodashka says to Kade, likewise rising. "A lot of money."

Bodashka's father is *derzhatel obschaka* in St. Petersburg, head accountant just like my father. He has connections at all the major banks, so Bodashka's assertion rings with truth.

"Are you making an accusation?" Kade says.

The three older boys have all stood up from the mats now and formed a half circle around him.

"I'm not the one saying it," Vanya informs Kade, his voice low and insinuating. "It's everyone in Moscow. They say your father is overstepping. Doesn't know his place. Just like Adrik when he was at school, thinking he was an Heir when he's only an Enforcer."

"Don't talk about my brother," Kade hisses, tendons standing out in his neck. "Or my father either."

"I'll say whatever I like about them," Vanya scoffs.

"Leave him alone," Ares says sharply.

He's crossed the gym to intervene, which is strange because he generally avoids conflict at all costs, unless Leo Gallo drags him into it. This is the first time I've seen Leo tagging along instead, following his typically peaceful friend.

Kade doesn't appreciate the rescue. He throws Ares an angry look as if he'd prefer him to stay out of it.

"My father is an honorable man," Kade spits at Vanya. "You know nothing about my family."

"I know more than you think," Vanya says with an air of holding back some secret.

The threat only makes Kade angrier.

"My father has run St. Petersburg flawlessly while Uncle Ivan's been in America. The business prospers as it never has before. And the dispensaries in America are raining money!"

"Yes, so *your father* says," Vanya hisses, his eyes narrowed to slits. "It's him making the reports, after all."

"If you have something to say, then say it!" Kade cries. "And I'll break your fucking jaw for you!"

"Alright, I will. I think your father is a lying fucking thie—"

Kade rushes at Vanya, and I run forward at the same moment, intersecting the two before they meet. I put my back to Kade and shove Vanya so hard that he stumbles backward, falling on his ass on the mats.

Instantly, Bodashka and Silas surge forward, as do Leo and Ares.

I find myself in the bizarre position of facing off against my own friends with my enemies by my side.

The truth is I like Kade Petrov better than Bodashka, and I fucking despise Vanya and his father, who are conniving rats, always trying to improve their own standing within the Bratva by tearing down those above them.

I only met Dominik Petrov for a moment, but he seemed like a man of honor. Besides, Ivan Petrov is one of the most feared bosses in all the Bratva. He controls the entirety of St. Petersburg as well as massive holdings in America where he capitalized on the legalization of marijuana to open seven of the largest dispensaries on the West Coast. I highly doubt his brother would be stupid enough to embezzle money from him or whatever the fuck Vanya's trying to imply.

"Back off," I snarl at Vanya. "If the high table has a problem with Dominik Petrov, they'll convene a council."

"They are," Vanya smirks. "My father is heading it."

"Then let them decide if there's been any malfeasance. It's not up to you to make accusations."

"Why are you defending him?" Bodashka says, glaring at Kade. "He and his brother are both the same. Arrogant. Grasping. Above their station."

"You're just mad because Adrik beat *your* brother in the Quartum Bellum three years in a row," Ares says, staring down Bodashka.

The petty rivalries among the Bratva are almost as vicious as those against their foreign foes. There's antipathy between St. Petersburg and Moscow, between the Paris Bratva and London, and intense jealousy against our brethren in the States.

I'm not familiar with the drama Ares is referencing, but I'm sure he's right.

It doesn't matter. I've gotten enough shit from the children of Bratva over my own family's standing. I'm not gonna watch Vanya heap the same abuse on Kade's shoulders.

"Keep your ignorant opinions to yourself," I say to Vanya, who has climbed to his feet once more, his handsome features distorted with anger. "It's none of your concern how the Petrovs run their business."

"It's you who should watch yourself, *Dmitry*," Vanya sneers. "You ought to learn where to make allies. The Antonovs are rising in Moscow. If you pay your respects, I might find a place for you when Danyl makes me lieutenant."

I snort. "I'll find a place for you shining my boots when *I* earn that spot."

Vanya opens his mouth to retort, only to be interrupted by Snow clapping his hands sharply, calling the class to order.

"My apologies," he says. "I was delayed by the chancellor. I hope you all took the opportunity to warm up, because we're going directly into drills. Pair up."

I nod to Kade Petrov. "Want to join me?"

"Sure," he says, surprised but gratified. I haven't voluntarily sparred with him before—it's usually Snow who rotates the more experienced fighters through the younger students.

Snow orders us to grab pads. I slip the targets on my hands so Kade can go first for the drill.

I take him through a jab, hook, cross combo. Kade punches the pads viciously, exorcizing his residual animosity against Vanya.

"Never mind him," I say to Kade. "He's a fucking asshole. Everyone knows it."

Kade throws me half a grin. "I thought that's what everybody says about *you*. How come you stood up for me?"

"I may hate everybody, but I hate Vanya the most," I say with a shrug.

Kade laughs. He hits the pads in combination again, hard enough that my palms sting. His punches are getting cleaner.

"You drop that right shoulder too much," I tell him.

Kade tries again, this time keeping his shoulder in better alignment. His punch pops the center of the pad with a satisfying *thwack*.

"You're a good teacher," Kade says. "Like Snow."

"I'm not like him," I say. "I'd never have the patience to teach a bunch of degenerates."

Particularly Bodashka and Vanya, who are lazily going through the drill with sullen glares in our direction.

Glancing at Kade again, at his clear, youthful face, I think how passionate he was in defending his father and brother.

"I liked your father," I tell him. "He was faithful to your mother."

"He's always been faithful to her," Kade says proudly. "And he's loyal to Ivan. Vanya doesn't know what the fuck he's talking about."

"He never does." I nod. "If you could capture half the shit that comes out of his mouth, you could fertilize Siberia."

Kade laughs. "He wouldn't dare talk that way if Adrik were here."

"No, he wouldn't," I agree. "You remember he didn't say fuck all at the Bolshoi Theatre."

Kade snickers. "He and his father were much too busy with their lips pressed firmly against Abram Balakin's ass."

Now I'm the one laughing. "*I brought you one of those cigars you like so much... God, they suck.*"

We're not talking loudly enough for Vanya to hear, but he sees us laughing. His scowl darkens until he looks like a petulant toddler. A petulant toddler who drew his own eyebrows on with a pen.

A question strikes me that Kade could probably answer.

"Why isn't Ivan Petrov's son at Kingmakers?"

Kade shrugs awkwardly. I regret asking—I hadn't meant to pry into family business.

"He didn't want to come," Kade says. "He's very popular in America. Very...you know...occupied with his life there."

"Of course," I say, nodding.

A common problem when Bratva allow their children to grow up in the wealth and glamour of the States. They get into the playboy lifestyle, fucking and partying, and they don't want to learn the business.

Kade and I swap positions, Kade donning the pads so I can take my turn with the drill. I hit the targets harder and faster each round until Kade is wincing and has to remove the pads to shake out his hands.

"Fuck, you've got a hammer for an arm," he says.

I usually feel annoyed by compliments because my skill is obvious. Today, however, I simply say, "Thanks."

"My father says your dad is a brilliant bookkeeper," Kade says.

"He likes to organize," I say.

On the page. Not in our fucking house, unfortunately.

I wait, expecting Kade to follow that up with some comment on my father's appearance. It never fails. People can't help themselves.

But Kade says nothing at all. He just holds up the pads again, waiting for me to take my next turn.

That blessed silence is the best part of our conversation.

After class, as the students file out, Snow calls, "Dean. Wait a moment."

I wait, sweat drying on my skin. It was an intense session.

Snow stands silent with arms folded until everyone else is gone. Then he says, "You worked hard today."

I smother the impulse to tell him that I work hard every day.

"Thank you," I say instead.

Look at me, becoming humble and well-mannered. At least for a day.

"You've taken Kade Petrov under your wing."

"I don't know about that." I shrug. "I don't mind sparring with him. He's not the best in the class, but he's improving."

"So are you," Snow says. "I want you to come here Tuesdays and Thursdays when class is done. I'll work with you one-on-one."

The idea of boxing five days a week is daunting—my back is already knotted up harder than an oak tree from the current sessions. But I understand how valuable a gift Snow is offering me. I don't think he's offering it to anyone else.

"Thank you," I say. "I'd like that."

"Good." Snow claps me on the shoulder. His hand is heavy and warm. "Hurry on then, Dean. I don't want Professor Graves to lock you out again."

Was that Snow's version of a joke?

He's not smiling. But I've yet to see him smile—he may not be capable of it.

"Don't worry. I'll run," I say.

"See you tomorrow." Snow nods.

I jog across campus with long strides, my body sore but strangely light.

CHAPTER 8
CAT

Dean leaves me alone for an entire week.

Those days are oddly blank.

I had grown used to running around campus, meeting him between classes and over meals.

I had gotten used to his tall frame always beside me and that tense, electric energy he radiates.

Dean does everything efficiently. I've memorized the way he lines up his fork and knife beside his plate, how he butters his bread, and how he sets his water glass down in precisely the same place after taking a drink.

I find myself setting out my own dishes in the same way, even though I'm eating lunch with Rakel, Anna, and Chay today and not Dean.

"Nice to have you back," Chay says to me, spreading out her own generous lunch, which includes three chocolate chip cookies.

"Are those keto?" Anna teases her.

"No," Chay replies with great dignity. "I stopped doing keto over the summer when I went to Tasmania. I wanted to try the local food. And anyway, Ozzy says he likes me with a little more ass."

"I bet he does," Anna laughs. "You can have my cookie too—for Ozzy."

"Are you guys still dating?" I ask Chay, pleased to hear an update.

"Yes," she says happily. "I met his dad and cousins. We went bow hunting and cliff diving. Took a three-day trip to the barrier reef and swam with whale sharks. His dad is just like Ozzy. I felt like I knew him already. I think it was a good distraction for him. For all of us. Ozzy showed me his mom's rose garden. I rode her favorite horse… He's still sad, really sad. But he's also himself, funny and playful and…"

Chay breaks off, pink-cheeked, thinking she's said too much.

She's clearly head over heels for Ozzy, despite the fact that they're now long distance.

"Are you going to Tasmania again when school lets out?" I ask.

Chay shakes her head. "No. Ozzy's coming to Berlin. I mean, if he still wants to in the spring."

"I think he'd swim there if he had to," Anna laughs.

"You can't swim to Berlin. It's landlocked," Rakel says.

"Don't ruin my joke with geography." Anna pretends to scowl at Rakel, stealing one of her grapes.

"Make more accurate jokes," Rakel sniffs, snitching Anna's apple in return.

Rakel and Anna have formed their own brand of friendship, where they're free to be as grouchy with each other as they please.

"Where's Leo?" I ask Anna.

"Finishing up a history paper with Ares."

"I wanted to congratulate him. I saw he's captain again for the Quartum Bellum."

The vote was posted this morning. It was no surprise that the juniors chose Leo once again after he led them to victory the two years before.

"I think he regrets ever wanting to be captain in the first place," Anna laughs. "The challenges are so goddamn grueling, and the pressure's sky-high. Everybody expects us to win."

"You will win!" I say with full confidence.

"You're not supposed to cheer them on. You're supposed to help *our* team win," Rakel reminds me.

"No, I'm on Miles's side about this," I say, taking a bite of my sandwich. "The sooner we're eliminated, the sooner I can stop worrying about something horrible happening to me in that cursed competition."

As I set my sandwich down once more, Dean carries his tray of food past my table, flanked by Jasper Webb and Bram Van Der Berg. Our eyes meet as he passes, but he doesn't speak to me.

I watch him cross the dining hall and take his seat on the opposite side. He's facing me, and his eyes hold mine as he spears a carrot on the tines of his fork, placing it in his mouth.

Chay clears her throat.

"So..." she says. "What's going on with our friendly neighborhood sociopath over there? You're eating with us, yet I can't help but notice that Dean seems more interested in you than his carrots."

"It's not like that," I say, dropping my eyes to my plate. "He doesn't...like me or anything like that."

Even as I'm saying the words, I'm remembering the way Dean kissed me up against his bedroom wall. I've never imagined that a kiss could be so ravenous.

Anna is watching me, not with anger or jealousy but with something very like understanding.

"Dean has his good points," Anna says. "I understand that better than anyone. Just be careful, Cat. He can be cruel—and dangerous."

Chay leans across the table to rest her hand on my arm, her blue eyes seeking mine out.

"He tried to kill Leo," she tells me. "In our freshman year."

"Is that true?" I ask Anna.

She nods, her expression somber. "Yes, it is. Dean tried to drown Leo. And it almost worked."

I look across the dining hall again, at Dean's stern and unsmiling face. He's still watching me. Does he know we're talking about him? Does he care?

I can't imagine Dean ever apologizing. Ever showing remorse.

I pick up my tray, ready to return it to the kitchen staff.

As I walk toward the kitchen window, I hear steady footsteps intercepting me. I know without turning that Dean is standing behind me. The tiny hairs rise on the back of my neck, like the charge in the air before a lightning storm.

"Did you enjoy your lunch?" he says quietly.

I return my tray and turn to face him.

We haven't stood this close since our kiss.

He hasn't spoken to me since then.

The memory is like a hologram shimmering in the air between us. I can see the two of us locked in an embrace, and I'm sure he can too.

"I have a proposition for you," Dean says.

"What kind of proposition?" I reply warily.

"Meet me in the bell tower tonight. Nine o'clock."

I chew the corner of my lip, considering.

The last time I was alone with Dean, things took an unexpected turn...

There's been a constant throbbing curiosity in the back of my brain ever since. A strange, dissatisfied yearning, like a melody cut off midnote.

Dean and I have unfinished business.

"Alright," I say at last.

"Nine o'clock," he repeats, his low voice vibrating in my bones. "Don't be late."

All afternoon in class, I'm thinking about Dean and what sort of "proposition" he might offer me.

He already has all the leverage he needs to coerce me into doing what he wants.

Which can only mean...he's about to ask for something more.

Dean terrifies me. I just learned that he's a would-be murderer himself, that he tried to drown his own cousin out of jealousy over Anna and whatever other grudges he holds against Leo.

Still…I can't deny that there's something magnetic about Dean.

I've never met someone so intense, so consuming. He's like a fire running wild through dry brush, swallowing up everything in his path.

He wants what he wants. He does what he pleases. He doesn't care if he's liked or hated.

I have to admire that to a degree. Because I absolutely care what people think of me. I'm easily embarrassed, easily intimidated.

If Dean were to leave me alone…I'd still think about him all the time. The last week has shown me that. When I lie in bed at night, unable to sleep, I slip my hand beneath my covers and touch myself, trying to recall the exact texture of his rough, strong fingers against my skin. My small, soft hand is nowhere near as satisfying.

After class, I find myself showering and shaving every inch of my skin, making myself clean from top to bottom. Dean is obsessed with cleanliness. The thought of him finding me dirty or unkempt is intolerable, though the idea of him touching me again is hardly any better. I'm a bundle of raw nerves.

I put on fresh clothes: knee socks, Mary Janes, a green plaid skirt, and an oversize knitted jumper. I pile my curls up on my head, pinning them in place, or at least attempting to—little corkscrews always escape, dangling down around my face and the nape of my neck.

I look at my face in the mirror, wondering if I should put on makeup or not. Dean made me wash it off that one time, but I think he was just being an ass.

I take a liquid liner and draw a wing on either eye, tilted up at the outer edges. It makes my eyes look bigger than ever, very like a cat. I blink slowly, pleased with the effect.

Why am I dressing up for Dean?

I don't know.

I only know that my heart is racing long before I jog across the open expanse of grass between the undercroft and the ruined bell tower on the northwest corner of campus.

The bell tower looks as if it was hit with a lightning blast. It may well have been—the stones are charred and blackened by fire, with large gaps in the wall where the inferno raged through. Only half the roof remains in place, the other half gaping open to the stars like a missing eye. The edge of the bell peeks through, the metal tarnished from sun and rain.

No one comes in here because it's a death trap. It looks like it might crumble at any moment.

I stole stones from this tower.

I carried them up on the wall. I stuffed them into a canvas sack and hung that sack as a counterweight. Then I looped a noose around Rocco's wrist, kicked the pin free, and sent both stones and Rocco plunging five hundred feet down to the jagged rocks below.

So in a sense, the bell tower was my instrument of murder.

I don't know if Dean is aware of that fact.

Guilt eats at me as I climb those loose and blasted steps once more.

My steps echo in the dark tower. I didn't bring a candle, and I can barely see five feet in front of me.

I fail to notice a gap in the steps. My foot plunges through the empty hole into the blackness below. I stumble, hitting my knee on the next step above and banging my elbows for good measure.

"*Fuck*," I mutter.

So much for staying clean. I try to dust off my soot-smeared knees, wiping my palms on the sides of my skirt.

The wind blows through the holes in the tower, making a creepy moaning sound. I hear the echoing bounces of rubble dislodged by my feet, tumbling down the stairs behind me.

Shivering, I scale the last few steps.

Dean is waiting for me at the top of the tower. He leans up against the vast bronze bell, arms folded across his chest. The bell no longer hangs suspended with a rope dangling from its clapper. It crashed down at some point, now tilted at an angle on its side, half its mass supported by the creaking wooden floor and half protruding over open space.

Music plays from a speaker in the corner, quiet and low. I can barely make out the lyrics, but the beat crawls under my skin like a burrowing insect.

"Why did you ask me to meet you here?" I ask Dean.

"So we can be alone."

"Aren't you afraid the whole place is going to collapse?"

"No." A careless shake of his head.

I don't know if that means he thinks a collapse unlikely or if he doesn't give a damn if it all falls down on our heads.

I lick my lips nervously. Whatever part of me wanted to see Dean tonight has abandoned me entirely. Now all I'm seeing is the malevolent glint in his eye and the cruel set of his mouth. And those bone-white hands, shapely and beautiful but capable of horrible things.

Quietly, I ask him, "What's your proposition?"

Dean uncrosses his arms, taking a step toward me. The dropping of his hands is like a bird of prey unfolding its wings. It makes him infinitely more dangerous.

"It's simple. I want one month."

I swallow hard.

"A month of what?"

"A month of true slavery."

I fidget in place, the ancient wooden boards creaking under my feet.

"I'm already doing all the things you asked."

He closes the space between us, looking down into my eyes.

"I want more."

My heart is in my throat, like a bird in the hand, trying to escape.

"Tell me what you want."

Dean reaches into his pocket and pulls something out. He holds it between his thumb and index finger, letting it drop and hang suspended from his hand.

A strip of leather with a single metal ring in the center.

A collar.

"I want you willing," he says softly. "I want you obedient. And I want you completely under my control. For one month. From now until Christmas."

"And after that?"

"Then you're free. I'll never bother you again. And your secret is safe forever."

I consider this carefully, the collar swinging before my eyes like a hypnotist's watch.

I don't take his offer lightly.

Dean's games are not like other people's games.

Everything he does is deadly serious.

If he wants a pet, then that's exactly how he'll treat me. As an animal that belongs to him.

On the other hand, if he says it's over at the end of a month…I believe that too.

Whatever else he may be, Dean is not a liar. He'll keep his word.

"Yes." The word is barely more than a breath of air.

Dean hears it all the same, and his eyes gleam with triumph. It's the look in the devil's eyes when some poor soul accepts his bargain.

I almost snatch back my agreement, but it's too late. Dean is already drawing the collar taut between his hands.

"Take off your clothes."

"Wh-what?"

"Strip," he orders. "I want to see what I'm getting."

I gape at him in horror.

The music throbs from the speaker, ordering me to obey just as much as Dean's imperious stare.

He's not joking. He's never joking.

Slowly, I obey.

I pull the sweater over my head, dropping it down on the dusty floor. Then I begin to unbutton my blouse. My heart is jittering in my chest, yet somehow, my fingers are steady. I unfasten each button in turn, then take off the blouse and drop it down on top of the sweater.

I unzip my skirt and let it fall. I step clear of the puddle of fabric, standing in my underwear before a man for the very first time.

My bra and panties are plain cotton, unmatched—the bra gray and the underwear blue. I'm still wearing my knee socks and shoes because there's nowhere to sit, and I don't want to hop on one foot trying to take them off.

Dean doesn't seem to care about the socks. His eyes are fixed on my body alone.

"Underwear too."

I have never been naked around another human in my adult life. I don't use the communal showers, and I don't even strip down fully in front of Rakel—we face the opposite wall while changing.

Yet what I feel isn't embarrassment. It's curiosity.

What will Dean think of my body?

Am I beautiful?

I don't even know.

We can never really see ourselves except reflected in other people's eyes.

I unclasp my bra and let the shoulder straps fall. Then I drop it on the ground.

My breasts are small but ripe, like peaches. The nipples stand out from the flesh, delicate and stiff.

I watch Dean's face closely to see his reaction.

His eyes widen, and his jaw twitches. His nostrils flare like a stallion scenting a mare in heat.

It's lust, pure lust. He likes the way I look.

Emboldened, I drop my panties too, stepping clear.

Now I'm standing naked in only my socks, my pussy bare to his view. Slowly, I turn on the spot, showing him that round, full ass that he spanked so recently.

I'm displaying myself to him.

I want his stare.

I want his approval.

And Dean wants to inspect me.

He walks around me like a buyer at auction, looking me up and down, evaluating my body.

His eyes are a hundred pairs of hands passing over my flesh.

I stand still, shoulders back, chest thrust out to his gaze.

Dean cups my ass in his hand, squeezing my buttock as if examining the firmness. Then he circles around to the front and touches my breast. He tests how it fills his hand, tilting his head approvingly as the curve of my breast lines up perfectly with the curve of his palm.

I shiver as his thumb slides across my stiff nipple.

"Very good," he says softly.

A rush of heat, and my mouth salivates at his approval.

I'm discovering something about myself in this moment.

I'll do anything for a compliment.

I want praise. I want it badly. And I especially want it from this man, who doesn't like anyone or anything.

"Lift your hair," he orders.

I lift up the curls that have fallen loose, baring the base of my neck.

Dean takes the leather collar and wraps it around my throat with the ring in the front. He fastens the clasp behind me.

Then he steps back to admire the effect—my figure naked but for a pair of socks and the leather circlet around my neck.

"Perfect," he breathes.

My heart is thundering. I can feel the aching wetness between my thighs. I had hoped Dean would touch me there too.

"Down on all fours."

I drop to my knees and then place my palms on the dusty boards. He says, "Crawl."

I crawl in a slow circle before him, my face burning with embarrassment. It's degrading and humiliating. My ass and pussy feel horribly exposed as I turn around. I can feel Dean looking down on me, and I wonder if he's laughing at me in his head.

But he doesn't laugh. When I chance a glance upward, I see his cock straining against the fly of his trousers, so thick that it looks like a soda can shoved down the front of his pants. A tiny wet spot soaks through the material where the head is pressed.

My mouth waters even more.

Quietly, Dean asks, "Do you know how to suck cock?"

I sit back on my heels, looking up at him, and shake my head.

"You're going to learn."

He pulls off his own sweater and lays it on the dusty ground. He sits down and whistles for me, pointing to the space next to him.

I start to stand up, and he barks, "No!"

Understanding, I crawl over to him on hands and knees.

He grabs the ring of my collar and pulls my head down so I'm curled up next to him with my head in his lap. Then he unzips his trousers.

His cock springs out, as pale as the rest of him. The shaft is thick and white, veined like marble, while the head is smooth and faintly pink. Clear fluid beads at the tip. I want to taste it.

"Suck it like a Popsicle," he tells me. "Gently. Don't scratch me with your teeth."

His cock is bigger than any Popsicle I ever put in my mouth. But I want to try.

I close my lips around the head. I lick it with my tongue, tasting the sharp spark of salt from that leaking fluid. More saliva floods my mouth, and I'm able to run my lips and tongue smoothly over his cock while I suck gently.

My head lays in his lap, my ear pressed against his thigh. Only part of his cock fits in my mouth, but Dean doesn't force it any farther. He lets me suck on the head while he strokes his fingers in my hair.

His touch is incredibly soothing. The sucking and his strong fingertips against my scalp put me in a trance state.

Dean takes the pins out of my hair so the curls are loose. He runs his fingers through the hair in slow, lazy swirls, sometimes with pressure, sometimes with light swoops.

Warmth floods through my body. Every muscle relaxes.

He's petting me.

And I like it.

I keep sucking his cock.

After ten or twenty minutes, Dean reaches down between my thighs and rubs my pussy. He rubs me in time with my sucking. The harder and faster I suck his cock, the more pressure he applies against my clit.

I moan around his cock, grinding my pussy against his hand.

The dual sensation of his warm flesh in my mouth and his warm hand against my clit is phenomenally satisfying. I want to keep sucking, and I want to keep grinding against him.

I feel half-asleep, floating in this erotic dream state where I'm a good little pet earning my reward.

After all, is it so bad to be a pet?

All it means is that someone loves you. Someone's taking care of you.

I've always been a good girl, eager to please…

Maybe I needed a master all along.

Dean's breath is speeding up. He rolls his hips, pushing his cock a little deeper into my mouth. He thrusts his hand into my hair, gripping the back of my skull, manipulating the angle of my head so he can push his cock farther in.

Now I'm gagging a little, and it's harder to keep pace, but he's still rubbing my pussy with his other hand, pushing his fingers inside me while he pushes his cock down my throat.

I'm starting to feel that building pressure again, that ball of heat expanding in my belly. My mouth is extraordinarily sensitive from all that sucking, my lips and tongue and even the soft flesh of my throat all engorged and throbbing like the inside of my pussy. My mouth is as erogenous as my clit, and the dual sensation of penetration, orally and vaginally, is bringing me to climax.

I start to come, waves of pleasure flowing through me with each thrust of Dean's fingers. I moan around his cock again. The vibration of my throat tips Dean over the edge. His cock begins to twitch, and thick, warm spurts of come hit the back of my throat, coating my tongue.

Dean lets out a long, tortured groan, a sound so primal that it scares me. And yet…I like that too. I like having that effect on him.

His come is slippery and hot. It startles me. He holds my head down, ordering, "Swallow it. Every drop."

I gulp and swallow, trying to obey.

The taste isn't bad—it's the volume that makes me struggle. He keeps coming, at least five or six spurts, until I think I'm going to drown in it.

At last, he releases my head, and I sit up, wiping my mouth on the back of my arm. My whole body is loose and warm, suffused with shivers that pass over my flesh without warning.

Dean leans back on his elbows, his eyes heavy, his body drained. I've never seen him so relaxed.

I'm waiting for his judgment. I want to know how I performed.

He looks at me, then takes my chin in his hand. He pulls me forward so he can kiss me, not giving a fuck that I still have his come in my mouth.

"Good girl," he growls.

CHAPTER 9
DEAN

IF I THOUGHT I WAS FIXATED ON CAT BEFORE, IT'S NOTHING compared to my obsession with my own personal pet.

I tell her to wear the collar everywhere she goes, all day long.

And then I see her walking to class dressed as innocently as ever, backpack over her shoulders, oversize shirt hanging down above her knee socks, with the mark of my authority wrapped around her neck.

It drives me insane.

My cock is hard as steel all fucking day.

I can't stop thinking about her. Can't stop trying to catch glimpses of her. Can't stop imagining what I'll make her do when we're alone at night.

I have one month to take full advantage of this.

I had considered a longer timeline—after all, I'd planned to torment her for two more years until I graduated from Kingmakers. But in the end, I decided she'd never agree to it if it seemed like it would last forever. You can do anything for a month.

Sure enough, she consented without much convincing.

Because I had already discovered the crucial truth about my little kitten—she fucking likes it.

I just need to show her how *much* she likes it. She doesn't even know. She has no idea what I can make her do. Or how good it will feel.

Meanwhile, I've started my private classes with Snow.

I walk into our first session feeling like the king of the world. Like nothing and no one could touch me.

Snow quickly reminds me that if I'm the king of the world, then he's Thor Odinson, and he can smite me any time he likes.

His fists are thunder and lightning. They beat me with pagan fury, reminding me of the difference between a god and a mortal.

"You're telegraphing your punches," he says, bouncing lightly on his toes, not even winded from our sparring. "Why can I dodge your punches when I'm twenty years past my prime? Because I can tell what you're going to throw just by the position of your feet."

I attack him again, determined to move my body as one unit without my toes betraying my fist a split second before it can land.

"Better," Snow says as one of those punches clips his jaw. "But you have to maintain it. As you get tired, you fall back on bad habits. This is true of all fighters—any tendency or pattern they hold, they try to stamp out. But as the body grows weary, they slip back into routine."

Snow's voice is deep and gravelly, ringing with truth. It's become the voice inside my head, pointing out my flaws, reminding me of his lessons long after class is over.

His bulky frame is firm and immovable as a mountain. He never loses his temper. He never makes mistakes.

Snow is what discipline has made him. Forty-eight years beaten against the refiner's anvil—now he's harder than any sword.

I admire him.

I hated him at first, the day he humiliated me in front of the class.

Now I want his approval. And this is strange to me because I never truly cared what Abram Balakin or Danyl Kuznetsov or my professors thought of me. Not as long as I got what I wanted.

I'm not sure I even care what my father thinks. After all, he's never pleased, no matter what I do. And I have my own resentments against him for how he drove my mother away and how he allowed our house to fall into ruin. He raised me in a garbage heap, so all my life I've had to struggle against the shame of our past, the shame of our home, and the shame of who I am.

Snow is a man worth impressing.

He knows nothing of my family, and he doesn't care.

He only cares how I perform here and now in this gym.

I attack again, harder and faster than ever before. This time, I can see that he has to hustle to block my punches, and he *is* breathing harder. I strike him on the ear with a glancing blow.

"Good," Snow says. "You hit me once in our first fight. That was a good combination. You were desperate, and it was the only time you didn't telegraph what you were about to do. It was a strong blow. You've always been talented, Dean. I can see that. But you have to be more than talented. You have to be the best. To be the best, you have to become a student of your craft. You cannot win through fury. Anger will never be enough. You need knowledge, mentorship."

"That's why I'm here," I pant, striking out at him again.

"Yes," Snow says, hitting me with a hard right cross that knocks me on my ass. "But I'm not sure you're listening."

After we spar, Snow brings out his phone so we can watch old tape of his fights.

"You attack hard in the first round, Dean," he says. "Sometimes, it's a good strategy. But not always. See this boxer—Ivo Chavez. I watched hours of tape on his old fights. And he did the same with mine. Both of us studied our opponent. When we fought, you can see in the first round he altered his strategy. We circled each other, seeing what each of us had changed. But look…as the fight wore on, he tired. And what do you see?"

"Jab, jab, cross, hook," I say, spotting the other boxer's pattern.

"That's right. Sometimes it's better to wait and allow your opponent to make his mistake."

Dinner is chicken and dumplings, a particular favorite among the students. The dining hall is packed. I see Kade Petrov and Tristan Turgenev struggling to find a seat, and I wave to them to take the empty spots next to Bram.

Kade sets down his tray, grinning.

"Dumplings and apple pie for dessert," he says. "Must be my birthday."

Bram gives Kade an appraising look. He's heard Bodashka talking shit on Kade Petrov in our boxing classes, but he's also seen that Kade is clever and a good fighter. For all Bram's faults, he prefers skill over pedigree in his friends.

"I heard you were chosen as freshman captain," he says to Kade.

"Yeah," Kade says, coloring a little. "Probably just 'cause of my brother. He won three times, so maybe the freshmen hope it's genetic."

"Sorry," Valon says, stuffing a dumpling in his mouth. "Ya got no chance, kid. We're sweeping all four years. Gonna beat your brother's record."

"Yeah, I know you're a bunch of all-stars. I've heard about Leo Gallo." Kade grins, brash and unconcerned. "I've got nothing to lose. If he beats me, that's what everyone expects. But if I win…"

"Then you'll wake up in the morning and realize it was all a dream," I say, laughing.

Kade laughs along with me, not offended. "Maybe so," he agrees. "Can't fault a guy for trying."

I like Kade's easy confidence. A year ago, it would have irritated me—it would have reminded me of Leo. But somehow it doesn't bother me on the younger boy. Maybe because I wish I had been more like him my first year at school. Less angry—looking for friends instead of foes.

Foes come all on their own.

Bodashka stops at our table, staring angrily at the seat he usually takes, currently filled by Kade Petrov. Without a word, he stomps off to join Vanya and Silas instead.

"Is this his spot?" Kade says guiltily.

"Don't worry about it," I tell him. "It doesn't have his name on it."

Bram raises an eyebrow but doesn't argue. Bodashka is pompous and not that bright. Kade is better company and a lot funnier.

"How about you?" Bram says to Tristan. "How come you're not sitting with the Frenchies?"

"I like the Paris Bratva," Tristan says in the surprisingly soft voice that does not at all accord with his large frame. "But Jules is kind of a dick."

Bram laughs. "Yeah, he is. His room's right next to ours. He's moodier than a girl."

Tristan chuckles. "The only person who can keep him in line is my sister. And she's in the library right now."

"Your sister's Claire Turgenev?"

"That's right." Tristan nods.

"Fucking hell, she's gorgeous," Bram groans in a tone of deepest longing. "No offense."

"I'm not offended," Tristan says, shrugging. "She is beautiful."

Claire Turgenev has long been the standard of beauty and class at Kingmakers, one of the few female Heirs beloved by almost everyone. When she graduates at the end of this year, a hundred male hearts will break, and probably some female hearts too.

Not mine.

I'm not as captivated by stunning blonds as I once was.

In fact, what I'd like to see right now is a shock of black curls, thicker than fox fur and darker than a moonless night…

As if I summoned her with my thoughts, Cat Romero walks into the dining hall with my collar around her neck.

She locks eyes with me, standing still for a long moment.

She looks like she might join me voluntarily until she sees the lack of empty chairs at my table.

I curse the impulse that led me to invite Kade Petrov over.

Cat sits with Anna, Leo, and Hedeon instead.

Hedeon pulls her chair back for her because her hands are occupied by her tray.

That simple chivalrous act sends a bolt of fury down my spine. I've never thought about Hedeon Gray for two seconds, but all of a sudden, I think he might be my mortal enemy.

He takes a bite of his roll and makes some comment to Cat.

Cat answers back politely.

I want to know what they're saying.

No, fuck that—I want to rip out Hedeon's voice box. Can't he see, clearer than day, that Cat belongs to me?

The evidence is wrapped around her neck.

Cat can feel me watching her. Her eyes flit up to meet mine. Her cheeks flush deeply pink, darker than her lips. Instinctively, her fingertips fly up to touch the metal ring in the center of her throat.

"*One hour*," I mouth.

Cat nods slowly.

That's the time we set for her to meet me in the bell tower.

Blood surges into my cock.

"What are you looking at?" Bram demands.

"Nothing," I say, returning to my food.

Bram glances across the room, but he can't follow my gaze across the crowded dining hall.

I've been making improvements to the bell tower. I've brought up cushions, blankets, and candles, stolen from all over the castle. Other things too. Ropes. Chains. And a tool of my own invention…

I wait for Cat, blood pumping through my veins with the pressure of a fire hose.

If she's one fucking minute late, I'm going to punish her...

I hear a pebble tumbling down the steps.

It's the only hint that Cat is coming.

She's quiet and light on her feet. Small and unobtrusive.

She really is a talented Spy in her own way.

After all, even that consummate predator Rocco Prince had no idea that she was stalking him.

She stands just out of sight in the shadow of the stairwell. But I know she's there, watching me.

I light the candles one by one until they form a half circle around the fallen bell, like the precursor to a séance. What will Cat and I summon tonight?

I start the music.

A playlist of my choosing, selected specifically for Cat.

Only once my preparations are complete do I speak.

"Why are you still dressed?"

Cat steps out of the shadows into the candlelight.

Her face is still, but those big dark eyes never stop communicating with me. They betray all her secrets.

She begins to disrobe.

Something I've noticed about Cat: when she forgets to be nervous, she moves with surprising grace. She slips out of those oversize clothes, baring the tight body beneath.

And what a body it is.

Her small, round breasts stand at attention on her chest. Her waist is so slim I could close my hands around it. But she isn't skinny or childish. Those curving hips and that full ass add a satisfying sensuality to her figure.

Her bronze skin glows in the flickering light. Every inch of her is smooth and unmarked. For now...

"Come here," I bark.

Cat crosses the space between us, silent and obedient.

"Stand against that wall," I order. "Put your hands over your head."

Cat stands with her back to the curving stone wall. She raises her hands over her head, wrists crossed. The movement lifts her breasts even higher, tilting the nipples up invitingly.

I've already passed a length of rope through the holes in the wall. I loop the rope around Cat's wrists, tying them in place.

Cat's lips part. I catch the sharp scent of adrenaline rising off her skin.

She's already frightened, and we haven't even started.

"Spread your legs," I order.

Cat widens her stance so her feet are shoulder-width apart. I tie her ankles to the wall so she can't close her legs.

Now her whole body is taut and trembling. She knows she's trapped in the most vulnerable position possible. Completely at my mercy.

Yet she allowed me to do it. Which means she trusts me to some degree.

She really shouldn't.

I stand before her, looking at her stretched frame, pinned to the wall like a butterfly. All that soft, tender flesh completely under my control.

Searching through my backpack, I pull out a leather scourge.

I made this myself, just like I made Cat's collar, in the workshops adjacent to the old forge.

It took several hours to knot the leather thongs and attach them to the carefully wrapped handle. The leather is soft and supple, but it can sting. I tested it out on my thigh.

I grip the handle loosely, letting the leather threads trail.

Cat watches my every movement, eyes wide.

With her hands up above her head, her breasts are bare and completely unprotected. I swing the scourge, letting the leather thongs nip at her left breast. Cat jumps and lets out a little shriek. A dozen pink lines mark her delicate chest.

I trail my fingers along the leather strands, letting the anticipation build. Then I whip her again, on the other side. The knotted leather flicks her nipple sharply, and Cat shrieks even louder.

I step closer, trailing the scourge gently up her inner thigh.

Cat shivers, her knees weak, held up mostly by her arms bound over her head.

I bend to whisper in her ear. "I saw you sitting with Hedeon at dinner."

I caress her left breast in my hand, feeling the warmth of the whipped flesh.

I seize her nipple between my thumb and index finger and squeeze it hard. Cat moans.

"I saw him talking to you."

I grab her face and force her to look me in the eye.

"What did he say?"

"Nothing!" Cat cries. "He just asked about my programming class."

I grab her nipple again and pinch it even harder.

"Don't lie to me."

"I'm not!" she gasps.

She's sweating slightly, from fear and pain.

I grab her chin and run my tongue up the side of her throat, from collarbone to ear, passing over the leather collar, tasting the salt on her skin. Then I kiss her hard on the mouth, shoving my tongue through her lips, making her taste it too.

"I've seen him walking with you. Talking with you. He's barely friends with Leo and Ares. Why is he friends with you?"

"I don't know!" Cat tries to twist her chin out of my grasp.

She's not quite meeting my eyes.

She's lying. I know she's lying.

Her resistance infuriates me.

I whip her again, across both breasts and her belly. I whip her lightly at first, to bring the blood to the skin, and then harder, until I can see the marks of the lash everywhere.

Cat squirms and twists against the rope until it bites into her wrists.

She's not crying out anymore. Stubbornly, she bites those pink lips with her sharp white teeth, glaring up at me.

I kiss her again, and this time, I reach down and slip my fingers between her pussy lips. Her sweet little cunt is open and unprotected. She can't even close her legs. I rub her clit roughly, and she does cry out, half plea and half moan of pleasure. Her wetness drenches my fingers.

"Let's try this again."

I grab her face and make her look at me. I drill down into those beautiful eyes, so dark that it's hard to find the intersection of pupil and iris. Eyes that reflect only the tiniest flecks of light, like a glimmer of stars across a deep, black pool.

"What does Hedeon want? Does he like you? Does he want to fuck you?"

"No!" Cat cries.

I rub her pussy again, pushing my fingers inside her the way she likes. I've already learned the perfect technique to bring her to the edge in seconds. It's not hard when the blood is already rushing through her body, whipped into a frenzy by the scourge and her own fear and arousal.

I know I have her right where I want her when she tries to press her hips against my hand, hindered by how tightly she's bound to the wall.

She pants and groans, needing just a little bit more.

"Tell me," I growl in her ear. "Tell me what he wants."

"He's trying to find his parents!" Cat cries out.

I pull back to look at her, surprised.

"What?"

Cat tosses her head angrily, making her dark curls fly.

"He wants to know his biological parents. You know he was adopted by the Grays. He doesn't have a crush on me."

Her tone is disdainful, like that should have been obvious. She's so irritated at me wringing this piece of information out of her that it must be true.

"Why didn't you just tell me that?" I say, sliding my fingers inside her warm wetness once more.

Cat groans.

"Because he doesn't want anyone to know," she mutters.

"I don't care what Hedeon wants," I hiss in her ear. "I only care what *I* want. And you'd better share that attitude. Or I won't be so nice to you."

I pump my fingers in and out of her until her whole body starts to shake. She's trying to squeeze her thighs together, but she can't. She can't do anything except bite down hard on my shoulder with those sharp teeth.

"*Argggghhhh!*" she screams as I make her come.

A rush of fluid runs down my hand.

I think I just made her squirt.

I wipe my palm off on the thigh of my trousers, for once not giving a fuck if my clothes are dirty.

I only care to look at Cat, at the sheen of sweat on her chest, at the lingering marks of the lash across her breasts.

Her head lolls limp against her shoulder, wrung out by the strength of her climax.

We're not finished.

Not even close.

I cut the ropes binding her to the wall. Cat falls into my arms. I lift her easily, one arm supporting her back with her knees draped over my other arm. She weighs almost nothing, even limp and exhausted.

I carry her over to the stack of cushions I stole from the gallery on the ground floor of the keep. I throw her down on the cushions, watching her legs splay apart.

Her little pussy is like a soft pink shell, delicate and inviting.

I've never eaten pussy before. I always thought it was beneath me.

But I tasted Cat on my fingers, and I want more.

I strip off my clothes and lie between her legs, pushing her thighs apart. I dive my tongue into her cunt, seeking the source of that enticing flavor, wanting it to fill my mouth. I lick her like an animal, ravenous and wild. I explore every part of her with my tongue.

When I find a sensitive spot, Cat purrs like a kitten. She lets out a long exhale that makes her teeth chatter together like she's shivering cold. But she's not cold—her body burns at a thousand degrees, and her pussy is the furnace generating that heat.

I lick her pussy over and over, bring her back to the edge again, until her back arches and her breasts thrust up in the air and she's grinding against my tongue with all her might.

Then I sit up, my cock jutting out from my body like the prow of a ship.

I look down at her, and she looks up at me, panting and desperate.

"Beg me to fuck you," I growl.

Her little pink tongue slips out to touch her upper lip. Her cheeks are flushed, her eyes bright.

"Please," she whispers. "I need you."

She opens her legs all the way, inviting me to thrust my cock into the softest, most sensitive part of her.

I need you.

No one has ever said that to me before.

I put the head of my cock at her opening, and I push inside.

She's wet, slicker than an oil spill. Still, it's so tight that I have to brace myself with my arms on either side of her face so I can drive into her.

My cock plunges into her tight embrace. Her wet, hot grip is beyond anything I imagined.

"Oh god!" she cries.

I silence her with my mouth.

I kiss Cat long and deep while my cock fills every millimeter of space inside her.

I'm falling into pure liquid pleasure.

Fucking hell, I might actually be dying. Can a man live through this?

I want to blow inside her instantly.

The only thing holding me back is the far greater drive to make Cat come first.

Nothing arouses me more than controlling her orgasms. Denying them when she wants to come and forcing her to climax when she tries to resist.

I made her come with my fingers and almost with my tongue. Now I want to see if she can come all over this cock.

I take both her hands, her fingers entwined with mine, and I pin them over her head. I suck and nibble on her breasts while I drive into her over and over.

Cat is in an ecstasy of pleasure and pain. My cock tears into her. She was a virgin until this moment, I'm quite sure of it. She's killed a man but never fucked one.

Yet she's urging me on with frantic movements of her hips, panting and gasping. Trying to grind that sensitive little clit against my body.

I bear down on her, giving her the friction she needs. Fucking her deep and steady.

Cat turns her face toward me, sucking the side of my neck. She licks and sucks all the way up to my ear, then bites the lobe hard between those sharp teeth. Her tongue dances over the edge of my ear, sending waves of pleasure down my spine.

She rubs her nose in my hair and inhales deeply.

"*Me encanta tu fragrancia,*" she moans as she starts to come.

I've never heard Cat lapse into her native language. Her English is perfect and unaccented.

That's how I know she's lost all control.

And so have I.

Her voice echoes in my head.

Me encanta tu fragrancia.

I need you.

I need you.

I need you.

The dam breaks. I explode inside her, a torrent of come pouring out of me. Cat's teeth are chattering again, and I'm yelling out, a cry that sounds like a sob.

CHAPTER 10
CAT

I LOST MY VIRGINITY TO DEAN.

I guess I knew it was coming.

I agreed to be his pet for a month and then sucked his cock on the very first day. So I was unlikely to make it all the way to Christmas intact.

Still, I'm not sure how I feel about it.

Zoe gave her virginity to Miles, the love of her life.

I gave mine to an enemy. I wonder if I'll regret it.

The truth is I don't regret it at this moment. I can't regret it because I'm already craving doing it again. And I don't honestly view Dean as any enemy anymore.

Maybe I never did.

He's frightened me from the day I first laid eyes on him outside Miles's Halloween party, just over a year ago. And he's frustrated me a hundred times since then.

But did I ever actually hate him?

No. I don't think so.

My terror has always been accompanied by a strange fascination with Dean. He intrigues me, like a dark pathway into the woods. I want to see what's inside.

No, I definitely can't regret fucking him. It felt too good. The most pleasurable moments of my life have come in our last several encounters.

But I am confused about one thing. The thing that makes me feel a squirming sense of guilt and shame when I think what I allowed Dean to do to me. And how much I liked it…

There's only one person I can ask.

I call my sister.

Miles told me where to find his cache of hidden cell phones so I could call Zoe any time I like, not just on Sundays.

I go to the very farthest point of campus, in the northwest corner of the fortress walls, tucked behind the prison tower and the edge of the ruined cathedral. Here, in a thicket of hemlocks, no one will see me using a forbidden piece of technology.

Zoe answers at once, pleased and breathless.

"Cat! How are you?"

I don't have to ask how she's doing. I can hear the pure joy in Zoe's voice. That's how she always sounds since she moved to Los Angeles with Miles.

"I'm good," I say. "Or at least I think I'm good."

Zoe laughs. "What does that mean?"

"Well, I…uh…had sex for the first time."

"What?!" she shrieks. "With who?"

"With…Dean, actually."

There's a long silence on the other end of the line.

"What are you doing, *conejita*?" Zoe murmurs. There's no judgment in her voice—only concern.

"I…might like him. A little bit," I admit.

Another silence. Then Zoe says, "He's bitter, Cat. Bitter and twisted inside. Do you know what he tried to do to Leo—"

"Yes," I interrupt. "I know."

"Then how can you *like* him?"

I can't answer her question because I know I'm in the wrong. You're not supposed to like someone who tried to kill your friend.

But after all, he *didn't* kill Leo, and I don't think he'd try again. In fact, in all the time I've spent with Dean, he's never said one thing about Leo Gallo. Or about Anna either. Maybe he's keeping his hatred locked inside. I've never seen any hint of it.

"I think...he might have changed since then," I say to Zoe. "Changed a little at least."

Zoe lets out a disbelieving sigh.

I know I sound ridiculous.

It doesn't matter. I didn't call Zoe so she could waste her time trying to talk me out of a situation in which I'm far too deeply embedded.

I have a different question to ask.

"Zo," I say. "You like sleeping with Miles, don't you?"

She laughs, and I can almost picture her shaking her head at my change of subject.

"Of course," she says.

"Do you ever have sort of...uh...aggressive sex? Violent, even?"

Zoe hesitates, her irrepressible honesty forcing her to answer.

"Sometimes," she says.

"Why do people like that?" I ask.

Even though I'm alone and out of sight of anyone, including Zoe, I'm still blushing with all my might.

People means me, and Zoe knows it.

"Well." Zoe considers. "I suppose it's because it shows a man's masculinity and strength."

"Do you ever...let Miles tie you up?"

I want the earth to swallow me up, but I also need to know.

"Yes," Zoe says. "But, Cat...the reason we can do kinky shit is because I trust Miles. He knows my limits. He pushes me to the edge, but he would never hurt me."

"Right. I understand."

Zoe sighs, and I know she's probably biting the edge of her lip, just like I'm doing thousands of miles away.

"I'm not going to tell you what to do, little sister. But please... be careful."

"I will be," I promise.

"I miss you," Zoe says.

"I love you," I reply.

I end the call.

Even though Zoe doesn't approve of me dating Dean—how could she?—she loves me and supports me no matter what.

And she did answer my question without entirely meaning to.

The reason why I'm willing to do all these things with Dean, the reason I let him tie me to that wall…is because I *do* trust him. As much as he scares me, I've come to believe that he won't actually hurt me. Not in any real or lasting way.

The pain of whipping and spanking is nothing compared to the pleasure that comes after.

I get up earlier than usual the next morning, so only a dozen other students are scattered throughout the dining hall when I grab a bowl of oatmeal and a pot of mint tea.

I prop my Extortion and Racketeering textbook up against an earthenware milk jug, intending to study and eat simultaneously. All the time I've been spending with Dean is undermining my efforts to improve my grades this year.

I've only read through a single page before Hedeon plops down in the seat next to mine, saying, "Who in the hell decided that oatmeal's an acceptable breakfast food? If the Victorians ate it, that should be reason enough to chuck it off the menu forever."

"It's actually pretty good. It's got blueberries and cinnamon and—"

Hedeon shoves away his untouched bowl.

"It's still slop," he says.

He hasn't shaved in a week or two, and his thick, dark stubble is halfway to a beard. It makes his eyes look all the more blue.

I can't help casting a nervous glance around the dining hall in case Dean sees us sitting together all alone. He's obviously touchy about Hedeon, which is laughable because there's never been the slightest spark of romance between us.

Hedeon just wanted me to use my access to the computer lab to search through old student records. He never explicitly told me that he was looking for his parents—that was my assumption. I think I'm right, though, because Hedeon seems to hate the Grays, despite the fact that they named him heir over his brother Silas.

I feel guilty that I let that secret slip to Dean. I didn't mean to. He quite literally tortured it out of me, however pleasant that torture might have been.

Even though I wasn't able to access the student records, I did suggest to Hedeon that he might find paper copies among the detritus of cast-off filing boxes, broken furniture, and abandoned sports equipment in the old stables.

He never told me if he found what he was looking for.

I ponder if I'm brave enough to renew the topic now.

Hedeon sits sullen and silent, his expression as unwelcoming as I've ever seen it. If I wait for him to be in a good mood, I might as well wait for the Second Coming.

Clearing my throat, I say, "Uh, Hedeon, did you ever…find that thing you were looking for?"

"What?" he says, startled out of whatever moody thoughts were swirling around in his head.

I can feel myself blushing, but I persist. "In the boxes…in the stables…"

His jaw clenches, and I think he's going to tell me to fuck off and mind my own business. Instead, he says, in a low, defeated tone, "No. I found a box of records from around the right time, but the files didn't say anything useful. It was stupid to think they would."

"Do you know your parents' names?" I ask hesitantly.

He shakes his head, his dark hair hanging down over his eyes.

"I don't know anything about them. I only assumed they came here because a long time ago, I found a gray envelope crumpled up in the back of a drawer. It had half a wax seal on it—the Kingmakers seal. At the time, both Silas and I were too young for school, so it wasn't for us. It's the only clue I have. The Grays won't tell me anything, not even my mother's name. I have no pictures. I have nothing at all."

I frown, considering that.

"Did your parents—the Grays, I mean. Did they go to Kingmakers?"

"Yes, but decades ago. They're old. They spent a long time trying to have their own children."

I'm wondering if the envelope could have been from one of their acceptance letters. People don't always clean out their drawers.

Perceiving this, Hedeon says defensively, "The envelope didn't look that old."

I'm not sure how accurately one can discern the age of paper, but I don't want to argue with Hedeon. So I only say, "Maybe they know someone who works at the school. Maybe a teacher wrote to them."

"You don't think a student could have gotten pregnant?" Hedeon demands in an undertone so no one around us can possibly overhear. "People sneak off to fuck all the time around here."

That hits a little too close to home. I have to pretend to be very interested in the blueberries on my oatmeal.

"Hard to hide something like that," I say quietly. "Besides, you know what Mafia families are like. They might be mad about an accidental pregnancy, but at the end of the day, if two kids fucked up, the parents would still want the grandchild."

"You don't know that," Hedeon hisses back at me.

He's angry and impatient, not wanting to hear any arguments against his only lead.

I take a breath, mulling it over.

"You're right," I say after a moment. "I don't know anything for certain. I'm just making guesses. And that's not really helpful."

Hedeon's shoulders drop as he lets go of some of his frustration but also some of his conviction.

"All I have are guesses," he says unhappily. "I want them to have gone here. Because then I'd be where they were. I'd feel like I knew them a little."

His hands clench on the table. His shirtsleeves are rolled up to the elbow, and I can see a long, twisted scar running up his forearm. Most Mafia children have scars. Hedeon's aren't normal—they're too numerous and too strange. There's nothing accidental about them.

"Does Silas know anything?" I ask.

"No," Hedeon says. "And he doesn't care."

Silas has never struck me as having much curiosity or feeling.

Hedeon, while equally ill-tempered, does have flashes of kindness and humor.

I don't blame him for his bitterness. It's clear that his upbringing among the Grays was far from pleasant.

"I'm sorry I couldn't help," I say.

Hedeon sighs.

"Just…don't tell anyone," he says.

I squirm guiltily in my seat.

"I won't," I lie.

———————

The universe seeks balance in all things.

Now that Dean has stopped tormenting me between classes, restricting his dominance to our nightly sessions, it seems that Lola Fischer is determined to fill the void.

She and Dixie have been steadily ramping up their harassment so that Rakel and I can barely step foot outside our dorm room without one of the southern belles slamming us into the wall.

Rakel wants to poison them or at bare minimum sneak into their room in the middle of the night and steal all their clothes.

"No," I say flatly. "I'm not interested in escalating."

I've already experienced the sickening dread that comes from breaking the worst rule at Kingmakers. I got away with it once, and I have no interest in tempting fate again.

"But we're not doing anything at all!" Rakel cries, infuriated. "We're acting like weak little bitches!"

"I don't care," I say. "I've got enough on my plate with the Quartum Bellum and first term exams."

The first challenge of the Quartum Bellum takes place the following Friday.

Kade Petrov was chosen as captain for the freshman team. He's extremely popular among the freshman students, who of course hope that he's the second iteration of the record-setting champion Adrik Petrov.

However, Kade seems to have drawn the ire of several upper-classmen, including Bodashka Kushnir and Vanya Antonov. I saw them get into some kind of confrontation in the dining hall before Dean and Bram intervened.

I didn't quite understand what I was seeing. After all, Dean and Bodashka used to be good friends. I have to assume Dean was motivated by his hatred of Vanya because he's not usually a defender of younger students. If anything, Dean's usually the one bullying them.

It was all very strange, and I'd like to ask Dean about it, but we don't spend much time talking. As soon as I step foot into the bell tower, I become his little pet. My orders are to obey, not to question.

Our interactions are raw and primal.

That's the way I like it.

When I'm with Dean, I don't have to think or plan or worry.

All I have to do is give in to my natural desires. However *unnatural* they may be.

It washes away the confusing complications of how I feel about Dean, what I did to Rocco, or the highly inconvenient fact that the sophomore captain is none other than Lola fucking Fischer.

She looked like the cat that swallowed the canary when her name was posted in the commons. I hoped it would at least put her in a good mood. Unfortunately, it's only emboldened her and Dixie in their tyranny.

Leo, of course, will be junior captain.

Claire Turgenev was chosen by the seniors.

"They should have picked her last year over that idiot Simon," Rakel says.

"Leo says he bribed people to vote for him."

"Plus, they're just plain sexist," Rakel says. "The Enforcers always vote for the biggest dude."

"It's gonna be stiff competition," I say nervously. "All the captains are good."

"Don't call Lola 'good,'" Rakel sniffs. "It's like calling an atom bomb 'pretty.' Just doesn't sound right."

"She's smart, though."

"I think you mean conniving."

"Talented."

"Obsessive," Rakel corrects me.

"Motivated." I'm trying not to laugh.

"Unhinged," Rakel says, and we both give in to giggling.

We're less amused when we see the actual challenge.

The students file out onto the sprawling field outside the stone gates, where we see four large piles of lumber waiting for us. High overhead, a thin wire stretches from the castle wall all the way down to the tree line at the edge of the field. From that wire hangs four flags: white, green, gray, and black. The flags flap in the breeze, suspended fifty feet over our heads.

"Oh, dammit," Rakel mutters.

We already know without Professor Howell's explanation

that this challenge is definitely going to involve retrieving those flags.

Sure enough, the professor waits until the students have assembled, then uses his theater-level projection skills to shout out, "Welcome to the first round of the Quartum Bellum! As most of you are aware, this is a single-elimination competition. The last team to finish the challenge will be eliminated. Those who finish first and second may win an advantage for the next round, so do your best to finish quickly, even if another team has already achieved the objective!"

We nod, as these are always the base rules. It's only new information for the few freshmen who don't have older siblings to enlighten them.

Professor Howell continues his instructions. I wish I weren't standing so close to him, because even though he's only a few inches taller than me, his bellow is deafening.

"The objective today is to retrieve your team's flag. The tool at your disposal is the lumber you see waiting. You can build any apparatus you like to reach the flag. But you have no hammer or nails—only the wood. There will be no sabotage of the opposing teams in this particular challenge."

Lola pouts, clearly disappointed by that rule. Sometimes sabotage *is* allowed and even encouraged.

"Gather with your team, and we'll begin!" Professor Howell shouts, raising his pistol overhead.

I bunch up with the rest of the sophomores, all dressed in identical olive-green T-shirts. Lola is hissing instructions to our team before Professor Howell can pull the trigger.

"The strategy is speed," she says in an undertone so the freshmen and juniors on either side of us won't hear. "We need to build a tower as quickly as possible. August, Joss, Carter, take the biggest students and start hauling the wood over. Lyman, Sadie, you're in charge of engineering. Tell the others how to build."

Much as I dislike Lola, I have to admit she seems to know exactly what to do. The other sophomores ready themselves, motivated by her confidence.

Professor Howell fires into the clear blue sky.

We all take off running toward the stacks of lumber.

The pieces of wood are irregular in size, rough and untrimmed. Rakel and I grab a log between us, instantly filling our palms with splinters.

"Couldn't give us any gloves, could they?" Rakel complains.

"At least it's not raining," I say.

The one and only challenge in which I competed last year was a morass of mud. Jogging over the springy turf on a sunny day is positively pleasant by contrast, even if I do have to carry this damn log.

By the time Rakel and I haul our burden over beneath the flag, August and Joss have already run to the woodpile and back three times.

"Move your ass!" Dixie Davis bellows at us on Lola's behalf.

"I'd like to shove this log up *her* ass," Rakel mutters to me.

I snort, then wipe the smile off my face as Lola glares at us.

"You think it's funny that the two of you are worse than worthless?" she snaps, tossing back her mane of shining caramel-colored hair.

"Sorry, Great Leader," I reply in a tone of utmost politeness. "I didn't know barking orders required both your hands and your mouth. Why don't you pick up a log and help us?"

Lola's pretty face contorts with so much venom that she barely looks human.

"You're a parasite," she hisses at me. "A worm under my feet. You don't belong here. And you'll get what's coming to you."

Rakel pulls me in the direction of the woodpile once more.

I'm quiet, thinking to myself how strange it is that whether Lola tells me I don't belong at Kingmakers or Dean tells me that I do, I feel offended either way.

Maybe it's because *I* don't know who I am, so how can they?

I thought I knew.

Until I killed Rocco, shattering my own image of myself.

Now I'm trying to pick up the pieces and glue them back together, wondering what form they'll take.

Thinking of Dean makes me search for him over in the horde of juniors. I easily spot his white-blond head and the rigid muscles of his back straining against the fabric of his gray T-shirt. He's working next to Leo and Ares, already building the base of their tower. The three boys move in unison like a clockwork machine, swiftly and expertly stacking the logs in a tower formation that reminds me of da Vinci's self-supporting bridge.

The tower Lyman and Sadie are building looks a lot less stable. Driven on by Lola's relentless demands for speed, they're not matching the size of the logs with much care, and the tower is already starting to lean to the left.

Claire Turgenev's tower is the tallest of the three and looks reasonably stable until a half-rotted log snaps, sending her structure crashing down.

I can see the fury on her face, but she doesn't give in to panic, swiftly reorganizing her workers to repair what fell.

Kade looks decidedly more stressed, but he's holding up under the burden of leadership, building a tower that is wide and sturdy, though the smallest of the four.

Despite my annoyance with Lola, I really am working as fast as possible, following her orders as best I can. I'm not as invested in winning this competition as the rest of my teammates, but I don't want to let anyone down.

I'm willing to do whatever I can to help.

Until Lola seizes me by the back of the shirt and yanks me over.

"Up you go, *Cat*," she orders.

"Up where?" I say blankly.

"Get that fucking flag," she says, jerking her head toward our spindly tower.

I stare up at the fluttering green flag, which looks impossibly distant, bobbing on the flimsy wire.

"But…I don't think the tower is ready," I say.

Our tower is little wider than a ladder at the top. Its angle resembles the Leaning Tower of Pisa, and it seems to be swaying with the breeze almost as much as the flag itself.

"It's a fucking race!" Lola barks. "You're the smallest and the lightest. Get your ass up there and climb!"

Lola is correct that I'm the smallest student in the competition— including the freshmen. But I still don't think this rickety pile of kindling is going to support me.

On the other hand, I'm supposed to obey the captain.

The rest of the team is staring at me expectantly, except for Rakel, who fixes me with narrowed eyes and gives a small shake of her head.

The other teams haven't finished their towers. If I can make it up there and snatch the flag, we'll win the first round.

"Can you at least have somebody hold the base steady?" I ask.

"Cameron, Belkie—stabilize the base," Lola orders.

The two burly Enforcers rush to obey.

Their efforts help a little. I can still feel the entire structure swaying with my every movement as I begin to scale the side.

I've never been rock climbing in my life. Haven't even climbed a tree. I try to keep my gaze pointed upward at the enticing green banner overhead.

My fellow sophomores shout up instructions and words of encouragement. I can barely hear them over the blood thundering in my ears. This tower feels more and more like a floppy, makeshift Mount Everest, and I can't help wondering if Lola would prefer me to grab the flag and win or break my neck falling down.

I don't think karma's on my side.

I sent Rocco off a ledge ten times this height.

Stuffing that thought down, I keep climbing steadily upward.

The tower sways like a tree in the wind. I pause, afraid to go any higher. I reach up as far as I can, trying to grasp the fluttering tip of the flag. It dances just out of reach. I feel the material tickling my thumb and index finger, but I can't quite grip it. My arm isn't long enough.

I'll have to climb up just a little farther.

I set my foot on the next log up.

Then I hear shouting below, and the tower beings to tip.

I lose my grip and plunge down into its center with all the logs collapsing on top of me.

CHAPTER 11
DEAN

I HADN'T NOTICED THAT THEY WERE MAKING CAT SCALE THE tower because I was too fixated on my own work.

Under Leo's clear direction and with Ares and Anna's design, our tower rose straight and sturdy, a marvel of engineering.

It pleased me to see how clean it looked compared to the pile of matchsticks the sophomores were throwing up or the squat square Kade Petrov had commissioned.

Claire's tower almost matched ours in elegance, until an unlucky log snuck in the mix and set her back by several minutes.

I felt sure we would win.

Winning feels good. Quality work feels good.

For all the conflict I've had with students in my own year, I have to admit that the juniors are unstoppable. We work well together: Leo, Ares, Anna, Chay, Hedeon, Jules, Bram, Kenzo, and me. We've got the cream of the crop from the other divisions too: Bodashka and Silas, Ilsa Markov, Pasha, Motya, Shannon Kelly, Gemma Rossi, and Isabel Dixon.

For the first time, I catch the vision of how glorious it would be to be the first team of students to win the Quartum Bellum all four years.

It might even be worth the fact that Leo's ego will need its own zip code.

I work feverishly to make that happen until I hear the sophomores shouting and the snap and crash of a forty-foot pile of logs tumbling down.

I catch one glimpse of a small, dark-haired figure poised at the top of the pile before Cat plunges down in the center of the collapse.

"Move!" I roar, shoving my way through the mass of students around me.

Despite how close we were to finishing our own tower, I can hear Leo and Ares likewise dropping their work, dashing along after me.

I don't care if they're following. I'm shoving everyone out of my way, sprinting to the place where I saw Cat fall.

She'll be crushed under the mass of wood. I can't believe she survived, but I know I have to find her, right this fucking second.

I'm ripping up logs bigger than my body, flinging them out of my way, not giving a damn who they might hit.

I'm digging her out, the flesh tearing off my palms, my every muscle straining as I hurl those logs like fucking kindling.

Leo and Ares are digging too. The only reason I don't shove them away is because they're helping.

It's me who finds her, though—me who sees the small, pale figure huddled beneath two crossed beams, blood covering her face.

Had the logs fallen otherwise, they would have crushed her. As it is, I have no idea how bad the damage might be. I scoop Cat up in my arms. Her featherlight weight terrifies me, as if there's no soul inside that body.

"I don't think you should move her—" Leo starts, but I shoulder him out of the way and sprint for the infirmary. Cat's weight is nothing at all to me, I'm running faster than Leo and Ares can keep up.

Professor Howell intersects us, his silver whistle bouncing on his chest as he runs.

"Keep her steady," he instructs me.

I'm already doing that, carefully cradling Cat's neck with my right arm, supporting her legs with my left, using my hand to press her face gently against my chest.

I've never seen her so pale and ashen, all the beautiful color bleached from her skin. The blood and dust make it difficult to tell if there's any movement of her lashes against her cheeks.

I press my fingertips against the side of her throat, careful not to jostle her.

I think I feel a pulse fluttering against my ring finger.

Leo dashes ahead, hammering on the infirmary door.

I expect Dr. Cross to open it with his usual ill humor. Instead, an elegant blond woman stands in the doorway. In my panic, I'd forgotten that Snow's wife is the medic now.

"Get her inside," Sasha Rybakov says at once. "Lay her on the bed."

I carry Cat into the long, low building, which now smells of soap and fresh flowers instead of like antiseptic and Dr. Cross's chai tea. I only notice the change subconsciously, occupied by the far more pressing task of laying Cat carefully on the clean infirmary sheets.

"Thank you," Sasha says. "Now I'll need you to leave—"

"No!" I bark. "I'm not going anywhere!"

"Fine," Sasha says, unwilling to waste time arguing. "The rest of you, out. There isn't room for six in here."

"I'm going back to the challenge," Professor Howell tells me with a concerned glance at Cat. "Report to me as soon as you can."

Leo and Ares seem even more hesitant to leave, but Sasha shoos them out unceremoniously, closing the door in their faces.

Then she turns all her attention on Cat, swiftly checking her pulse and her pupil dilation, lifting Cat's shirt to examine her abdomen and listen to her breathing, then gently running her hands down Cat's limbs, checking for breaks or sprains.

By this point, Cat is coming to, letting out a groan of such pathetic softness that my heart clenches up in my chest. I'm sick and furious. What the fuck was Lola thinking, making Cat climb up on that rickety pile of sticks?

"Is she alright?" I bark at the doctor. "How bad is it?"

"I think…" Sasha says, gently feeling Cat's head and neck, "that we have a very lucky girl here."

"That didn't feel so lucky," Cat moans, those thick black lashes fluttering against her cheeks.

"Get me a basin of warm water," Sasha orders, pointing to the cabinets.

I hurry to obey, testing the temperature of the water, then filling the basin. I bring a clean cloth as well. Sasha adds a little disinfectant that makes the water foam, then begins to gently clean Cat's face. The dirt comes off but not the freckles, which stand out more than ever against her pallor.

I was worried that she'd broken her nose or knocked all her teeth out. But it seems like the blood is all coming from a gash along her hairline.

"Why is it bleeding so much?"

"Head wounds always do," Sasha says calmly. "You know that, Dean."

I look up at her sharply.

She gives me a small smile. "Oh yes. Snow has told me all about you."

"You call him Snow?" I ask, curious.

"Sometimes," Sasha says.

I search Cat's face, wanting her to open her eyes all the way so I'll know she's alright.

"Don't squeeze her too hard," Sasha says.

I look down at my hands, which are tightly clasped around one of Cat's. I hadn't realized I was gripping her hand.

"Is this your sister? Cousin? Lover?" Sasha says, noting my intense concern.

"She's my…" I look at Cat, and now those dark eyes do open

and fix on mine. "She's my friend," I say, squeezing her hand once more.

The corner of Cat's mouth twitches in quiet amusement.

"Her name is Cat Romero," I tell the doctor.

"Cat," Sasha says gently, "do you feel any sharp pain or pressure anywhere on your body?"

Cat takes a deep breath, eyes half-closed, focusing on what must be a thousand aches and pains.

"No…" she says after a moment. "Just a lot of dull throbbing."

"You're going to have quite a few bruises," Sasha says. "And I'll probably have to stitch this." She nods toward the cut on Cat's forehead.

"That's fine," Cat sighs. "I had a couple of those last year."

I bite back the urge to demand why she needed stitches last year and who fucking caused it.

"Are you really alright?" I ask her, trying not to let her hear how anxious I am inside.

"Yes," she says, a little color coming back into her cheeks. "Just sore."

"I'll give you something for that," Sasha says. "Then the stitches won't hurt either."

She fills a syringe with clear fluid and inserts the needle into the crook of Cat's arm. She pushes down the plunger, and almost immediately, Cat lets out a long sigh.

"Ohhhh, that's really good…"

Sasha chuckles. "That's Professor Lyons's own blend. We have to keep it under lock and key, or all the teachers would be knocking on my door."

The doctor begins to organize the instruments needed for the stitches.

Cat rolls her head to the side to look at me, her eyes large and liquid, the pupils dilated.

"Don't worry," she says. "I'm not that injured. You'll still get your month's worth."

"I don't care about that!" I retort angrily.

Then I see Cat's teasing smile.

I hadn't realized that she could be funny. There's a lot about Cat I still have to learn.

"Dean…" she says softly.

My heart hits against my ribs, not yet calmed from the mad race over here.

"Yes?" I reply.

"Did you catch me?"

"No." I shake my head. "But I did dig you out."

"Maybe next time…try to catch me," Cat says.

I know she's joking, but I feel an uneasy guilt that makes my laugh sound strange.

"Next time, give me a little warning," I say.

"You're so fast," Cat whispers, her voice drifting across the space between us.

"Not that fast," I say.

"You could catch me…" Cat says, her eyes half-closed.

I know she's high as balls on whatever Professor Lyons cooked up, but her confidence in me fills me with warmth all the same.

Her hand is no longer cold and limp in mine. Instead, she intertwines our fingers.

Sasha brings over her tray of sterilized instruments.

"You want to stay for this too?" she says.

"Yes." I nod. "Blood doesn't bother me."

Cat's breathing is slow and steady as she drifts off, heedless of the doctor's needle and thread stitching her skin.

Sasha's hands are wonderfully capable. Everything about her is calming, from her gentle voice to her clear blue eyes. She wears her blond hair in a long plait down the back of her white lab coat.

"What did Snow say about me?" I ask her, unable to stifle my curiosity.

"He said he was very proud of your progress," Sasha tells me.

For some reason, this makes my throat feel thick.

"That's good," I say after a moment. "He's an excellent coach."

"The best," Sasha says proudly. "He trained our son Zane, and he's sure to become a champion as well."

"Where is he now?" I ask.

"In New York with our daughter, Faye. They share an apartment together. She's in med school."

"Both of them follow in their parents' footsteps," I say.

Sasha nods. "We didn't expect it. They could have done anything. It didn't matter to us."

I think about that.

My father has very clear instructions for what he expects from me. He won't accept anything else.

Yet Snow and Sasha's children choose to emulate them willingly. Because they look at their parents and they see a life worth imitating.

So do I.

Only when I look at Snow—not at my own father.

"She's probably going to sleep for a couple of hours," Sasha tells me, nodding toward Cat's peaceful figure beneath the thick infirmary blankets.

"I don't care," I say. "I want to stay."

CHAPTER 12
THE SPY

I WALK ACROSS CAMPUS TO THE LIBRARY. IT'S LATE ENOUGH THAT I know nobody else will be there. Not on a Friday, and especially not on a night when there's at least two parties planned to celebrate the seniors winning the first round of the Quartum Bellum.

I want to speak to Ms. Robin.

It's so ridiculous calling her that. But she insists. In fact, she gets furious if I ever slip and call her what she really is to me. She says we have to convince even our own selves of these identities. That's the only way to be sure that we won't slip up. One mistake could be fatal. It could undo two long years of work.

Sometimes I start to believe my own lies.

My old life seems like a dream, like it happened to someone else. And this new life…

Sometimes I enjoy it. I want to believe it's real. The part I play is so much easier than the truth.

It's so lonely wearing this mask.

That's why I have to go see her. Because she's the only one who knows. The only time I can be myself is with her, even if she uses this name, and I have to use hers.

The library tower is a dark silhouette against the purple sky, shaped like a chess rook. Ms. Robin's apartments are at the top. I've seen them, of course. It's a scrupulously neat space, plain and unadorned. She's never cared for knickknacks or sentimental things.

She does love art, however, and history, which has helped her play her role so well.

She's thrown herself into her work here with a passion that only a true connoisseur could muster.

I expect to find her poring over papers and documents as usual. No one is as tenacious or as tireless as her. I've never seen her falter. Never seen her give up.

I pull open the metal-strapped door and enter the dim spiraling space, treading the slanted floor that always makes me feel slightly off balance, as if the library is a parallel dimension, part of another world.

I hear a soft, gasping sound, distant and muffled.

For a moment, I'm confused, because while I know what it sounds like, I don't think it can actually be true.

Already my feet are sprinting up the ramp, and I'm looking around wildly, trying to find her.

She isn't at her desk. I have to run all the way up to the topmost level, to the last and most distant table. Then I find her slumped over a pile of books, her head on her arms.

Her shoulders shake with near-silent sobs.

I sit down next to her, putting my arm around her.

She knows it's me without even looking.

She turns toward me, letting me encircle her in my arms, letting me hug her, though I'm not supposed to.

"I can't find it," she sobs. "I've looked everywhere."

I don't know if I've ever seen her cry.

It scares me.

She never breaks. She never gives up.

She's the bedrock of my life. If that rock is splitting apart...

"If I can't find it—"

"You *will* find it," I tell her, hugging her with all my might.

"If I can't—"

"You *will*. When have you ever failed when you were determined to succeed?"

She laughs, the tears still gleaming on her cheeks. "There was that one time…"

"Yeah, well, there won't be another. You won't fail. You can't."

She lets out a long sigh, leaning heavily against me. She looks exhausted.

"It's been so long. What if it's all for nothing?"

I hold her by both shoulders so I can look her in the eye.

"Then we kill them all."

CHAPTER 13
DEAN

Cat stays overnight in the infirmary.

I was only able to sit beside her for an hour before Professor Howell came and hollered at me for not reporting back to him, then booted me out of the infirmary and sent me out to the field to clean up the mess left from the competition.

Due to the interruption of the sophomore tower delaying our team, the seniors retrieved their flag first and the freshmen second. It doesn't matter. We still beat the sophomores and secured our place in the next round.

By all accounts, Lola Fischer threw a tantrum over her elimination, blaming Cat for their loss.

I'd like to fucking strangle her for sending Cat up there in the first place.

By the time I've helped the grounds crew haul off every last scrap of lumber, it's fully dark and too late to try to visit Cat again.

When I return to the infirmary in the morning, Sasha tells me that Cat left early so she could clean up and attend class as normal.

I track Cat down between first and second period.

She looks relatively revived, other than the scrapes and bruises all down her arms and the bandage on her forehead. Her uniform is nicely pressed, and I can't help but notice her leather collar peeking out from the neck of her blouse. The sight gives me a Pavlovian thrill.

"Why didn't you come find me?" I demand. "I was worried about you."

Cat smiles. "I figured we'd see each other tonight."

"You want to meet me in the bell tower?" I say in an undertone because I don't want the passing students to overhear. "I thought you'd take a few days off."

"I'm fine," Cat says. "I don't need any days off."

My pulse quickens, and I feel my cock swelling, aroused by the fact that Cat isn't using her accident as an excuse to avoid me. She *wants* to meet me tonight.

"Nine o'clock?" I say.

"Of course." Cat nods.

Then, to my astonishment, she winks at me and heads off to class with a flirtatious little flick of her skirt.

It occurs to me that when I first met Cat, I mostly observed her while she was stressed or scared. Often due to my own behavior toward her. Now that she's relaxing a little...she's actually quite playful.

I like it. She's teasing me and even flirting with me like she's trying to get a rise out of me.

If she wants to poke the bear, I'm happy to show her how beastly I can be.

All in good time, however. I don't believe she's fully recovered. I'll have to be careful tonight, even if the sight of her in that plaid skirt and collar has already whipped me into a fever pitch with hours yet to go before I'll see her again.

I'm in such a mood of anticipation that I don't immediately snap Vanya Antonov's neck when he deliberately slams into me in the hallway of the keep.

"Watch it!" I say, more annoyed than infuriated.

"It's you who better watch yourself, *Dmitry*," Vanya sneers as Silas and Bodashka join him in crowding around me. "It's your fault we scrubbed the challenge. If you hadn't been distracted by your little pet—"

"Say one more word, and I'll knock your teeth down your throat," I snarl back, getting right in Vanya's face, not giving a fuck that it's three-on-one in the otherwise deserted hallway. I'll fight all three of these assholes and every other friend they've ever met.

"Where do you get that arrogance, Dmitry?" Bodashka hisses. "When your father's a gargoyle and your grandfather's a fucking disgrace?"

I switch my attention to Bodashka, seizing the front of his shirt and pulling back my fist to execute my threat on his face instead.

Until I hear the sharp sound of someone clearing their throat.

Vanya and Silas step back, as if they weren't just about to leap on me from all sides.

"Let go of him," a low voice orders.

Snow's hulking figure fills the hallway. Slowly, I release Bodashka.

"Get to class," Snow commands the other three boys.

Sullenly, they obey—not without Silas making a derisive hissing noise as he passes me and Vanya muttering, "We'll finish this conversation later."

Snow watches them move out of sight, then says to me, "Aren't you getting enough practice already, Dean?"

"Might as well hit Bodashka as the heavy bag," I say. "They're equally useless at fighting back."

Snow shakes his head at me, but I think I see a hint of amusement in that frosty stare.

"You're late again," Snow says.

"I know," I sigh. "I'll miss chemistry."

"Why don't you come with me, then?" Snow says.

"Where are you going?"

"Conditioning," Snow grunts.

He's already dressed in the gray sweat shorts and white T-shirt that form our standard gym uniform. Since that's what he wears every day, I hadn't thought anything of it.

"I'll have to change," I say. I don't want to fuck up my trousers and sweater vest.

"Meet me outside the gates," Snow says and nods.

I hustle back to the Octagon Tower to change, then run across campus to the heavy stone gates that allow exit from the castle grounds. I'm already starting to sweat by the time I meet up with Snow. He gives me no rest, immediately breaking into a steady jog across the field.

That's fine with me. I'd put my stamina up against a racehorse. I can fight, fuck, or run for hours.

I fall into pace beside him, impressed as always that his fitness matches that of a man twenty years his junior.

"I met your wife," I tell him.

"I know," Snow says.

I picture Snow and Sasha convening in the apartments attached to the infirmary, telling each other all the events of their day.

What would it be like to share all that had happened to you with another person instead of keeping it locked inside yourself?

"She's very beautiful," I say.

Snow chuckles. "The most beautiful woman in the world. Yet that's only my tenth-favorite thing about her."

I don't know how to respond to that. I'm not used to men speaking of their wives that way. It's very sentimental for someone as stern as Snow.

We're crossing the field, heading south toward the river bottoms. I've run all over this island, usually alone. It's pleasant to jog with someone else. I've trained with Snow enough times that there's no awkwardness between us.

"Sasha told me you were very concerned about your friend," Snow says.

I can't tell from his measured tone if he's implying anything.

"I thought Cat might be seriously injured," I reply stiffly.

"It's good to care about someone," Snow says.

"It's not like that."

"You don't care about her?" Snow says, turning his head to fix me with that cool stare.

It's impossible to lie to him. He sees everything, from my smallest mistakes to the rebellious thoughts in my head.

"Maybe I do," I admit. "A little bit."

"That's good," Snow repeats. "Love is not weakness."

"I don't *love* her."

"Love is not just for a wife," Snow says.

I'm not sure what that means.

We jog on in companionable silence.

I shower in the Octagon Tower, heading back to my room with a towel wrapped around my waist. I pass Leo going in the opposite direction, likewise wearing a towel.

He grins. "Hot date tonight?"

I frown back at him. "Why do you say that?"

He shrugs amiably. "Post-dinner shower. That's usually the reason."

I suppose that means he has a date with Anna himself, but I don't think he's trying to rub it in my face. Honestly, I don't care. I already have my head full of plans, and I'm thinking about only one girl.

"Hey, I wanted to thank you," Leo says.

"For what?" I ask suspiciously.

"Well, for all the work you put in on the challenge for one thing."

"We came in third."

"Made it to the second round. That's all that matters." Leo shrugs. "But mostly I wanted to thank you for helping Cat."

"Why would you thank me for that?"

I bristle at the idea that I was helping Cat *for Leo*, as if she belongs to him. I helped her for my own benefit, if anything.

"Miles is gonna marry Zoe," Leo says as if stating the obvious. "So Cat is family."

"Oh," I say.

"Well." Leo grins and gives me a friendly parting nod. "See ya around."

"See you," I say.

It's the least aggressive encounter Leo and I have ever had together. One might almost call it pleasant.

I don't know when I stopped hating him. I didn't mean to. The realization slowly came over me that hating him wasn't getting me anywhere. It was a festering rot, eating away at me from the inside.

That's not to say we're friends. But I don't seem to have the energy to burn with fury in his direction. Not with boxing five days a week and Cat in the evenings. My focus has shifted.

I hurry back to my room, having no intention of being late.

I dress and comb my hair in front of the mirror hanging on the wall.

Bram lounges on the bed practicing tricks with a battered deck of playing cards. His black hair has grown all the way down past his shoulders. I don't know if he's cut it once since freshman year. The scar across his eye makes it look like he's squinting in a suspicious way. Which he usually is.

"Where are you going?" he demands.

"Out," I say.

"I gathered that. Where?"

"Gonna study," I say vaguely.

I look at my reflection, stone-faced. I resemble my father. Which means I probably look like my aunt Yelena too. They were twins, after all.

I wonder if Leo sees his mother when he looks at me.

Probably not, since it was hate at first sight with both of us.

But perhaps there was an alternate reality where we could have been friends.

I've been plagued with thoughts of what could have been all my life.

How do people accept the one and only path they find themselves on?

No one else seems to suffer this endless anger at the hand fate has dealt them. Not even Bram, who looks like he's about to push Mufasa off a cliff.

"I'll come to the library with you," Bram says, tossing down his cards and making as if to get up from the bed.

"No," I say rudely.

Bram scowls. "What's the deal with you lately?"

"You're the one acting strange," I say dismissively. "Pretending like you study."

Bram is still throwing a few choice curses in my direction as I grab my book bag and exit our room without him tagging along.

I don't mind bringing my books. Cat and I do study sometimes, when we're finished with our other activities. And despite what she said, I'm not sure how many other activities there will be tonight. She can't be more than half-healed.

Still, once I've climbed the fire-blackened steps of the bell tower, carefully avoiding the gaps in the stone, I set up my portable speaker so we'll have music, and I light the dozen half-melted candles.

Then I pull out my contracts textbook, settle myself on the pile of cushions I stole from the keep, and begin to read. Only two weeks remain before end of term exams. I still intend to place first in my year. It will take all my focus to beat Anna, not to mention Ares, Isabel, and the other academically inclined juniors.

I'm so absorbed in contract law that this time, Cat does manage to sneak up on me unaware. Her stealthy shadow crosses the curved stone wall, and she stands before me, firelight dancing on her glistening black curls. Her skin glows copper bright, and her dark eyes shine.

"There you are," I growl. "Why aren't you naked yet?"

Obediently, Cat begins to strip.

Once she's down to her socks, I order, "Leave those on." I've come to like those knee socks even better than full nudity. "Turn around," I say.

Cat rotates slowly on the spot, assuming that I want to examine her.

And I do—but not for the usual reason. I'm tallying up every cut and bruise on her slender frame, assuring myself that there's no crucial injury I hadn't yet seen.

Cat spins gracefully on the ball of one socked foot. Her naked skin has a rosy glow, as if she's some unearthly creature summoned from the fire. A fire sprite bewitched and put under my control—until I loosen the collar from her neck.

"Come here," I say in a low voice.

Cat sinks down to her knees and crawls over, keeping her eyes fixed on mine.

She's become so much more comfortable around me that she really does move as sinuously as a cat. She lays her head in my lap, curling up next to me.

"Stroke my cock while I read," I order. "Don't put it in your mouth."

I want it in her mouth, of course, but I'm taking my time.

Cat plays with my cock using both hands, like it's her toy. She strokes the shaft gently with her fingertips, then cups my balls and gently tugs. She dances her fingers around the ridge separating head from shaft and rubs light circles around the tip.

Her touch is exquisite. She's very good with her hands, probably from all her time spent painting and drawing. I've seen her sketchbook—she's quite talented. But what I told her was true: she would have been wasted at art school. The more I get to know Cat, the more I see that her talents are far more varied than charcoal and paper could fulfill.

I keep studying. Cat's touch makes the words float through my brain, light and ephemeral. My eyes unfocus from the page, and instead I watch the flickering candlelight, my whole body warm as that flame.

"Don't speed up," I order, leaning back against the cushions.

Cat continues stroking her hand up and down my shaft, increasing neither the pace nor the pressure. Her hands are delectably soft and her touch gentle. The pleasure increases even though the pressure doesn't. I feel right on the edge of climax, but it's not quite enough to tip me over the edge.

"Just like that," I groan. "Don't change a thing."

Cat continues to stroke me, steady and unhurried. In fact, she seems to be enjoying the sensation of the smooth skin of my cock against her palms almost as much as I am. Her eyes are half-closed, her breathing steady.

She sighs. Her warm breath against my cock makes me shiver. The orgasm begins.

It's no ordinary orgasm. I feel the waves of pleasure and the deep, satisfying sensation but not the accompanying contraction of my balls. I don't actually ejaculate. It's just the climax; nothing comes out.

I moan all the same from how good it feels. My head lolls back, and my toes curl up.

When it's over, Cat examines her hands, mystified.

"Did you...come?" she asks.

"Yes," I say.

"But...where is it?"

"I don't know," I reply. "Keep going. Same pace."

Cat keeps stroking my cock, just as light as before.

In the aftermath of the orgasm, her touch is almost too intense. Each stroke of her hand seems to run over bare nerves. But it's still intensely pleasurable, and I begin to experience that sense of building again, as if the orgasm reset and is starting over. My cock has stayed hard the entire time. In fact, it might even be stiffer now than it was before.

"Keep going," I moan. "Exactly like that."

Cat obeys. She seems intensely curious to see what will happen. We're both in uncharted territory.

Sure enough, the climax builds and builds until it tips over once more, Cat carefully maintaining just the right level of stimulation. In fact, this time, she squeezes the head of my cock slightly harder as I come, which increases my pleasure without forcing the ejaculation.

Tremors run down my body in waves.

"What in the fuck is that?" I say as my whole frame shakes.

"You're like a girl," Cat laughs. "Having multiple orgasms."

"If this is being a girl, then sign me up," I say. "Do it again."

Cat sits up so she can adjust her angle. This time, she cups and strokes my balls with one hand while lightly jerking off my cock with the other. She's pulling my cock so it's pointing downward instead of standing out from my body. That feels even better and makes me harder than ever as the blood rushes down.

She increases the pressure a fraction, never too much. The third orgasm is already beginning, less and less space required between them. I've never come three times in less than ten minutes. The flood of oxytocin through my body suffuses every cell. My head floats above my shoulders like a soap bubble.

I've dropped my textbook god knows where, and I don't care. All my senses are focused on Cat's hands on my cock, on her expert rhythm.

"Oh my fucking god…" I moan as the third climax rolls over me.

Cat's eyes are bright with interest. She gives me no time to recover but keeps stroking. She seems to view this as a challenge, like she's trying to set a record.

I'm sure as fuck not going to stop her.

As the next climax builds, she closes her mouth around the head of my cock and gently sucks, the warmth and wetness ten times better than her hand.

"Fuuuuck me!" I cry, pushing her head down on my cock.

I thought that would make me blow all the way, but now that I've discovered this strange trick of orgasm without ejaculation, it seems like it will go on forever. Cat makes me come twice more with her mouth in rapid succession.

The orgasms aren't as strong this way, but they're intensely pleasurable and relaxing.

I feel blissfully weak, and I don't protest when Cat climbs on top of me, straddling me with her strong thighs and lowering herself down on my cock.

Her pussy grips me, wet and ready. She starts to ride.

She seems to enjoy me in this wrung-out state, too exhausted to boss her around. I let her ride my cock at any pace she likes, and she experiments with leaning forward and back, riding me fast and slow. I come inside her just like I did in her mouth, with a long, slow climax that feels intensely warm and relaxing.

Cat starts to come too, and it really is funny how both of us can ride the waves of orgasm several times in succession.

It makes me feel connected to her in a new way. I can see that she loves making me come over and over—she doesn't tire of it. In fact, each of my climaxes seems to motivate her to seek another. She seems to be counting them up in her head, highly pleased with herself.

I understand that, because I feel exactly the same when I'm making her come. It gives me a sense of accomplishment. It fuels my competitive drive. As she shivers and moans on top of me, I think to myself, *No one could fuck her like I do. No one could make her feel like this.*

I've never experienced anything like this. It's sex on a whole other level. I wonder if this is some bizarre one-time occurrence or if we could learn to do it again.

If this is my only chance, I'm going to make the most of it. I never want it to end.

Or at least that's what my brain wants. My body is feeling the effects of an unprecedented number of orgasms. I'm tiring, but I want at least one more. I can feel the come boiling in my balls, as if all the loads that should have been released are clamoring to get out.

I roll over on top of Cat, pinning her down in the pillows.

"I'm gonna put the biggest load inside you," I growl.

"Do it," Cat whispers. "Give it to me."

She wraps her legs around my waist, pulling me in tight.

Her pussy feels warmer and wetter than it's ever been. I know I'm going to have to fuck her hard to get this last orgasm.

I drive into her with all my strength, grunting, "You okay?" because even in this state of insanity, one small part of me still wants to be sure she isn't injured.

"Fuck me hard, and don't stop," Cat says, looking up into my eyes.

She's feral, cheeks flushed and curls wild around her face.

I fuck her harder than I ever have before, my hips slamming against her. I fuck her and fuck her until the last orgasm rips through me, carrying along that entire load of come that goes pouring out of me, deep into Cat instead. It's wet and sloppy and primal and intensely satisfying. I'm making sounds I've never made before.

And Cat is loving it. I can see that on her face. Her eyes gleam with triumph, like this is the biggest accomplishment of all, making me come as I never have before in my life.

Cat lies on my chest.

I stroke my fingers through her hair.

I always pet her like this when we're finished.

It's her reward, and she's never earned it as thoroughly as she did tonight.

Her steady, satisfied breaths are the sighs of a sleepy little kitten.

I don't think of Cat as a pet that is disposable or beneath me. I think of her as an exotic, unearthly creature that I've captured and tamed. Far more valuable than an ordinary human.

She was so frightened by me at first.

I remember the day she saw me crying in the school bathrooms.

I had never felt rage like that. I honestly could have killed her.

Looking back on it now, I realize it wasn't anger that drove me... it was shame.

"Dean?" Cat says quietly. Her head shifts slightly on my chest as she looks up at me.

"Yes?" I say.

"Why do you always want everything to be so clean and organized?"

"I like it that way. I hate mess. When something doesn't smell good, I can't stop noticing. It nags at me, distracts me, drives me insane."

"Do I smell good?" Cat asks.

"You smell better than anyone," I tell her honestly.

"Really?" she says, pleased.

"It's one of my favorite things about you. It's like catnip. I can't get enough."

I can tell she's smiling, even though I can only see the edge of her face illuminated by the candlelight.

That's all I had planned to say, but relaxed and in a strangely candid mood, I find myself continuing:

"My father's house in Moscow...it's filthy. Nobody can come inside except me, and I hate being there. He didn't use to be that way, but it's gotten worse and worse. I can't stand it. I've always been... ashamed of it."

"Oh," Cat says.

That one syllable carries so much sympathy and sadness that it pains me. I don't want her to feel sorry for me.

"Anyway," I say gruffly. "My house will never be like that."

"I'd like to have a studio," Cat says dreamily. "A big, open room full of sunshine, with lots of plants hanging down, greenery everywhere. That's where I would paint."

"You still want to be an artist?" I ask her.

Cat hesitates. "Well…I don't know. But I'll always want to draw."

"That sketch you made of the girl by the well…it was beautiful. Not just beautiful…it made me feel things. It was the sketch that made me sure of what you'd done."

We haven't spoken of Rocco in several weeks.

I don't bring it up because I know Cat feels guilty, even though she shouldn't. It was necessary. I would have eliminated someone far more innocent than Rocco if my sister were in danger. If I had a sister, I mean.

"Sometimes sketching is the only thing that makes me feel better about something," Cat says softly. "That's how I used to deal with my dad being an asshole. "Well." She laughs. "It used to be the only thing that made me feel better."

"What do you mean?" I say.

"This has been strangely cathartic too," Cat says, sitting up on her elbow to look at me.

"You like it?" I say.

"I think you know that I do."

We look at each other for a long time.

This is the most honest Cat and I have ever been.

So when she asks her next question, I feel compelled to answer, even though I never talk about this, ever.

"What about your mother?" she says.

"She left me when I was ten years old." I take a breath, wanting to stop but compelled to tell her what I've never told anyone before. "My father was drinking. He was becoming more and more angry and violent. Breaking things in the house. Throwing things at her. I don't think he'd struck her yet, but he shoved her down and she hit her head on the dining room table. He regretted it afterward. He tried to pick her up, tried to apologize, but she ran and locked herself in her room and didn't come out for hours."

"I'm so sorry," Cat says, her big, dark eyes fixed on mine.

"They were happy once. They loved each other, and they loved me. But he was in pain. He was bitter. He drove her away. And she left. Just packed up and disappeared while he was out. She didn't warn me. I came home from school, and the house was dark and quiet. I knew. I just knew."

Cat's eyes glitter with tears. She blinks, and they run down her cheeks in parallel tracks.

"Dean…" she says.

"I don't care!" I say, suddenly embarrassed that I laid open this wound for her to see.

Cat knows I'm lying.

"Can I ask you one last thing?" she says.

I don't know if I can take any more questions. But she interprets my silence as assent.

"Why were you so sad the day that Ozzy's mother died?"

I can tell she's afraid to ask that question, but it must have been eating at her all this time.

I have to really consider it.

I know why I was angry—I had never allowed anyone to see me cry. I had never lost control like that.

But why was I crying in the first place?

I take a deep breath, trying to still the miserable pounding of my heart.

"I just…I just realized that no one would do that for me," I tell her quietly. "Ozzy's mother laid down her life for him. My mother left, and she didn't even take me with her."

I try so hard to keep my voice steady, but it cracks at the very end.

I'm grateful when Cat puts her arms around me so I can hide my face against her neck.

"I'm sure she didn't want to leave," Cat says. "She must have been frightened."

"I know," I say hollowly. "I think he found her and killed her after. She hasn't called or written in years."

"Zoe says our father killed our mother too," Cat murmurs. "She says he let her bleed to death after her last baby."

Cat holds me tight, squeezing me with all her might.

She's small but strong. It's a good hug.

She draws back and looks at me.

"Your father was drinking…because of what Leo's father did to him. Because of the burns."

"Yes."

"Do you hate him still?" Cat asks.

I know she means Leo, not my father.

"No," I sigh. "I'm tired of hating him."

"It's so sad," Cat says. "That your father did love your mother once…"

"The more he loved her, the more he felt he wasn't worthy of her," I say.

"That's just wrong!" Cat cries.

I nod.

But deep inside, I fear that I might feel the same.

CHAPTER 14
CAT

I'M AMAZED AT MY OWN BOLDNESS IN ASKING DEAN PERSONAL questions.

Even more amazed that he answered.

To me, that interaction was more shocking than Dean's apparent superpower for multiple orgasms.

He looked like the same devastated ten-year-old he must have been the day he came home to that empty house. He struggled to keep his face stern and composed, but I could see the awful pain in his eyes.

Dean's past does not justify his actions. However, it certainly explains them.

He's never known anything but shame and abandonment.

I understand the torment of a cold and demanding father and the absence of a mother. But unlike Dean, I had Zoe by my side, always loving me, always keeping me safe.

Dean was completely alone.

My heart aches for him.

I wish I had Zoe here to tell me what the fuck to do about Lola Fischer. If Lola disliked me before, it's nothing compared to her hatred of me after her disgrace in the Quartum Bellum. Eliminated after the first round, she's biting the head off anybody who even mentions it.

And she's harassing me every chance she gets.

Which is very inconvenient with exams right around the corner.

I'm trying to study in the library when she attacks me yet again.

Rakel and I have our textbooks and half-finished papers spread out across our table. Rakel is arguing with me over the benefits of a wireless security system. We're so engrossed in quiet debate that I don't even hear Lola and Dixie creeping up behind me until Lola dumps an entire bottle of milk over my head.

My textbooks and papers are drenched, not to mention my hair and blouse. The milk is cold and sickly sticky, dripping down into my eyes. The papers are all ruined, the ink smeared into oblivion.

"Oops," Lola giggles, shaking out the last few drops all over my history textbook.

Rakel leaps up from her seat, immediately shoved back down by the burly, freckled Dixie Davis.

I look up at Lola with cold fury.

"It's your fault you lost," I tell her. "You're a shit leader."

Lola's smirk turns into a snarl of rage. She has such pretty, doll-like features that anger distorts them to a disproportionate degree. She's like a harpy, transformed by fury.

She opens her mouth to attack me in return, only to be interrupted by Ms. Robin's surprisingly sharp voice.

"What happened here?" she demands.

Lola instantly reverts to her innocent smile and singsong voice.

"Cat spilled her milk," she says sweetly. "I told her food isn't allowed in the library."

"She spilled it on her own head?" Ms. Robin says coldly. "How ingenious of her."

Lola shrugs shamelessly. "She's so clumsy."

"You're banned from the library," Ms. Robin says without hesitation. "For one month."

"What!?" Lola shrieks. "How am I supposed to study for our exams?"

"I really don't give a shit," Ms. Robin says. "Now get out before I make you mop up this mess with that fancy little blouse you're wearing."

Lola is white with anger, her expression venomous.

The usually shy and gentle Ms. Robin faces her unafraid, her hazel eyes snapping and her arms crossed over her chest.

Lola is wise enough not to argue further. She and Dixie skulk off down the ramp while Rakel tries to gather up the sodden textbooks.

"Sorry about that," I say to Ms. Robin.

I really do feel awful about soaking the table and rug in milk, even though it wasn't exactly voluntary.

I'm still dripping milk right now, which makes it difficult to help clean up. Also, my soaked white shirt is now transparent, a fact the boys at the neighboring table have not failed to notice. Corbin Castro mutters something to Thomas York, and they both laugh. My face burns.

"There's paper towels over by my desk," Ms. Robin tells Rakel kindly. "Cat, why don't you come upstairs with me? I've got a sink. You can clean up. You can borrow a cardigan too."

"Thank you," I say gratefully.

I follow Ms. Robin up the spiraling ramp to the topmost level, trying unsuccessfully not to leave a trail of droplets along the rug.

The library is always chilly, which is probably why Ms. Robin wears three or four sweaters layered over top of each other, the sleeves long enough to hang down over her hands. The milk was fresh out of the dining hall fridge, and I'm shivering.

Ms. Robin stretches up on tiptoe to pull down the ladder that leads to her private loft.

I feel a little awkward following her up. I've never been inside a teacher's quarters before.

The compact, circular space sits directly under the pointed roof. I notice at once how tidy and organized she is, not a single cup or book out of place. Despite the fact that the library is stuffed with thousands of books, Ms. Robin keeps dozens more on her personal shelves. A low couch, a narrow bed, and a hot plate all share the same space.

No art hangs on the walls. Instead, I see dozens of the weathered maps and schematics upon which Ms. Robin labors in pursuit of her doctoral thesis on ancient monasteries. She has them pinned up all around, several marked with Post-it notes.

"Don't tell the chancellor about those," Ms. Robin says with a conspiratorial smile. "I don't think you're supposed to stick a Post-it to a seven-hundred-year-old document, but to be frank, they were hardly in pristine condition when I got them. The archives are an absolute mess. Half those charts were soaked in mouse urine and god knows what else."

She opens a hobbit-size door leading to her bathroom.

"Watch your head," she laughs. "I think they expected all the librarians to be pocket-size."

"I am, so I'll be fine," I assure her.

I head into the bathroom, which is just as scrupulously clean as the rest of Ms. Robin's space. A fresh bar of soap sits on a pristine dish, and the hand towels are freshly laundered, folded neatly over their bar.

I can smell Ms. Robin's perfume. I can't resist locating the glass bottle sitting on the toiletry shelf. Givenchy *L'Interdit*—orange blossom, jasmine, and dark vetiver. Exotic and rather thrilling for a librarian. But of course, I've long suspected that Ms. Robin has hidden stores of adventurousness inside her. After all, she came to this lonely island to work, and she certainly had no trouble telling Lola to fuck off.

I grin, remembering Lola's livid face, as I carefully set the bottle back on its shelf.

Then I strip off my sodden shirt and rinse it out at the sink. Wringing it dry as best I can, I hang it over the rack and then wash the milk from my hair and face.

I hope Ms. Robin doesn't mind me using all her towels.

As I straighten up, I see something that even Ms. Robin's careful cleaning must have missed—a splash of red on the tiles behind the faucet.

It looks like blood.

I rub my fingertip across the spot. It stains the skin red. I inhale a faint chemical scent.

Frowning, I wash my hands again.

A faint patch of red remains on my fingertip.

I don't mean to be so nosy. Whether it's my Spy training, or whether I've had this incessant curiosity inside me all along, I can't help feeling that I'm missing something here. Something tantalizing, just out of reach…

I don't want to be suspicious of Ms. Robin. She's always been kind to me. In fact, she saved me from Rocco just last year. I don't think it was any coincidence that she snatched my book bag out of Dax Volker's hands right when Rocco was about to discover me hiding in the shelves.

Quickly, I carry my damp shirt and the used towels out to Ms. Robin.

"Better?" She smiles.

"Yeah, thank you," I say, standing there shyly in my bra.

Ms. Robin doesn't make me feel weird about it. Instead, she passes me a soft, warm cardigan that smells as freshly laundered as the towels.

"Keep it as long as you need," she says, smiling. "As you can tell, I have quite a few of them."

"Really, thank you so much," I say. "You always look out for me."

"Well, I liked Zoe. And I'm glad to see you following in her footsteps."

"What do you mean?" I ask.

"Zoe wasn't afraid to go after what she wanted," Ms. Robin says. "I see that in you too."

I have the distinctly uncomfortable sensation that for all I guess about Ms. Robin, she sees far more about me.

"Right…" I say hesitantly.

"How is Zoe, by the way?"

"Very happy. She moved to Los Angeles with Miles."

"Good." Ms. Robin smiles. "I'm glad Rocco is no longer an impediment."

Now I feel a distinct chill. Ms. Robin looks as sweet as ever, but there can be no doubt that she feels not the slightest particle of sympathy for the untimely demise of Rocco Prince.

"Well," she says, "I'd better get back to work. I'll walk you down, Cat."

I follow Ms. Robin back down the ladder, uncertain how much I've enjoyed the added intimacy between us.

When I meet Dean that evening in the bell tower, he confronts me at once.

"What the fuck is this I hear from Corbin Castro that Lola Fischer dumped a bottle of milk on your head?"

"Yeah, she sucks." I shrug, not really wanting to discuss it.

"Does she have a problem with you?" Dean demands.

I hadn't told him that Lola was harassing me. Since Dean and I don't share any classes, he hadn't witnessed her aggression firsthand.

"She a little bit hates my guts," I admit.

"Why?" Dean says.

I sigh. "No good reason."

Dean's eyes glint with that electric gleam I know so well. He says, in his deadliest voice, "I'll deal with her."

"No!" I beg. "Seriously, Dean, please don't. She's just an asshole. I don't want it to turn into a whole thing."

Dean looks at me, stern and unsmiling. He grabs the ring of

my collar and pulls me close so I'm pressed against his furnace-like chest, having to tilt my chin all the way up to look into his face.

"She should know that you belong to me, little kitten," he says softly. "That means she has no right to fuck with you. Because when she fucks with you, she fucks with me."

Dean kisses me.

He's still gripping the collar. The compression on my throat makes my head spin.

He releases me.

"Strip," he says as he selects the next song he wants to play.

I remove my clothes with trembling fingers. The closer it gets to Christmas, the colder the bell tower becomes, the chill let in through the gaps in the walls. But I know the minute I'm touching Dean, his blazing heat will warm me to the bone.

I'm shivering with anticipation more than with cold.

I can hardly stand the hours leading up to when I see Dean each night.

Our encounters in the bell tower have become more real than actual life. Everything else feels like a floating dream compared to the intense sensation I experience here. I'm asleep in real life. I'm only truly awake with him.

"Kneel," Dean orders once I'm naked.

I sink to my knees on the rough wooden boards, looking up at him.

Dean has likewise stripped off his clothes. He towers over me like a god. I want to be on my knees before him. I want to worship him.

His cock is already heavy and swollen, anticipating the touch of my lips.

"Suck my cock like you did last time," he orders. "Softly."

I know what he wants. He wants to see if we can replicate what we did last time.

I'm equally curious.

I run my fingers lightly down his shaft and flick my tongue gently around the head of his cock. As it begins to reach its full thickness and length, the pale skin stretching tight over the head, I take it in my mouth. I keep the pressure light, soft, and steady. I start to bring him to the edge, but slowly…holding him back as long as I can.

Dean breathes deep and slow, using his substantial powers of concentration.

I've never met anyone as disciplined as Dean. He has an intense level of willpower—I believe that's the key to him taking control of this usually involuntary process.

His legs begin to shake, and he throws his head back and groans. His cock twitches and spasms in my mouth. Only a little clear fluid comes out on my tongue—he's held back his actual load. I smile around his cock, knowing that means he's going to be able to come again.

Sure enough, his cock only grows harder, and I keep sucking it slowly, hardly able to hold back my grin.

I fucking love this.

I love making him come over and over.

I increase the pace just a little, having learned last time that I can increase the intensity of each subsequent orgasm as long as I ramp it up gradually.

Dean thrusts his hands in my hair and fucks my face, even and slow.

I love when he lets me work, but I also love when he takes control like that, pushing his cock in deep until it hits the back of my throat and then pushing it even a little farther. It's rough and dominant. It makes all the muscles stand out on his chest and arms. I grip the backs of his thighs, gagging helplessly.

He comes again, holding his cock in the back of my throat while it pulses. He gives out a deep, guttural moan, a primal sound that makes my pussy soaking wet.

Dean releases me.

"Come here," he orders.

I follow him over to the stack of cushions.

"Get on all fours," he says.

I obey, waiting while he moves around behind me, gathering up some unseen objects.

Every time I come up here, Dean has some new plan in store for me. I can never guess what he'll do to me. That endless inventiveness and endless pushing of boundaries are what keeps me in a fever pitch of anticipation.

Dean kneels on the cushions next to me, running his hand possessively down my spine and groping my ass. I wait, mentally begging him to take his hand down lower and rub me where I really want.

He knows. He knows exactly what I'm silently pleading for.

He slips his hand between my thighs, cupping my pussy. I groan softly. He parts my pussy lips and slides his fingers back and forth across my clit.

"Ohhh," I moan.

"You like that, little kitten?"

"Yesss," I sigh.

"What about this?"

He slips his finger inside me. I'm already so swollen and sensitive inside that his finger feels as big as a cock. I groan even louder.

He soaks his fingers in my wetness, and then he rubs his thumb a little higher, over the bud of my ass.

I stiffen up, instantly uncomfortable.

"Shh," Dean says, his other hand on the small of my back, holding me in place.

He rubs circles around my asshole, then applies gentle pressure.

My whole body is rigid. I can feel my face flaming.

Dean has never touched my ass before. I know how much he hates anything dirty. I showered right before I came, but I'm paranoid that I might still be unclean somehow.

"Stay still," he growls.

He begins to push his thumb into my ass.

The pressure is intense. I try to squirm away, but he's holding me still with that heavy hand on my back.

I'm embarrassed, almost panicking.

The sensation is like nothing I've felt before. It feels totally wrong, yet at the same time…it also feels good. Which only humiliates me all the more.

I close my eyes, unable to even look at the floor in front of me.

Dean's finger is all the way in my ass now. It's so intense that I can hardly stand it. It seemed to take ten minutes to push it in and ten minutes to pull it out again.

Finally, my ass can relax again, but I keep my eyes squeezed shut, too embarrassed to look at him.

I hear Dean moving behind me. I hope that was the end of it.

Instead, I feel something else pressed up against my anus. Something bigger and colder.

"Dean!" I squeal in protest.

"Quiet," he growls.

He pushes the plug against my ass. It's too big to go in, despite the fact that he's lubricated it.

"Relax," he orders.

Immediately, without conscious thought, I obey him. My ass relaxes enough for him to begin to push the plug inside.

If I thought his finger was intense, it was nothing compared to this. The plug feels the size of a fist. I'm impaled.

"It's too big!" I squeal.

Dean gives a low laugh. "It's tiny," he says.

Dean never lies, yet I can't believe that. Every nerve in that highly sensitive area is screaming from this unprecedented friction.

Dean reaches down with his other hand to rub my clit while he pushes the plug inside.

The pleasure of his touch helps so much. As I've already learned, sexual pleasure can override an immense amount of discomfort.

The sexual sensation seems to confuse my brain, convincing it that not only are Dean's fingers on my clit pleasurable but also the plug itself. It seems to rewrite the neuron response.

The plug stretches and stretches me, until all of a sudden, it sets in place as if it were made for me.

I sigh with relief.

"How does that feel?" Dean asks.

I consider. The plug gives me an acute sense of fullness and pressure. But there isn't any pain—it fits perfectly.

"It's…strange," I say.

"Good," Dean growls. "Now climb on my cock."

"Right now?" I squeak. "With this?"

"That's right," he says. "This is for me, not you. I want to feel it while you ride me."

Dean lies back against the cushions, his cock jutting upward, expecting me to climb on.

Swallowing hard, I shift positions.

Every tiny movement makes the plug move inside me, reigniting the nerves, reminding me of its existence.

It's a little uncomfortable.

But also…it feels good in a way I've never felt before. An entirely new sensation.

I straddle Dean, worried that the plug might fall out.

No chance of that—the flared shape keeps it exactly in place inside me.

Slowly, I lower myself down on his cock.

"Oh, fuuuck," I groan.

Dean's cock has never felt so enormous, not even the first time.

There's no space inside me for both his cock and the plug, yet I'm forcing them both in.

The tightness is insane.

Dean groans simultaneously, feeling the pressure and grip as intensely as I am.

"God, yes," he moans. "I can feel it rubbing against my cock."

I slide all the way down on him. Then, carefully, I begin to ride him.

The sensation is so extreme that we can barely breathe, let alone speak.

It feels good. I mean really fucking good.

I'm ashamed how good it feels, but it's too pleasurable for me to care. I want more.

I increase the pace, and Dean instantly begins to come. He grips my waist, making a desperate moaning sound, his whole body shaking beneath me.

I fucking love being on top of him.

I love riding a man like Dean.

Every tendon stands out on his neck, his chest and shoulders swollen with the effort of fucking me. He looks more powerful and muscular than ever before.

Yet he's completely at my mercy.

I'm the one dominating him now. I'm the one in control of his pleasure.

I can ride him faster or slower. I can grind or bounce on his cock.

I can tease the pleasure out of him at my will. He's shaking beneath me, kissing me ferociously, utterly obsessed with me in this moment.

I think I could ask him for anything, and he'd give it to me.

I could never get this rush fucking a lesser man.

The more violent and vicious Dean behaves, the more of a thrill it is to see him like this: gasping, vulnerable, and totally wrapped up in me.

I'm high on it.

I make him come over and over, and every time he does, I

come too, because I'm drunk with the eroticism, with this sense of omnipotence.

I will never be physically strong, not like Dean.

But I feel powerful when I have power over Dean.

"You like that?" Dean growls, his hands gripping my waist. "You like riding me with that plug up your ass?"

He said it was for him, but he knows how good it feels for me too. It's a doubling of pleasure, like I'm being fucked twice over.

"Yes," I admit, blushing with the taboo of it. "I fucking love it."

"Good girl," Dean says.

I come again, melting with pleasure and satisfaction.

"I want to see it," Dean says.

He flips me over and shoves my face down in the pillows, pulling my hips up so my ass is in the air. He drives into me from behind, fucking me hard and fast.

I know he's looking at the plug in my ass. I should feel embarrassed by that.

But right now, I don't give a fuck. We're way past shyness. I want Dean to take his pleasure out of me any way he likes. I want my body to be his plaything.

"Harder," I beg. "Fuck me harder."

I want more, more, more.

There's never enough.

Dean roars as he explodes into me, what feels like a gallon of come pumping out of him.

I turn my face into the pillows, grinning with delight.

CHAPTER 15
DEAN

ONLY A WEEK REMAINS BEFORE CHRISTMAS.

That means I only have one more week with Cat as my pet.

That's a problem, because I'm completely fixated on her. She occupies my mind night and day.

An additional problem: I fucking need her to come.

I tested it on Saturday morning when Bram walked down to the village with Valon.

I stayed alone in our dorm room, setting myself up in my bed, planning to try to stroke my cock light and steady like Cat does. I wanted to prove to myself that I was the one in control of my orgasms. That I could make myself come over and over just like she does, that I didn't need her.

I lay back and tried to think of things other than Cat. I didn't even want to use her for mental stimulation.

But no matter what kind of woman I tried to picture, tall or short, thin or curvy, I couldn't get hard. They all seemed bland and insipid, as plastic as dolls.

I only felt that spark of lust when I pictured Cat on her knees before me, with that wild mane of dark curls all around her face and those big, innocent eyes looking up at me above her mischievous smile.

Then my cock swelled to life. I couldn't help but picture her crawling around in that sinuous way, the candlelight gleaming on her tight body.

I scowled, thinking that I would use her for fantasy but I'd come all on my own, without her touch.

I stroked myself, imagining it was Cat's small hand wrapped around my cock, making it look enormous.

My hand was too big, too rough, too clumsy. It felt wrong.

Far from coming multiple times, I couldn't bring myself to climax at all.

I wanted her, not myself.

Disgusted, I flung the covers off and went to shower, pent-up and furious.

I can't be this dependent on her. Especially not with so little time left.

It's dangerous and weak. I told myself I'd never make this mistake again, wrapping up my desires in a woman.

That night in the tower, I fucked Cat viciously, telling myself I was only using her, that I didn't care about her at all.

I never should have told her about my mother.

I never should have told her anything at all.

Cat didn't seem to care that I was in an awful mood. She didn't mind that I was rough with her. She bit and scratched me back until we had scattered the cushions and rubbed our backs raw on the floor.

When we lay there after, panting and sweating…I felt nothing but peace.

———

Sunday, I go hunting for Lola Fischer.

I find her lounging in the common room of the gatehouse, with Dixie Davis and a half-dozen other members of the Dixie Mafia.

They're a motley group, all ages and appearances. The Dixie Mafia is one of the only Mafia groups not connected by family or country of origin. They recruit out of prison, and their members include both wealthy entrepreneurs who run the businesses along the strip in Biloxi as well as decidedly less-reputable members operating riverboat casinos, strip joints, and bingo parlors all through the Appalachian states.

Which is why Lola dresses like a dolled-up debutante while her henchmen Carter Ross and Belkie Blintz look like they've never encountered indoor plumbing.

She notices me at once as I enter the large and cluttered common room, messy with abandoned shoes and pullovers and the detritus of forgotten snacks. I can see from how she sits up a little straighter and tosses back her fair hair that she knows why I'm here.

"Dean Yenin," she says, batting those big blue eyes at me. "What a pleasant surprise."

"I doubt it's pleasant or a surprise," I reply coolly.

"Oh, it's both, I assure you." She smiles sweetly. "After all, when have you ever broken that brooding silence of yours to speak to me before?"

"I'd prefer to keep it that way," I say flatly. "But you've been putting your hands on something that belongs to me."

Lola pouts. "You can't possibly mean Cat Romero."

"That's exactly what I mean."

"That shy little mouse...she's not worth the time to walk over here."

"And you're not worth the breath that sentence took. So let's cut this short. Cat is under my protection. You don't talk to her. You don't touch her. Is that simple enough for you?"

A flicker of anger crosses Lola's face. She quickly smooths it away, putting out a hand to still Carter and Belkie, who shift menacingly in their seats.

"And what do I get in return?" she inquires. "After all...Cat lost the Quartum Bellum for us."

"You did that to yourself," I say coldly. "In fact, I should break your fucking neck for trying to break hers. As for what you get—how about I let your henchmen keep their arms? Unless they try to stand up from those seats again, in which case, I'll use Carter's fist to beat Belkie's fuckin' head in."

Lola toys with a lock of her shining hair, her eyes bright with interest, as if she'd enjoy watching that happen, even to her own friends.

She stands up, crossing the space between us with an unnecessary swaying of hips.

"I've always thought you had a certain spark that I find quite… fascinating," she says, trailing her fingers up my arm.

Her floral perfume fills my nostrils. It stinks.

I shake her off roughly.

"There's nothing interesting about you."

Now Lola isn't smiling at all. Her face is pale and pinched, her lips disappearing in one thin line.

"Stay away from Cat," I warn her. "Or suffer the consequences."

I turn away from Lola and stride off, feeling certain that if she had a knife close at hand she'd fling it between my shoulder blades.

Trying to focus on my exams is torture when all I want to think about is Cat.

Our last week is slipping away faster than I can believe.

Next Monday is Christmas Eve. The end of our agreement.

I'm determined to make the most of the time I have left by executing every dark fantasy I've had on Cat's willing body.

There's one thing in particular I'm aching to try.

I want to fuck her in the ass.

I can't stop thinking about it, ever since I put that plug in her.

I've never tried it before. Never wanted to.

But the way Cat responds to being touched there is so fucking enticing…it's like I discovered this secret button that overrides every other impulse. She can't resist it, no matter how uncomfortable it makes her feel.

That delicious combination of resistance and submission is irresistible to me.

I've been having a hell of a time getting the supplies I need on the island. With Miles Griffin gone, I've had to go to the much less effective Louis Faucheux for contraband and pay his goddamn outrageous prices. He charged me $400 for that steel plug.

Doesn't matter. So far, it's been worth every penny.

Tonight, I tell Cat to meet me earlier than usual up in the bell tower. I want to have plenty of time to work on her.

She arrives precisely on time, knowing the consequences if she's late. Without me even asking, she begins to undress until she's fully naked.

"What do you want me to do?" she asks quietly, her dark eyes looking up at me.

"Get in position."

Obediently, Cat sinks to her knees in the middle of the floor. She sits on her heels, shoulders back, chest out, hands clasped lightly behind her.

I circle her slowly, examining her body from every angle in the guttering candlelight.

Her beautiful breasts have a rosy glow. Her slim waist flares out to a full, heart-shaped ass resting on those bare feet.

Yet it's her face that draws my gaze—delicate, soft, with a hidden wickedness that flickers in and out of being like candlelight.

Her nipples stiffen, and I know that when I touch her pussy, it will already be wet.

I strip off my clothes slowly, folding them and laying them in a neat pile. Cat's dark eyes watch my every movement. They slide over my skin. Now her nipples are pebble hard.

My cock hangs down heavy and swollen. It swings as I walk toward her.

I grasp it in my hand and trail the head across her lips.

Cat's mouth opens slightly.

"Put out your tongue," I order.

Cat extends her soft pink tongue.

I rub the head of my cock across it until a little clear fluid runs down onto her tongue.

"Swallow it."

Cat closes her mouth, and her tongue darts out to lick the last drops of precum off her lips before she swallows.

"Good girl. Go lie on the cushions."

Cat crawls over to the cushions, giving me a deliberate, sensuous look at her perfectly shaped legs and ass as she glances back at me over her shoulder.

She rolls over onto her back, her thighs parting automatically.

I drop down between them, thrusting my tongue directly into her pussy. Cat squeals with pleasure, her fingers plunging into my hair as she grabs the back of my head, her nails scratching pleasantly against my scalp. I lick her pussy up and down, swirling my tongue around her clit until she's moaning and writhing against the pillows.

I dip my fingers inside her, wetting them thoroughly, and then I rub that wetness all around her ass. Cat squirms, knowing what's coming next. Sure enough, I start to apply pressure against that resistant little bud, pressing and rubbing gently until it finally begins to relax.

All the while, I'm licking her clit steadily, warming her up, awakening every part of her to sensual pleasure.

I spend an achingly long time eating her pussy, bringing her to the brink of orgasm again and again but not allowing her to tip over. I keep fingering her ass until she's relaxed enough that I can slip a finger in and out with relative ease.

Then I turn her over.

Cat knows what's coming, and she instantly stiffens up, the muscles going rigid all the way down along her spine.

"Relax," I growl.

Cat tries to obey, but she's too nervous.

I massage that tight back, pushing my palms up her lower back and down again, kneading the globes of her ass, even rubbing her hamstrings. When Cat is sufficiently soothed, I lube up my fingers and start penetrating her ass again, slowly and gently.

She lets out a long moan of helpless pleasure.

Now I know she's ready.

My cock is an iron bar, red hot and standing straight out from my body. It looks enormous as I place the head between those tight, round ass cheeks.

I hold Cat pinned down with my knees on her hamstrings. I lube up the head of my cock, press it against her anus, and begin to push it inside.

"Oh my god," Cat groans. "Oh fuck…"

"Shh."

I put barely an inch inside her. Then I wait.

The pressure and tightness are phenomenally intense around the head of my cock. I can only imagine how it feels for Cat.

As her ass relaxes, I push my cock in a little farther. Millimeter by millimeter, I keep going, with long pauses to let her get used to it.

When it seems like she can't handle any more, I slip my hand under her hip and rub her clit until her ass relaxes again.

"Take it," I growl, pushing in farther.

I don't stop until my cock is all the way inside her, squeezed in a vise grip that's like nothing I've ever known.

It takes every ounce of my willpower not to explode. I'm holding still as much for my benefit as hers. I don't want to spoil the party too soon.

Cat is making noises like I've never heard. Squeals and groans but also little whimpers of pleasure. After a moment of holding still all the way inside her, she starts to rock her hips just the tiniest bit, feeling the insane friction of my cock stuffed deep in her ass.

This is the ultimate submission.

Me taking the ultimate prize from her and Cat giving it to me.

Enduring the discomfort for me because I want it.

Slowly, carefully, I fuck her ass with shallow thrusts.

Cat moans, low and desperate. She grinds her pussy against my hand, her ass squeezing around my cock.

I fucking love it.

But I want more.

Very slowly, I withdraw my cock from her ass.

Cat sighs with relief as I pull all the way out.

"I'm not done," I tell her. "Get on top of me."

"You mean…"

"Yes, that's what I mean."

Cat straddles me while I lube up my cock even more. It has to be fully slippery to slide into that tight little ass.

This time, Cat positions my cock and slowly sinks down on it. I watch her face, delighting in every wince as my cock impales her ass all over again from this new angle.

"Do it," I growl. "Ride me with my cock up your ass."

Slowly, Cat rocks her hips, accustoming herself to this brand-new sensation. Her clit rubs against my lower belly, as it always does in this position. And just as I suspected, she finds her rhythm and begins to moan with every thrust, her cheeks flushing as the pleasure begins to mount inside her.

She can't ride me as vigorously, but the friction is so tight that neither of us could stand that anyway. Every tiny movement feels ten times as intense as usual.

Her breath quickens, and her whole chest flushes as pink as her face. She's panting. I know she wants to come, but something is holding her back—either the edge of discomfort or her own embarrassment at climaxing in such a taboo way.

"Do it," I order. "Come on my cock."

She groans, biting her lip and riding my cock.

"I can't…" she moans.

"Can't or won't?"

"I don't know!" she cries helplessly.

I seize her by the throat and grab her hip in my other hand, forcing her down on my cock.

"Do it," I growl, thrusting up inside her. "Fucking come."

"*Aghhhh*," she moans, her eyes rolling back.

The orgasm hits, her hips rocking against me, her ass squeezing around my cock in rhythmic pulses.

I've never felt so much power, forcing her to come with my cock rammed up her ass.

I own her body.

I own her pleasure.

She'll do anything for me.

With that thought, I explode inside her, coming deep inside the tightest, most forbidden place.

I ride the high of that encounter for several days, playing it over and over again in my mind.

I've never felt such a rush.

The wilder and more uninhibited I am with Cat, the better it feels.

And she feels the same. I know she does.

When she lay in my arms afterward, panting and sweating, looking up at the stars through the holes in the tower roof, she said, "That was the craziest thing I've ever felt."

In this new universe we've created together, crazy is good. Insane is even better.

That blissful state only lasts until Sunday, when I'm expected to call my father.

We haven't spoken in over a month.

I have to call him now, before Christmas, because I know he won't want to talk to me over the holiday.

He married my mother on December 26th. She had always wanted a snowy wedding, and the weather obliged—their photos are filled with swirling white flakes, as if the whole sky scattered confetti on their heads.

He hasn't celebrated Christmas since she left.

"Hello, Dmitry," he says when he picks up the phone.

His voice sounds dull and echoing, as if his office is empty, though I know it isn't.

"Hello, Father."

"Did you call to tell me the results of your exams?"

"We don't have all the marks back yet. But I'm in first place so far on the tests that have been scored."

"Hm," he grunts.

No compliment. No congratulations.

"How is work?" I ask him politely.

"As it always is," he says.

I grip the receiver tightly, alone in the bank of phones on the ground floor of the keep. I'm filled with the helpless misery that always overtakes me at the coldness of my father's voice.

Why does he speak to me like a robot?

You would never know he was talking to his one and only son.

Trying to force some response from him, I say, "I met someone, Father. A girl."

"I thought you learned your lesson last time," he says. "After that embarrassing affair with Anna Wilk."

Oh, so we remember Anna all of a sudden, do we?

The plastic receiver creaks as I squeeze it so hard it could almost break.

"This is different," I say.

"This is not the time for dating," my father briskly informs me. "You need to secure your place in the Moscow Bratva. Once you have done so, you can make an advantageous match among the daughters of our allies."

"You didn't," I say before I can stop myself.

We never speak of my mother. Ever.

A long silence follows in which I think my father might have hung up on me. Then he says, very coldly, "And look what a love match got me."

"Just me," I say bitterly. "Your son."

"Exactly," my father says, and he does end the call, without a word of goodbye.

I'm breathing so hard I think I might be sick.

I slam the receiver down, then snatch it up again and hit the display with it over and over, until the plastic splinters and half the numeric pads pop off.

Then I stalk out of the keep, walking so fast I'm almost running, my head a churning storm of fury and my fists clenched at my sides.

I don't know where I'm going until I pass the old wine cellar leading down to the undercroft. I wrench open its door, descending the dark steps into the earth.

Jasper Webb passes me in the hallway, skeleton hands tucked in his pockets. He gives me a friendly nod, which I ignore in favor of hammering on Cat's door.

She opens it a moment later, looking drowsy and startled. She must have been sleeping in. Her hair is a bird's nest, and she's wearing an oversize T-shirt with nothing underneath. Even in this state of fury, I feel my cock twitching in my pants at the sight of her small, bra-less breasts loose under the shirt and her bare legs extending beneath its waffled hem.

"Dean?" she says, confused. "What is it?"

"Do you want to go to the dance with me?" I say.

"The Christmas dance?" Cat asks, as if there's another one.

"Yes," I hiss, impatient and already regretting this.

Regretting it because…if she says no, I'm going to have to burn this whole school to the ground.

Cat hesitates.

The seconds stretch out torturously. I'm about to abandon this whole idea and leave when at last she says, very softly, "That would be nice."

I search her face, trying to see if she really means that.

Cat has grown up a lot in the time I've known her, but right now she looks just as young and scared as she did on the very first day of school.

"Alright," I say gruffly. "See you tonight, then."

"See you tonight," she whispers.

I leave, my guts still churning with anger.

But maybe just a little bit less than before.

CHAPTER 16
CAT

IT'S CHRISTMAS EVE.

I'm dressing for the dance with Anna, Chay, and Rakel.

We're in Anna and Chay's dorm room, which is one of the largest and prettiest in the solar, where all the female Heirs have their rooms. They have a stunning view over the cliffs straight down to the dark, rolling ocean.

Anna's battered ballet slippers dangle from the footboard of her bed, and several of Chay's tattoo designs hang on the walls. Chay's a master of classic pinup style, as evidenced by the large Bettie Page portrait on her right thigh.

On Chay's nightstand sits an eight-by-ten-inch photograph of her and Ozzy riding four-wheelers, both of them covered in mud, only recognizable by the white slashes of their smiles as they laugh together.

Rakel and Chay are poring over each other's substantial makeup kits while Anna unwinds her waist-length blond hair from a thousand straw curlers.

Chay's brought out a bottle of pear brandy, which she informs us is a crucial part of any Christmas celebration. I took one shot and that was quite enough for me—I'm already giggly and much more talkative than usual.

Music blasts from Anna's scratchy portable speaker.

"Why does that thing make every song sound like it's playing on the radio in 1942?" Chay demands.

"'Cause you've knocked it in the sand ten times over!" Anna scolds her.

"I'm not the only one who knocked it in the sand," Chay huffs.

"That doesn't make it play any better," Anna says.

"I've got a speaker down in our dorm," Rakel says. "I could grab it."

"Nah." Chay shakes her head. "Don't bother. This thing works alright, and it's balls cold outside. You don't want to walk all that way."

"You got a date for the dance?" Anna asks Rakel.

"Sort of." Rakel shrugs. "I told Joss Burmingham I'd go with him. Just as friends, though," she hastens to add.

Joss is in our Interrogation class.

"You didn't tell me that!" I cry.

"Because there's nothing to tell," Rakel says with a surly scowl. "I don't like him or anything."

"God no!" Anna says. "We would never suspect you of *liking* someone."

"Ares and I are going as friends too," Chay tells Rakel. "Just so neither one of us is a third wheel to Anna and Leo."

There's an awkward pause as everyone looks at me out of the corner of their eyes.

I know what they want to ask, and I'm already blushing.

"I'm going with Dean," I admit.

"Like an actual date?" Chay says, raising an eyebrow.

"Uh…I think so," I say.

Rakel knows I've been out every single night this month, so she has a pretty good idea that Dean and I have been seeing each other regularly. And from the state of my hair when I get home, I also think she knows what most of our previous "dates" consisted of. She looks even more skeptical than Chay.

Only Anna smiles at me encouragingly. "You know, Dean's been acting halfway human lately. Maybe he's grown up a little. Haven't we all?"

"Maybe…" Chay says slowly. "But you know, you can't turn a wolf into a puppy."

"That's alright." I shrug. "I don't want him to be a puppy."

All the girls spend an hour or more on their hair and makeup, Anna unleashing a torrent of curls from their wrappers and Chay twisting her reddish-blond hair up in a sleek chignon. Rakel puts hers in a spiky faux-hawk that makes her look more Viking than ever.

I wear my curls parted on the side and smoothed down into waves, a bit like one of Chay's pinup girls. My gown is a simple crimson silk, and I paint my lips the same shade.

The other three girls look utterly stunning by the time they're done. Rakel's dress is an electric violet color, short and punky. Chay's wearing a long white sheath with a panel down the back that looks like a cape. And Anna is dressed in black as usual, so gauzy and transparent that she floats along like an ethereal witch.

I feel plain next to all that beauty.

And I'm strangely nervous to spend an evening with Dean outside the bell tower.

Is he actually planning to talk and dance with me tonight like a normal couple?

I put the leather collar around my neck as usual.

It's a lot more noticeable with the low cut of my gown. I see Chay eyeing it, but for once, she doesn't demand an explanation.

There's a knock at the door. Anna answers, stretching up on tiptoe to kiss Leo.

"You're too gorgeous," he says. "I'm not gonna make it through the night."

"I'll resuscitate you," Anna laughs.

Ares stands just outside the doorframe, darkly handsome

despite the fact that his suit is neither as expensive nor as well-fitting as Leo's. He holds out an arm to Chay, who links her hand through.

Chay had a crush on Ares once upon a time, but it's clear from the platonic tone of their greeting that no lingering romantic interest remains. I don't think it was ever there on Ares's side. Actually, I thought he might have feelings for Zoe before Miles came along, but Zoe swore up and down that was never the case.

"He never flirted with me," Zoe had told me.

"Yeah, but he was at the library with you constantly…"

"Well," Zoe said, giving me a mysterious look, "if you want to know my secret theory…"

"Always," I laughed.

"Once, we were climbing the stairs of the library tower, and my shoelace came undone. I stopped to tie it, and Ms. Robin thought Ares came in alone…"

"And?" I said, giddy with the thrill that always comes over me when I learn a piece of information I'm not supposed to know.

"Well…she didn't say anything strange. But it was the *way* she talked to him."

"What do you mean?"

"Just so…familiar."

"Oh." I shrugged, disappointed. "He's in there all the time, just like you."

"I suppose," Zoe said stubbornly. "It just seemed so…intimate."

"You think they have a thing for each other?"

"I don't know." Zoe was losing confidence in her theory, realizing the flimsiness of her evidence.

"She's a lot older than him," I said.

"But she's so beautiful."

I had shaken my head, dismissing Zoe's idea.

But I've thought of it plenty of times since—almost every time I've seen Ares or Ms. Robin. They're both so reclusive and so carefully contained. Just the sort of people who could hide a secret affair. It does seem impossible that someone as handsome as Ares would resist so much willing female attention from his fellow students without a very good reason…

"I told Joss I'd meet him in the grand hall," Rakel says, snapping me out of my speculation. "You want to walk over with me?"

"Sure." I nod. "I'm meeting Dean there too."

We cross the long expanse of crunching, frosty grass separating the solar from the grand hall. Dozens of students in their dress clothes likewise hurry in the same direction, some paired up as couples and other bunches of boys left without a date in our gender-imbalanced school.

I spot Dean waiting outside the doors, instantly recognizable with his pale skin and hair ghostly white against his ink-black tux.

"Go on ahead," I say to Rakel.

She passes through the doors into the hall, while Dean pulls me to the side so we can speak in relative privacy.

"Sorry I'm late—" I begin.

"Never mind that," Dean says. "Why are you wearing that?"

He's looking at the collar around my neck.

"I thought…"

"The month is over. You can take it off."

"Alright," I say hesitantly. I reach behind my neck to undo the buckle, fumbling with the cold-stiffened leather.

Dean turns me around and deftly unbuckles the collar with his much stronger fingers.

My neck feels cold and naked without it. I've worn that collar almost constantly this last month. Dean slips it in his pocket. I feel strangely rejected, as if he's taken something from me.

"Our deal is done," Dean says, his purplish eyes fixed on mine. "You held up your end of the bargain. And your secret is safe. I'll never speak a word of it to anyone. In fact, you don't have to do this tonight." He nods toward the pale golden light leaking out of the heavy double doors. "We can go inside, part ways, and never speak again if that's the way you want it."

"Is that what *you* want?" I ask, looking up at him, his face like marble in the moonlight.

He flinches, and I see it—the crack in his armor. And the real person beneath.

"No," he says quietly.

"I don't want that either," I say, slipping my hand into his. "I want to dance with you tonight."

"Good," Dean breathes. "Because the way you look in that dress—I couldn't stand to see you dance with anyone else."

My heart is beating faster than it ever has before—even in Dean's and my most vigorous moments.

I think we're about to walk inside together, but Dean holds me back a moment longer.

"I did get you something," he says, his breath frosting on the air.

He reaches into his breast pocket and takes out a flat velvet box.

"I don't like to take something away without giving something in return."

Dean opens the lid.

I see a glimmering ruby on a spider-fine chain. Dean lifts the necklace aloft. The pendant hangs suspended from his fingers, the stone as rich and dark as a droplet of blood.

He drapes it around my neck, the necklace already warm from his body heat.

"It suits you," he says softly.

"You like how I look tonight?" I ask. This is my first time dressing as a woman, not a girl—sultry, sophisticated. I didn't know if it worked or if I look ridiculous.

"Cat," Dean says seriously. "There's no one more beautiful than you."

My heart soars up all over again, and I can't help saying, "So…is this a new version of the collar?"

Dean tries to hide his smile. "If you want it to be."

We enter the grand hall, decorated for the holidays with fresh fir boughs that fill the air with the smell of pine sap and deep, cold forest. A fire roars in the massive hearth, offset by the two double doors standing open.

Almost every student at Kingmakers is crowded in here. The Christmas dance is the only official school party of the year, and no one likes to miss it.

Even the chancellor is in attendance, dressed in a tuxedo that looks more like a smoking jacket with its velvet lapels. I have a deep-seated loathing for him after the way he executed Ozzy's mother. But I can't deny his powerful magnetism that draws the eye of everyone around.

His black eyes gleam as he chats with Professor Lyons, the "arsenic witch," dressed fittingly in a gown of poison green. Behind her, my combat teacher Professor Howell is sharing war stories with the expert in environmental adaptation, Professor Bruce. Literal war stories, I'm sure, as Professor Howell fought with the Israel Defense Forces and Professor Bruce was a Navy SEAL.

"I don't see Ms. Robin," I say to Dean.

"No surprise there." He shrugs. "I almost never see her outside the library."

"She usually comes to the dance, though," I say, disappointed. For all that Ms. Robin puzzles me, I like her very much. And a tiny part of me wanted to see if I could catch her admiring Ares in his suit. Or vice versa.

"Snow came," Dean says, sounding pleased. He points out the new boxing teacher with Dr. Rybakov on his arm.

I've heard plenty about Snow from Dean, who intensely admires him, and a little more from Sasha, who tended to me so kindly after I fell on my head at the Quartum Bellum. But I've never actually seen him in person.

He is, quite frankly, terrifying. Tall and brutal-looking, with several scars on his face and a nose that likely retains little resemblance to its original shape. Add to that a granite jaw, closely buzzed graying hair, and frost-colored eyes.

Even his suit can't conceal his rough and brutish physique. The set of his shoulders, the way he walks—everything about him says "street."

By contrast, Sasha Rybakov looks like she just put her name on a wing in the Guggenheim. She's elegant and refined, her blond hair sleek and shining, her pale blue gown in faultless good taste.

"Cat!" she says, waving and coming over at once. "How are you feeling?"

"Better than ever." I grin.

Snow claps Dean on the shoulder. "Glad to see you taking a night off." Then to me, "And this must be Cat. How come it's taken me this long to meet you?"

"I'm not a good enough fighter to be in your class," I say.

"I don't know about that." Snow smiles, closing his massive hand gently around mine. "Dean looks beaten into submission. The man's wearing a bow tie."

"So would you if I could find any that fit that neck," Sasha laughs.

Dean doesn't seem to mind Snow's teasing. In fact, he puts his arm around me and says, "Cat's a brilliant programmer. And an artist."

I struggle not to let my jaw fall to the floor.

Is Dean...bragging about me?

"I dunno about brilliant," I stammer.

Snow says, "You must be. Dean's nothing if not honest."

A smile passes between Dean and Snow, of understanding and perhaps a little embarrassment on Dean's side.

Sasha says, "I hope you two have a wonderful night." She gives my arm a friendly squeeze, and she and Snow carry on, only to be waylaid a moment later by the chancellor.

Awkward silence falls between Dean and me. I don't want to

presume anything, but that felt a lot like Dean introducing me as his girlfriend.

Grabbing my hand, Dean says quickly, "Should we dance?"

"I'd love to."

He pulls me into the space already crowded with swaying students, Joan Jett's "Crimson and Clover" blaring from the speakers.

I look into Dean's face, and I can't believe how open and relaxed he looks, his arms around me, his body swaying us both with that effortless grace he possesses.

He's smiling.

Dean doesn't smile very often. When he does, it makes him handsome on a level that should probably be illegal. So good-looking that it honestly scares me. It makes me wonder how I can be dancing in the arms of this boy who's always seemed more god than man to me.

"What are you thinking?" I ask him, half-fearful.

"I was thinking how different you look. You're fucking gorgeous, Cat. The most gorgeous woman I've ever seen."

"Oh, come on." I'm personally acquainted with several of the actual most gorgeous women at this school.

"You are!" Dean says ferociously. "Cat, you came here a scared kid. And now look at you—I wouldn't even recognize you. You're dark. Devious. And absolutely fucking stunning."

I bite the edge of my lip.

I'm not used to thinking of devious as a compliment. But it's clear Dean means it that way.

And in truth…the qualities I aspire to have indeed changed since I came to Kingmakers.

I'm not trying to be humble or gentle anymore. I don't believe in "turn the other cheek."

Maybe I do want to be devious.

Maybe I already am.

I look up at Dean, and he looks down at me. The music spirals down on us, *crimson and clover, over and over...*

I know Dean is twirling me around, but I feel like the room is spinning around us instead, as if we're the center of the world, the absolute axis.

Dean takes my face in his hands and kisses me.

We've kissed a thousand times in sex.

But never once like this, out in the open...as two people, falling in love.

CHAPTER 17
DEAN

CHRISTMAS MORNING, I LIE IN MY BED, THINKING OF THE NIGHT before.

I danced with Cat long past midnight.

I held her in my arms, spun her around, dipped her, and never took my eyes off that beautiful face.

Cat had never looked more captivating.

That scarlet silk gown clung to her figure, shimmering in the firelight. The pendant rested on her collarbone like a throbbing heart. Her hair lay in sleek shining waves. Her eyes looked up at me like burning coals.

She honestly intimidated me.

Cat has changed so much, and I don't think she's finished.

I feel like I witnessed the birth of a star, a creature that will burn brighter and brighter until she eclipses us all.

Our agreement is over.

I no longer feel like I own her.

But I still want to.

When the party ended, I walked her back to the undercroft.

I put my coat around her bare shoulders because the night was as cold as I've ever felt at Kingmakers.

Our breath rose up in smoky plumes.

We paused outside the old wine cellar, looking at each other. I was thinking it was the first night in a month that we hadn't fucked each other. And yet…it might have been my favorite night together, despite how much I had enjoyed all the others.

I touched her face gently, then kissed her once more, softly, carefully, as if it were the first time.

As I kissed her, I felt something cool against my face. Snowflakes drifting down, light as feathers.

When I pulled back, I saw them resting in Cat's hair and in her thick black lashes like a hundred tiny frozen stars.

"I've never seen it snow here before," Cat said in wonder.

I put out my hand and caught one perfect flake on my fingertip.

Cat brought my hand to her mouth and let it melt against her tongue.

I grabbed her and kissed her again, much harder.

I only released her when a crowd of Spies came along, wanting to descend down to their rooms.

Among them I saw Lola Fischer, tipsy on punch, leaning heavily against Dixie Davis, who had refused to wear a gown to the dance and was dressed in a tux instead.

"Look at the two lovebirds," Lola said, grinning at us maliciously.

I watched her pass, silent and irritated.

For all that Cat has grown, I don't like the idea of anyone holding a grudge against her. It makes me want to keep her right by me and not let her out of my sight.

"Do you want me to walk you to your door?" I asked her.

Cat shook her head, slipping my jacket off her slim shoulders and handing it back.

"Don't worry," she murmured. "I'm not afraid of Lola."

I'm not either. But I still watched Cat enter the dark yawning staircase with a feeling of unease.

I want to see her again today.

It's the first day in ages that I've been completely unencumbered, not a single paper to write, no studying to do. Exams are over.

I'm not even training with Snow, as he'll be spending the day with Sasha, probably calling New York to speak to their two children.

As I think of him phoning his son, Zane, the talented boxer on his own rise to fame, I feel that old spark of jealousy. But I crush it down at once. Snow has been good to me. I have no right to envy his son.

Besides, I'm much more interested in seeing Cat today than I am in receiving a phone call from my own father.

I shower and dress, trying to stay quiet because Bram is still snoring in his bed, then I head down to the dining hall to see if I can intercept Cat.

As I descend the stairs of the Octagon Tower, I find a fine layer of snow blanketing the grounds. The campus looks pristine and otherworldly, as if every inch of the grounds is clad in white marble. I almost hate to leave a trail of prints across the lawn.

I find Cat sitting at her usual table with Leo, Anna, Hedeon, Ares, Chay, and Rakel. The dining hall is packed with students. Everyone enjoys the Christmas brunch, which includes all the usual staples of pancakes, French toast, bacon, and eggs, as well as several regional favorites like German brown-butter skillet cake, Japanese egg custard, and Turkish poached eggs in yogurt.

I fill my plate, then carry it over to Cat's table.

She looks startled but not displeased as I set down my tray across from her, squeezing in between Hedeon and Chay.

"Hey," Leo says. "Merry Christmas."

"Merry Christmas," I reply politely.

Anna is watching me, wary but not hostile. I give her what I hope is a friendly nod.

"Did you enjoy the dance last night?" I say.

"I did," she says. "And you?"

I glance at Cat as I reply. "It was perfect."

A somewhat awkward silence follows until Chay breaks it by saying, "Did any of you see Professor Penmark harassing Professor

Thorn? He kept following her around and around the hall until she spilled her punch on his shoes. One hundred percent intentionally."

"Good. Fuck Professor Penmark!" Cat says, spearing a bite of French toast with unnecessary vigor. "I hope they were expensive shoes."

I love Cat when she's spiteful.

Grinning to myself, I likewise attack my French toast.

The strangeness of my presence at their table abates, and soon a pleasant hubbub of several simultaneous conversations arises as Chay shows Anna and Rakel the boots Ozzy sent her for Christmas, Ares asks Cat if Zoe and Miles went back to Chicago for the holiday, and Leo shouts something over to Matteo Ragusa at the neighboring table.

"I heard you've been training with Snow," Hedeon says to me. "Outside our normal classes, I mean."

"That's right."

"Lucky," Hedeon says enviously. "I've never had a better teacher."

"I agree." I nod.

Hedeon pokes at his food moodily. He's the only person at the table without a hint of a smile. I've always assumed he hangs around with Leo and Ares because nobody else wants to put up with his sulky silence. Even his roommate, Kenzo Tanaka, barely seems to tolerate him. And you'd hardly know that he and Silas were brothers for how rarely they're seen together.

"How come you never sit with Silas?" I say, indicating the table where Silas, Bodashka, and Vanya sit.

"Because I fucking loathe him," Hedeon mutters.

"He's not exactly a barrel of laughs, is he?"

Silas is the most humorless person I've ever encountered, and that's saying something after living with my father the last several years.

"You can't imagine what it was like growing up in the same house as him," Hedeon says quietly.

I look at Hedeon, really look at him for the first time.

I see his blue eyes, strangely lifeless, and his face that ought to be handsome but never seems to draw any girls toward him because of the anger and despair etched into every expression. He's like a reverse magnet, repelling anyone who would get near him.

It's far too familiar to me.

"What about the Grays?" I ask him. "Were they good to you?"

Hedeon laughs bitterly. "Is a butcher good to his knife?"

"I suppose he's careful with it."

"No," Hedeon says. "He sharpens it against stone and then uses it any way he pleases."

I think I finally understand.

"Silas is the stone."

Hedeon meets my eye for the first time. The understanding that passes between us is unhappy on both sides.

Cat watches me from across the table. I'm not sure if she likes me sitting here with her friends. It's a collision of worlds.

Especially when Bram passes our table, hair tangled and face still puffy from sleep, searching for somewhere to sit in the crowded hall.

"Here," Hedeon says, pushing down the bench to make room. "There's space for one more."

Bram grunts his thanks, dropping down beside me.

"Never seen the dining hall from this side," he says, glancing around.

"This is prime real estate," Leo says. "It's a straight shot back to the galley to refill your plate."

"Might do that a couple of times." Bram stuffs half a croissant in his mouth.

"You look like you already did," Chay says with a wicked smirk.

"What are you saying?"

"Oh, nothing. Just that you're a couple more croissants away from Father Christmas."

"Get the fuck outta town," Bram says, outraged. "Father Christmas couldn't gift himself abs like this."

He yanks up his shirt to display his stomach, which only makes Chay and Rakel laugh.

"She's just winding you up," I tell Bram.

"Don't you fuckin' test me," Bram says to Chay. "I'll strip all the way down, just like Leo."

"You'll regret it," Leo says. "It's breezy in here."

As the banter bounces back and forth across the table, Cat and I lock eyes. She smiles at me in a way that lets me know I'm more than welcome here.

After breakfast, I ask Cat if she wants to come for a walk with me.

"Sure," she says. "It's cold, though."

"I know a place we can go."

I take Cat to the south side of campus where the twin greenhouses stand.

To call them greenhouses hardly does justice to the vast iron and glass structures. Each one rivals the Crystal Palace built in Hyde Park for the London Great Exhibition. Much of the produce consumed at Kingmakers is grown here as well as herbs and Professor Thorn's collection of rare orchids.

"Oh!" Cat says, thrilled by our passage from the chilly day into the warmth and humidity of the greenhouse. "I didn't know we could come in here!"

"Nobody's stopped me yet."

The scent of leaves and blossoms is heady and overwhelmingly alive. It feels as if we've stepped into another world.

Cat removes her jacket and then pulls off her sweater as well, draping both over her arm. Her curls spring up tighter than ever in the humidity.

Condensed droplets run down the interior of the glass walls, and snow sits along the iron spines of the exterior. The plants look vividly green against the white snow.

"That was nice at breakfast," Cat says. "All of us sitting together like that."

"It wasn't bad," I say by way of agreement.

Cat looks at me with those dark eyes, always alive and curious, never restful.

"You don't seem to hate Leo as much as you once did."

"We're not friends," I say roughly.

"But you don't want to kill him anymore."

Ah. So he told her about that.

That's fine—I own my actions. Even those that might have been driven by a sort of madness at the time.

"Yes, I tried to drown him," I say, refusing to deny it.

"You must have been...very disappointed," Cat says, looking at her feet. "About Anna."

All the stiffness sweeps out of me in one breath as I understand what Cat is actually asking me.

"I respect Anna Wilk," I say very clearly. "But I don't love her, Cat. I'm not sure I ever did. What I felt—I think it was just the feeling of admiring someone for the first time. It was new to me."

"Isn't that what loving someone is?" Cat says quietly.

"It might be part of it. But it's not all of it."

"Do I sound jealous?" she says, looking up at me at last, her face open and vulnerable.

"I'm jealous," I say, seizing her arm and pulling her close. "Any time anyone looks at you or speaks to you, I'm jealous. I want all your minutes and all your words. I want all of you, all the time."

I see that mischievous delight spread across her face. Cat likes me best when I'm wild for her, when I'll tear anyone apart to get to her. She doesn't want me restrained and behaved. And I could never be that way when I'm around her.

She brings out the beast in me. And she likes it.

I kiss her roughly, bruising those soft lips.

"I want to keep seeing you," I tell her.

"What would you do if I told you no?"

"Tie you up in that tower and punish you," I growl. "Don't you ever tell me no."

"I never have yet," Cat whispers.

I throw her down beneath a bench loaded with tomato plants, and I rip her blouse open. We're only half-shielded by the trailing vines, but I don't give a fuck who might come along. I have to have her, and I have to have her now.

I pull her skirt up, unzip my trousers, and yank her underwear to the side. I thrust into her without warning, without foreplay.

I fuck her there on the dirt, with the scent of everything living and growing all around us.

I fuck her hard and wild as Cat sucks and bites on the side of my neck.

I've never felt more alive.

———————

School starts up again on Wednesday, which suits me fine. I don't like too much time off, and I'm especially itching to be back in the gym honing my skills with Snow.

So I feel as much irritation as confusion when one of the grounds crew interrupts my Extortion class.

"Dean Yenin is needed in the chancellor's office," he tells Professor Owsinki.

"What for?" I demand.

The man looks at me impassively, refusing to answer whether he knows the reason or not.

"Bring your things," he says.

I stuff my textbooks in my bag while Bram and Valon give me a questioning look.

I shrug impatiently, following the groundskeeper out of the classroom.

"Do you know where the chancellor's office is?" he asks.

"Yes."

"Then I'll leave you here."

He abandons me at the staircase, heading back outdoors.

I watch his retreating back, wondering if it's just my imagination that he doesn't want to accompany me to the top floor.

Foreboding creeps over me. I wonder if this might possibly have something to do with Cat.

It can't be. I'm the only person who knows her secret, and I haven't told a soul. Haven't written it anywhere. Haven't even whispered it to myself alone in the dead of night.

I scale five flights of stairs to the topmost floor, my stomach tightening with each step.

I've never been inside the chancellor's office before. I knock on the doors, hearing the terse response, "Come in," carry easily across the open space beyond.

I push open the doors, entering an expansive office that, along with the chancellor's private quarters, takes up the entire penthouse of the keep.

Banks of windows on two sides offer views over the cliffs and also across the campus grounds. I'm sure the chancellor's intimate knowledge of the goings-on among the students comes from his army of staff, but I can't shake the impression that he's constantly standing at those windows, watching us from above.

This office is more like an apartment, with a sitting area, a separate writing desk, shelves of books, and a globe big enough to break Atlas's back. The walls are covered in photographs of the chancellor with friends and allies from across the globe— some Mafia and others recognizable to any civilian. I'm instantly envious of the shot of Hugo and Mike Tyson on some sunny golf course.

My shoes sink into the thick rug as I make the endless journey toward the chancellor's desk.

No room I've seen inside the castle matches this one for wealth and luxury. The Hugos are immensely rich, one of the oldest and most successful of the ten founding families who first formed this school. From what I've heard, Luther Hugo has only increased his holdings. He's a brilliant investor. He could teach the finance classes better than Professor Graves if he cared to do it.

The chancellor waits for me behind his desk, dressed as usual in a double-breasted suit with a black silk cravat. I always find it difficult to guess his age. His thick mane of hair is still inky black, though threaded with silver. But his face is etched with lines as deep as hatchet marks. His spider-black eyes follow my every movement from the moment I stepped foot through his door.

"Dean Yenin," he says in his sonorous voice. "Sit." He gestures to the ornate chair set opposite his desk.

I take my seat, unnerved and trying not to show it.

I share Cat's antipathy for Luther Hugo after what he did to Ozzy's mother. I know it's the law at this school. But I don't care. There's no justice when the innocent pay for the crimes of the guilty.

"How did you enjoy the Christmas dance?" Hugo asks politely.

"I enjoyed it very much."

I don't know why I'm here, and I can't imagine it's for any positive reason. I don't want to give anything away.

"I saw you dancing with Catalina Romero," Hugo says.

My stomach clenches. This is what I was afraid of—that Cat had drawn his attention in some way.

"Yes," I say stiffly.

"Unfortunate that Zoe Romero and Miles Griffin chose not to complete their education at this school."

"I don't know anything about that," I lie, keeping my expression as bland as possible.

"We hate to lose our students. In any manner or for any reason," the chancellor says.

I can't tell if this is some sort of threat. His expression is impossible to read.

"Which brings me to the unfortunate business at hand…"

I keep my palms flat on my thighs, determined not to move or even flinch, no matter what he might ask me.

"Abram Balakin called me from Moscow this morning, Dean. Your father is dead."

This is so far removed from what I expected to hear that the words don't make any sense to me. A long silence follows while I try to rearrange the chancellor's sentence into actual English.

"My condolences," Hugo says. "I know this is hard to hear."

I can't hear anything right now because there's a loud rushing sound in my ears, like the ocean waves far below us are beating directly against my head.

"He can't be," I say slowly. "I just spoke to him."

"I'm afraid it's quite certain. There was a fire. Your father's house was destroyed. His body was found in his study. It appears he set the blaze intentionally. There was accelerant spread all through the house. The footage from the security cameras shows no other entry."

A vivid image arises in my mind of my father pouring gasoline all throughout our house—over the stacks of books and magazines, the boxes of unopened goods, the papers, the photographs. They must have gone up like kindling, blazing towers of fire. He burned the paintings, the vases and rugs and chandeliers purchased by my mother, their wedding photographs, and my old rocking horse up in the attic. My clothes and books and blankets in my room.

Then he sat in his office, his one safe place, and waited for the fire to finish the job begun twenty years earlier. The job of killing him.

"When did this happen?" I ask.

"The evening of the twenty-fifth," Hugo says. "I was not informed until this morning."

He killed himself on Christmas. The day before his anniversary.

"Did he leave a message for me?" I ask dully. "A note?"

"If he did," Hugo says, "it would have been burned. The fire spread to the neighboring houses as well. There's nothing left of yours."

I've never felt so much and so little at the same time.

A raging storm of emotion swirls around inside me.

And yet I'm as numb and dull as a corpse.

My body stands up without my order. I hear myself say to the chancellor, "Thank you for informing me."

"Usually, we do not allow departure and return to the school," the chancellor says. "But in this instance, with no other family to make the funeral arrangements—"

"There won't be any funeral," I say.

For the first time, Hugo's face shows a flicker of confusion.

"But surely you—"

"He made his own funeral pyre. Why should I go against his wishes?"

Hugo hesitates, watching me closely.

"If you would like a few days to consider—"

"That won't be necessary. I'll return to class now."

Another silence, and then he gives a curt nod.

"As you wish."

I cross that vast expanse of carpet once more, and this time, it seems only an instant until I'm out of Hugo's office, descending the stairs.

My pulse throbs in my ears, faster and faster, yet I feel oddly calm.

He left me. My father left me.

Just like my mother.

Everyone runs away eventually.

They get away from me, any way they can.

I check my watch—one of the only gifts my father ever bought for me. Plain and impersonal. Not any brand I particularly liked.

Snow's class is about to begin. If I hurry, I can make it still.

I take off the watch and drop it on the steps of the keep, stomping it with my heel until the face shatters. Then I keep walking, all the way to the armory.

I change clothes quickly, wanting to catch up with the class. My heart is beating faster and faster as I pull on the gray gym shorts and white T-shirt. My body knows I'm ready to fight. My hands start to shake as I wrap them in turn and don my gloves.

I'm almost running by the time I enter the gym.

Snow has already paired off the students for sparring.

He glances up as I enter, and I can tell from his expression that he already knows.

"Dean—" he says, moving to intercept me.

I push past him, looking for someone to fight.

"Who wants to spar?" I shout. "Who's got the stones? Jasper? Bram? Silas? Leo?"

I challenge them all, and I wish they'd all agree. I'll fight all four at once. I'll fight the whole fucking class.

"Dean," Snow says more forcefully, grabbing my shoulder.

I shake him off.

"Come on!" I shout. "Who's man enough to face me?"

Silas looks like he'll take the bait. He takes a step forward, and I'm already clenching my fists, ready to run at him until Snow intervenes.

"Everyone out," he barks.

The class stares at each other for one brief second before hustling off to the change rooms.

The impotent rage I feel might burn me alive.

I have to fight.

I need it.

I turn to face Snow, angrier than I've ever been in my life.

"I'll fight you then!" I howl. "I'm ready."

Snow holds up his hands, saying, "I'm not going to—"

But I'm already rushing him, swinging with all my might.

And I hit him. I fucking hit him, right in the jaw.

Then I hit him again and again and again.

I'm striking him with all my might, with all my fury.

I'm in such a blaze of violence that it takes me far too long to realize that he's not trying to duck or dodge. He's not trying to defend himself.

He lets me hit him, over and over, in the face and body, without ever even holding up his hands to block me.

He lets me exhaust my anger on him until I realize that I'm hitting the only friend I have, the only man who's ever been good to me.

And then all the strength goes out of me, and I would have sank down to my knees if Snow didn't wrap his arms around me and hug me tight.

I've never been hugged like this, by someone strong. Someone who could hurt me if he wanted to but instead is using his immense power to give me that sense of protection and support that I've never known in all my life.

I could have been a better man if my father had been more like this.

"Why couldn't he be happy?" I sob. "Why couldn't he live for me, for us?"

I'm thinking of my mother too, of all the years she tried to laugh with him and joke with him like they used to. He shoved her away, over and over. Until she couldn't smile anymore, not for him and not for me.

Snow doesn't try to answer. He just holds me, because somehow, he understands.

I'm crying again, and I'm so ashamed.

Cat saw me like this. And now Snow.

I'm weak and broken.

And that's the real truth that torments me.

The real reason I'm so angry and alone.

"Why didn't he love me?" I cry.

Snow puts his heavy hands on my shoulders and looks me in the face. His eyes are pale blue, clear as ice, but there's no coldness in them.

"When you become a man worthy of love, you will receive love," he tells me.

I search his battered face, trying to understand.

"I was alone," Snow says. "No parents, no family. They called me Snow because I fought so cold. But inside...I was dark and angry. An old boxer took me in. His name was Meyer. He was hard on me, and he was good to me too. He showed me friendship. Love came later when I met Sasha. I saw her for what she was: a treasure to be protected at all costs. To have her, I had to become the man she deserved."

"I don't know how to do that," I admit.

"It's always a step into the dark," Snow says. "No one knows the path they haven't walked before."

I look at Snow's face, cut and swollen from my fists.

"I'm sorry," I say quietly.

"Don't be sorry," Snow says. "Be better."

———————

I wait outside Cat's Security Systems class for a period of time that feels equally like minutes and hours.

I keep thinking of my father's house, burned to the ground.

It was the only address my mother knew. The only place we lived in Moscow.

If she's still alive, if she ever tries to send another postcard...it will have nowhere to go.

Of course, I don't really believe any postcard is coming.

It's been far too long for that.

Why did my father choose to die by fire? After all the pain he suffered, I can't imagine that anything terrified him more. Was he trying to prove to himself at the end that he wasn't a coward?

How could he destroy the only home I've ever known—the only reminders I had of our old life, the few good memories.

The one blow we struck against the Gallos was to burn their ancestral home.

Now he burned ours too, as if to wreak revenge upon us.

I don't understand him. I never did.

I hear the scraping of chairs and shuffle of feet as class dismisses.

I step to the side to let the exiting students pass, watching for Cat.

When she spots me, her eyes get bigger than ever, and her mouth opens in shock. I really must look like shit.

"Dean!" she gasps. "What happened?"

For me, the opposite effect occurs.

The moment I lay eyes on Cat, the maelstrom of sorrow, anger, and resentment swirling inside me finally eases. I throw my arms around her and hug her hard against me, pressing my face into her thick black curls, smelling my favorite scent in the world—the scent of this girl.

"What's going on?" she says, pulling back just a little to look up into my face.

"Something happened today. I had to come tell you."

"Tell me what?" she says.

"That I love you, Cat. I fucking love you."

"What?" Cat squeaks, sounding as terrified as the very first time we spoke.

I laugh, and then I kiss her, harder than I ever have before.

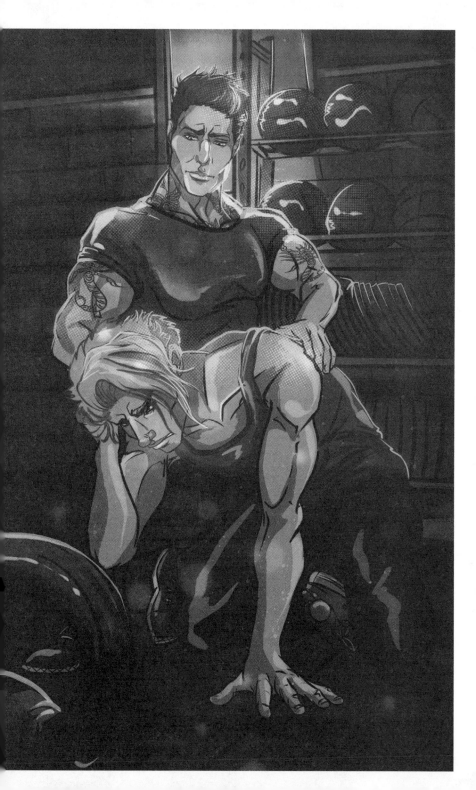

CHAPTER 18
CAT

DEAN AND I SKIP THE REST OF THE AFTERNOON OF CLASSES. WE GO up to the bell tower, and Dean spends two hours exercising his aggression on my body before we lie under a pile of blankets just holding each other.

It's freezing in the drafty tower, but Dean's body heat is always more than enough for both of us.

He tells me everything, from the moment he stepped foot in the chancellor's office, to his encounter with Snow, to his relief at seeing me afterward.

I barely recognize this man who speaks to me with such raw honesty. Just last year, Dean wanted to kill me for witnessing him in an emotional moment. Now he tells me all his darkest fears and deepest regrets.

"He died alone," Dean says, his deep voice vibrating against my ear as I lay my head on his chest. "I can't help but feel I'm bound to do the same. Everyone leaves me, Cat. They always have."

"I don't think your father wanted to die," I murmur. "I just don't think he knew how to live."

"I don't want to be like him," Dean says. "A prisoner to the past."

"You're already letting go of it."

"Only sometimes."

I wish I knew how to help him better.

I can hear his heart beating against my ear. A strong heart. A steady one. Not shrunken and twisted by time, despite all that's happened to him.

"You're wearing the necklace," Dean says, pleased.

"It's my favorite gift I've ever received," I tell him.

The necklace is the most beautiful thing I've ever held in my hands. I like it all the more for what it symbolizes between Dean and me: erotic connection and the violent secret that brought us together.

I don't feel the same guilt about Rocco Prince anymore.

It ebbed away, bit by bit, with every day I spent with Dean.

"I think our sex has been therapeutic," I say to Dean.

He chuckles. "For you or for me?"

"Maybe both."

He sits up on his elbow so he can look at me, his violet eyes keen and curious.

"Why do you like it?" he says. "The rough sex…the domination."

"At first, I liked it *because* I felt guilty. I felt like I deserved to be punished for what I did. At the same time, it felt *so good*. It heightened every sensation—I'd never experienced anything so intense. The stronger you were and the more aggressive, the more it made you seem godlike, superhuman. And that made me want to please you."

"Go on." Dean grins.

I can feel his cock stiffening again against my hip, though we only just finished fucking.

"There's this other part of it too," I say. "It's the way you focus on me when we're doing kinky shit. It's like I'm the only thing in the world. You'll spend hours touching and manipulating me. I love the attention."

"You *are* the only thing in the world," Dean says seriously. "You're all I have now, Cat."

I can't believe he's looking at me with that expression of utter focus. I can't believe he's saying those words to me.

For all the time I've spent with Dean, I still find it baffling that someone as ferocious as him could fall in love with someone like me. Some days, I think I've grown so much. But others, I still feel terrified inside.

Like right now.

I want this to be real.

I don't know what I'll do if it isn't.

I touch the pendant lying in the divot of my collarbones.

"I never got you a Christmas gift," I say.

"I didn't expect you to," Dean says. "The only thing I want is exactly what I'm getting. You, naked, obeying my every command."

He kisses the side of my throat, then slowly works his way down my body.

Before I lose myself in the sensation, I think to myself that there must be something I can do for him.

Saturday morning, I walk down to the village with Dean.

The village clusters in a half-moon around the harbor, the buildings green and mossy, the street unpaved because there's no cars on the island. The students like to walk down here in good weather to pick up letters at the post office, eat the fresh-caught cod at the fish and chips shop, or visit the tiny café for tea, biscuits, and handmade caramels.

Today is *not* particularly good weather, so Dean and I are two of the only people willing to brave the wind.

We stop in briefly at the secondhand bookstore where Dean has been trading in his well-read novels for any he can't find at the school library.

Upon better acquaintance with Dean, one of the many things that surprised me is that he reads at least one novel every week in addition to all his schoolwork. Or at least he used to before he started spending so much time with me.

I suppose I shouldn't have been surprised, since he places top in his class in marks. I knew he wasn't just a dumb boxer.

"There aren't any dumb boxers," Dean informs me as he picks through the pleasantly musty piles of books. "Or least not any good ones. Boxing requires strategy. It's not so different from chess."

"They might not start out dumb," I tease him. "But after all those hits to the head…"

"Careful," he growls, giving me a sharp little smack on the ass. "Don't think you're safe just because we're in public."

My bottom is already bruised from our last session. Dean has been especially aggressive this week, probably because he's still upset about his father, much as he tries to hide it.

I don't mind. I've never come more times than I did last night, and if an aching ass is the only price, then I'll gladly pay it. In fact, I'll probably do it again tonight.

The owner of the store clears his throat and gives us a stern look over the top of his glasses. I don't know if he heard us or if he just hates joviality. He's been watching us the whole time we've been in his shop, sighing with the air of someone forced to entertain unwanted visitors.

At least his big gray tabby cat is welcoming. It keeps winding itself in and out of Dean's legs, trying to trip him in the friend-liest way.

"What are you looking for?" I ask Dean.

"I dunno." He shrugs. "Whatever catches my eye."

"You ever read this one?" I hold up *Persuasion*.

"No," he says. "I read *Pride and Prejudice*, though. Actually, I kept thinking of a line from that book when I met you."

"What line?" I say.

Dean searches the Austen books, finding *Pride and Prejudice* and flipping through it until he locates the line in question.

"This one. 'No sooner had he made it clear to himself and his friends that she hardly had a good feature in her face, than he began to find it was rendered uncommonly intelligent by the beautiful expression of her dark eyes.'"

I slap him on the shoulder, earning another disapproving grunt from the shop owner.

"'Hardly a good feature in her face'!"

Dean laughs, grabbing my hands so I can't smack him again.

"Not that part. The bit about the dark eyes and how they show your cleverness. I can always see what you're thinking from your eyes."

"Oh yeah? What am I thinking right now?"

"You're thinking you want me to kiss you."

"That's too easy. I always want that."

Dean obliges, with zero care for the irritation of the shop owner. Then he buys *Persuasion* on my recommendation.

The shop owner wraps the book in paper as protection against the sleet. Dean tucks it under his arm, taking my hand with his other.

We have to push hard against the door to exit into the wind.

As we cross the main street, we overtake Ms. Robin leaving the post office.

"Morning, Cat!" she says, trying to hold back her frizzy red hair from blowing all around her face. "And Dean, of course."

"Good morning." Dean nods.

"Where are you two off to?"

"The café," I say. "Do you want to join us?"

"I won't interrupt your date. But I'll walk along with you so I don't blow away."

I take Dean's book so he can offer his other arm to Ms. Robin.

"Didn't think we'd see anyone else down here," Dean says.

"You almost didn't. That last gust just about carried me off." After a moment, she adds, "Dean, I heard about your father. I'm so sorry."

I suppose the chancellor told her. Being his niece, she might have been the first to know.

"It's fine," Dean says stiffly. "It won't distract me from my studies."

"It would be understandable if it did," Ms. Robin says gently.

We've almost reached the café. As I stretch out my hand to open the door, it bursts open from the inside. Fighting the pressure of the wind, Snow and Sasha tumble out, laughing at the awful weather.

"Oh, hello!" Sasha says before they can stumble into us. "How are—"

She breaks off, regarding Ms. Robin with a startled expression.

"Julia, have you met my wife?" Snow says. "Sasha Rybakov."

Ms. Robin holds out her hand to shake. Unlike Sasha, she shows no hint of discomfort.

Sasha takes her hand and grasps it briefly.

"Nice to meet you," she says.

"I won't keep you all in this." Ms. Robin nods toward the windswept street. "Enjoy your tea, Cat and Dean, and enjoy the rest of your day, Sasha and Snow."

Ms. Robin heads off down the street in the direction of Kingmakers, while Snow holds the door for Dean and me so we can enter the café.

I linger in the doorway, watching Sasha stare down the street after Ms. Robin.

After Dean and I have ordered and selected our table in the corner, I say, "That was odd."

"What?" Dean says, already attacking his scone.

"When Ms. Robin and Dr. Rybakov met."

"What about it?"

"You didn't think the doctor seemed…alarmed?"

"Why, 'cause Ms. Robin's pretty? So's Sasha. She's got nothing to worry about. Snow's crazy for her."

"It felt off somehow."

"Maybe because we were in the middle of a tornado," Dean laughs.

"Could be," I say, stealing his scone and taking a bite.

"Have the whole thing," Dean offers. "I'll order another."

That afternoon, I ambush Rakel in our room.

"I need your help," I say.

"I'd like to, but I'm extremely busy at the moment."

Rakel is reading her favorite graphic novel for the twenty-eighth time while eating oranges in bed. The whole room smells of citrus.

"Come on," I coax her. "It's a computer thing, and you're better at it."

Rakel holds her place with one long, dangerously pointed fingernail and glances over at me. "I haven't beaten you at a programming challenge in weeks."

"This is something different."

"You're being mysterious because you want to intrigue me."

I grin. "Is it working?"

"Maybe. I'll help you—"

"Yay!"

"—if you do something for me."

"What?" I say suspiciously.

"Go to the dining hall and get me four more oranges."

"What!" I groan. "It's hideous out there."

"I know. That's why it's a good trade."

"You already ate"—I try to count the towering stack of peels—"a whole fuck load of oranges."

"Nature's candy," Rakel says, returning to her novel and turning another page.

"I'm gonna freeze."

"You'll stay warm if you run really fast."

Grumbling, I sprint up the stairs and then dash across the lawn with my jacket pulled tight around me. I already froze my ass off walking to and from the village with Dean. After this second excursion, I'm going to need a solid hour huddled under a blanket just to thaw out.

I steal as many oranges as I can stuff in the pouch of my sweatshirt, then I run back to the undercroft, cursing Rakel's extortionary tactics the entire way. She's been paying a little too much attention in Professor Owsinki's class.

"Here, you fucking terrorist." I dump the oranges down on her lap.

"Great," Rakel says. "I'll help you when I'm done eating them."

"Rakel!"

"Alright, alright." She grins. "Tell me what you want."

I take a deep breath. "I need to find somebody. But I only have a small amount of information about her. And she might be in hiding."

Rakel considers. "Is Miles's satellite still working?"

"Yeah, as far as I know."

Miles and Ozzy set up their own private network on the island so they'd have constant internet access outside the limited and highly monitored connection available through the school computer lab.

Rakel keeps Ozzy's old laptop hidden under her mattress. It looks like it's been through a war but performs like a race car.

Though I've gotten pretty decent at my Code Breaking and Security Systems classes, Rakel is still the master at old-school hacking techniques. I hope she can put her skills to use on my behalf.

Rakel rolls off her bed so she can dig out the laptop, scattering orange peels everywhere.

Then she reseats herself, holding her fingers over the keyboard like a pianist about to play a concerto.

"Alright…what do you know about this person?" she says.

CHAPTER 19
DEAN

CAT AND I ARE OPENLY DATING NOW. WE SPEND MOST OF OUR TIME together, outside of our classes.

I need to be with her because when I'm not, I'm plagued with a sense of revulsion toward my own future.

I always knew the plan: graduate from Kingmakers, take a position under Danyl Kuznetsov, pay off my two years' service, then work my way up in the Moscow Bratva until I'm *pakhan*.

But now when I picture going back to Moscow, battling with Vanya Antonov for ascendency, forcing the rest of the Bratva to respect and support me, I just feel…blank.

I never liked Moscow. I always hated living there.

I ask Snow, "Did you like St. Petersburg?"

He shrugs. "Well enough."

"But you wanted to go to America."

"I wanted to fight at Madison Square Garden. To me, that represented the ultimate achievement in boxing."

"And you stayed in New York after."

"That's right."

He's taking me through a heavy bag workout with intense three-minute rounds. I can only question him during the brief rest period because otherwise I'm panting too hard to speak.

I pound the bag with all my might until Snow clicks his stopwatch, letting me know I can rest again.

"What's New York like?" I puff.

"Loud. All the time. Horns, sirens, subway trains, people shouting when they think they're just talking. It's constant stimulation—the color and diversity and the scent of the food. You could eat a different kind of food every day and never have the same thing twice. It's safe too—surprisingly safe. You can walk around any time, day or night. It's always busy, always people around."

He clicks his watch again, prompting me to launch myself at the bag once more, punching, ducking, circling, hitting again, until my three minutes are up.

I flop down on the mats, taking a hefty swig of water. I'm pouring sweat, and I've got four more rounds to go.

"My mother was from Chicago," I tell Snow.

"I've been there," he says. "Great city."

"I was born there. But I haven't seen it since I was little."

"Maybe you should visit," Snow says, clicking his watch once more.

I always thought of Chicago as the place from which we'd been exiled. Forced out by the Gallos.

But it is my heritage just as much as Moscow.

I have American citizenship, not just Russian.

I pound the heavy bag with both fists, enjoying the satisfying thud as it gives way before me.

The second round of the Quartum Bellum takes place in February. The sophomores have already been eliminated, so I don't have to worry about Lola Fischer endangering Cat again.

Instead, I have to endure the fiendish creativity of Professor Penmark, who organizes the competition for maximum discomfort. Usually Professor Howell sets up the challenges. This one has a sadistic flair that could only come from the master of Torture Techniques.

Professor Penmark orders the three remaining teams to form a horizontal line along Moon Beach, with our asses in the sand and our feet facing the water.

Then he strings a chain all the way down the line, looped around our wrists and ankles, with several different types of padlocks between each student. The challenge is to pick the locks before the tide comes in and drowns us.

This would be difficult enough if the water weren't freezing and the waves random and vicious, trying to tug us out into the ocean.

To add to the fun, each team receives only one lock pick that has to be passed along the line student by student.

As soon as Professor Howell fires his starter pistol, the pick begins to move down the line. Progress is in spurts, with some students easily popping their padlocks while others struggle for an agonizing period of time. Several of the locks are in hard-to-reach positions, and the padlocks quickly become jammed with sand and bits of seaweed.

The waves start washing over my knees before the pick is even halfway down the line. Each rush of frigid, salty water makes the students shiver until the chains clatter like castanets.

"I can't do it," Coraline Paquet sobs on my left. "My fingers are ice."

"Pass me the pick," Motya grunts. "I'll help."

Kade, Leo, and Claire have all stationed themselves at the very end of their respective lines, so they'll be the last to be unchained. Unlike most years, I'll be sorry to see any of the captains eliminated because I know how badly they all want to win.

The water is up to my chest by the time I get the pick. I have to work blind, trying to feel the tumblers when my numb fingers can hardly grip, let alone sense.

"I dropped it!" a hysterical freshman girl shrieks. "I dropped the pick!"

"Find it!" Kade cries. "Comb the sand."

Chained where he is, he's incapable of assisting.

"It's too late!" she cries. "The waves took it!"

I can see Kade gritting his teeth, furious and helpless.

"Find something else!" he cries. "Who has a bobby pin?"

"I do," another girl says, farther down the line.

"Pass it along," Kade orders.

The girl pulls the pin from her bun, straightens the minute metal rod, and passes it down the line.

It doesn't work as well as the lock pick formed for that purpose, but after a few minutes of struggling, the first girl manages to free herself. She passes on the bobby pin.

The freshmen are behind now.

I fumble with the last padlock on my right ankle, finally finding the appropriate angle and popping the hasp. I pass the pick along to Ares, glad to get the fuck out of the water.

Now only Ares, Anna, and Leo are left on our team.

Ares finishes quickly, taking only a few seconds to pop his locks.

Anna takes a little longer, as she has four separate padlocks on her length of chain. She grits her teeth, her slim shoulders shaking as the icy water hits her again.

"You've got this," Leo murmurs to her.

"Almost there…" Anna mutters, and finally the chains fall away. She passes Leo the pick.

The water is up to his neck now, and the next wave hits him right in the face. He holds tight to the pick, jamming it into the lock.

Meanwhile, the shorter Claire Turgenev is already almost entirely underwater. She has to tilt her head all the way back to catch a breath between the waves.

Stubbornly, she refuses to submit.

"Don't you fucking stop, Jasper," she says to the second-last senior, spitting out a mouthful of seawater.

Jasper Webb pops the last lock and presses the pick into her hand.

Claire takes one final gulp of air, then lets the waves wash over her as she blindly tries to pick her locks underwater.

I watch the place where she disappeared, wondering if she's really going to drown herself rather than give in.

"Got it!" Leo says, popping up like Harry Houdini with the chains dropping away.

Claire still hasn't emerged. I glance at Professor Howell, wondering what he's waiting for.

He watches the spot where Claire submerged, silently counting the seconds she's been under. A full minute passes.

Professor Howell frowns, unable to even see air bubbles rising in the rough surf. He uncrosses his arms, ready to intervene.

Right as he takes a step forward, his sneaker sinking into the wet sand, Claire jumps up, drenched and shaking.

"Done!" she coughs.

The waves tumble over Kade Petrov and the three remaining freshmen, dragging them out with the chains still wrapped tight around them. Professor Penmark and Professor Howell rush forward to haul them out of the water. One of the freshman boys retches up seawater, and one of the girls looks close to tears.

"No!" Kade sputters. "We weren't done!"

"You're out of time," Professor Howell says. "The other teams are done."

Kade stands on the beach, shaking with cold and acrid disappointment. He can't meet the eyes of his teammates.

I clap him on the shoulder, making him jump.

"You did well," I say. "There's nothing to be ashamed of."

"We lost," Kade says. "We're out of the challenge."

"Not everything is in your control."

"Then how come Adrik always manages to win?" Kade says bitterly.

"I don't know." I shake the seawater out of my eyes. "I'm not Adrik either."

Kade looks up at me, remembering who he's talking to—not a perpetual champion like Adrik or Leo. Just another person who sometimes takes it in the teeth, despite all he can do.

"Hey, I meant to tell you," Kade says awkwardly, "I'm sorry about your dad."

"He made his choice," I say, shrugging it off.

I hate that my father had to embarrass me one last time in such a public way. I've squashed the attempts of any of my friends to talk about it. The only person I've discussed it with is Cat. And Snow, the day I found out what happened.

We all have to make the long walk back up to school, shivering beneath the towels that Professor Howell handed out.

I walk with Kade, even though we're not talking, because I know how it feels to be alone with your failure.

CHAPTER 20
CAT

LOLA IS DRIVING ME BONKERS.

We share almost all our classes, and she won't get off my fucking ass.

I swear she's following me around campus just to give me shit.

She seems to pop up everywhere, especially if Dean isn't around. She accosts me in the hallways, the dining hall, and even the library now that her ban has elapsed—though she's careful to make sure Ms. Robin isn't around before she starts harassing me.

As I pass through the common room on my way out of the undercroft, she jumps up out of an overstuffed armchair, blocking my path.

"Where do you think you're going?" she demands, shifting in front of me as I try to sidestep her.

"None of your business," I say shortly.

"Are you going up to the bell tower to meet Dean again?"

I narrow my eyes at her. I think of the bell tower as belonging to me and Dean alone. I'm annoyed that she knows about it.

"What exactly is your fixation with me, Lola? Harassing me isn't going to get you back in the Quartum Bellum."

"I don't give a fuck about that stupid competition," Lola snarls, tossing her shining hair contemptuously.

"Then what the fuck is it?"

"It's *you*," she sneers, towering over me even in her flat shoes. "Mousy, sneaky, stupid little you. Everything about you irritates me."

"Then why can't we just avoid each other in peace?"

I try to step around her again, but she blocks me, her arms folded across her sweater-clad breasts. Lola always looks like she stepped off the pages of a Ralph Lauren catalog—nails manicured, skirt freshly pressed, not a hair out of place.

"I wish I could avoid you," Lola says softly, "but you're always strutting around with Anna Wilk and Chay Wagner and Leo Gallo like you're one of them, like you belong. They're not your friends. They just pity you. You're barely a mascot to them."

I can feel my face getting hot.

Lola is poking at my deepest insecurity, and she knows it.

But she's not invulnerable herself. In attacking me, she's letting her own weakness show.

"You're jealous," I say in wonder.

"Jealous of *you*?" Lola sneers. "Why would I ever be jealous of *you*?"

"I don't know," I say, moving to pass her again. "Maybe you just can't stand to see someone else happy—"

This time, Lola shoves me hard in the chest so I stumble back a step.

"And why are you so *happy*, exactly?" she demands. "'Cause of your new boyfriend? You don't actually think he likes you?"

Now she's really starting to piss me off. My hands ball into fists, my nails cutting into my palms.

"Just because he likes *fucking* you doesn't mean he gives a shit about you," Lola hisses. "I saw you chasing after him like a lost puppy, carrying his books to class… He's using you because you'll do whatever he says. When he's tired of you, he'll throw you away. And you'll be back to the lonely little loser you always were all along."

"You don't know anything about Dean and me," I spit back at her.

Lola laughs.

"I know everything," she says. "It's plain as day. You're the only one who can't see it."

With that, she shoves past me, heading for her room.

I cross campus alone, her words still ringing in my ears.

I do think Lola is jealous. With the exception, perhaps, of the Paris Bratva, Leo Gallo's group is the most popular at our school. Lola resents my place at their table.

But that doesn't mean she's wrong.

Dean's and my relationship started in a highly unorthodox way. How can I be sure how much of our connection is sexual chemistry and how much is something more?

Dean said he loved me. But he had just heard the news of what happened to his father.

He might only be attached to me because he has no one else.

I climb the cracked stone steps of the bell tower, a host of unpleasant thoughts swirling around in my head.

Dean is already waiting for me at the top. He seizes me and kisses me wildly, like it's been weeks since we saw each other.

Even the kiss fails to comfort me. I don't know how to discern between passion and love.

I feel low all the following week.

I shouldn't let Lola get to me, but the more I'm falling for Dean, the more I realize how miserable I'll be if this thing between us ends.

I've put myself in a precarious position.

After being with him, how could I care about anyone else?

Who else could seem handsome compared to Dean? Who else has a voice that sounds like sandpaper and silk, that vibrates on just the right frequency to make my whole body thrum?

Who could love or hate with his level of passion?

I'm in way over my head.

I'm crazy about Dean, and it terrifies me.

I don't know how to tell him how I feel or, better yet, how to show him. These are uncharted waters. I've never even had a boyfriend before—I skipped the training wheels and went straight to the Harley.

Until I figure it out, I'm trying to avoid Lola so she doesn't fuck with my head any further.

I'm heading down the stairs of the keep to our Security Systems class when I hear her coming up from the opposite direction, talking loudly with Dixie Davis. Their derisive laughter rings off the stone walls.

Not wanting to convene with them in the hall, I do an about-face and run up instead, all the way to the top floor.

I had planned to run down the long, carpeted hallway outside the chancellor's office, then descend the opposite staircase. Instead, the chancellor's door cracks open, and I dart into the nearest niche in the wall, crouching down behind a large and rather ugly Grecian urn.

The move is instinctive, driven by a desire to avoid being seen by Luther Hugo. I don't realize that he's accompanied by someone else until I hear a low female voice saying, "You're the one who let him come here."

"I had no choice," Hugo hisses. "It would have looked stranger if I didn't."

Peeking around the edge of the urn, I see Ms. Robin's brilliant red hair trailing down the hallway alongside the chancellor's broad back.

There's nothing unusual about the librarian visiting her uncle. Except for the complete lack of affection in either of their voices.

"He doesn't know anything," Ms. Robin says, haughty and dismissive.

"You'd better hope he doesn't," the chancellor snaps back at her.

"If you honestly think—"

They're getting too far away for me to hear. I lean out a little farther, trying to get a better angle.

The urn wobbles, drowning out whatever the chancellor replies.

I frantically grip its handles, preventing it from toppling over but grimacing at the noise.

There's a slight pause, as if Ms. Robin and the chancellor glanced back over their shoulders.

I hold my breath, worried that they might hear even an exhale.

After a moment, their motion resumes.

"Well, that's *your* problem," Ms. Robin says coldly.

Then I hear the light patter of her feet descending the stairs.

Luther Hugo comes stomping back down the hallway.

I shrink behind the urn, praying that he won't look in my direction. I'm only partly concealed by the oversize pottery.

Born along in a cloud of irritation, he sweeps into his office and slams the door.

I stay exactly where I am, too scared to move.

I only heard a fragment of the conversation.

But I can't help thinking they must be talking about Snow.

Finally Saturday rolls around again. I prefer the weekend—it's much easier to avoid Lola.

Rakel and I spend the morning as we've been spending all our weekends lately—searching for my missing person.

We have to take the laptop up to ground level because there's no connection down in the undercroft. We're holed up in the ice house on the west side of campus, Rakel tapping away on Ozzy's laptop and me keeping watch by the door so we're not caught with technological contraband.

Rakel has become even more obsessed with this task than I am.

She's been neglecting her homework in favor of chasing up obscure leads that inevitably conclude in more dead ends.

"People can't really disappear," Rakel says grimly, her eyes fixed on the glowing screen. "There's always some trace…"

"Unless they're dead," I reply.

"She's not dead."

"How do you know?"

"I just do."

I don't share Rakel's confidence. I told her from the beginning this might be a fool's errand.

"I found her sister easy enough," Rakel says. "She's a nurse too. Works at Evanston Women's Hospital in Chicago. Which is a little weird, 'cause the address on her tax return is Madison. That's a long commute."

"Could be an old address," I say, drawing idly in my sketchbook with a piece of charcoal.

"No, it's from January."

"Is that her only family?"

"Yeah, her parents are dead."

I'm drawing two sisters, both blond and dressed in nurse's uniforms.

Two sisters who look alike, not like me and Zoe.

The charcoal smudges on the page as my hand jerks involuntarily.

"Rakel…" I say.

"What?"

"Pull up the hospital directory."

Rakel finds the right page, scrolling until she sees the nurse in question: Lida Copeland.

"Look at that," Rakel says. "They could be twins."

I join her at the laptop, my eyes fixed on the blond woman facing the camera with only the ghost of a smile. Her face is angular and elegant, the austere lines of her jaw and her wide, full mouth offset by the heavy frames of her glasses.

The glasses can't disguise her beauty or the sadness in her eyes that is all too familiar to me.

"Not twins…" I breathe. "That's her. That's Dean's mother."

We found Rose Copeland.

CHAPTER 21
DEAN

CAT COMES RUNNING UP THE STAIRS OF THE BELL TOWER, FILLED with a nervous energy I've never seen before.

"You look excited to see me." I grin, grabbing her and trying to kiss her.

"I am!" she cries. "But not for—not just for that."

"What, then?" I say, my fingers slipping through her curls as she twists out of my grasp, too anxious to stay still.

She's pacing around the tower, nervy and almost hectic. Bright spots of color flame in her cheeks, her eyes glinting like black jet. She's grasping a folded piece of paper in her fist.

"I was looking for something. I didn't want to say anything in case I couldn't find it. But I did! Earlier this morning. And I'm almost certain of it."

"What?" I say.

Her agitation is infecting me. Not in a positive way—I've never liked surprises.

Cat twists the paper in her hand, her eyes as big as I've ever seen them.

"I think I found your mother."

I stare at her, uncomprehending.

"She's working at a hospital in Chicago. At first, I thought it was her sister, but her sister lives in Madison with her husband and kids.

I think your mother is using her name and social so she can work without anyone knowing."

Cat's words are a swarm of wasps swirling around me—too fast and too loud.

"It took some digging, but she has an apartment in Chicago too. You wouldn't need an apartment and a house if it was the same person."

I shake my head, trying to clear the cacophony.

"Cat!" I bark, my voice louder than I intend.

Cat breaks off, startled by my tone.

I try to speak softly, but my heart is racing in a sickening way.

"Are you saying my mother is alive?"

"Yes!" Cat cries happily. "Or, at least, I'm almost certain."

The uneven floor of the tower seems to lurch under my feet.

I really thought she was dead.

I thought that was why she never tried to contact me.

Now Cat is telling me my mom was alive all along.

She could have called me any time.

"She's in Chicago," I say dully.

"That's right." Cat nods. Her expression is eager and hopeful. It hurts me almost as much as her words.

I always wanted to move back to Chicago. I wished I lived there instead of Moscow.

My mother went without me.

"There's something else," Cat says, unfurling the paper she's been clutching so tight. It's a grainy black-and-white photograph, printed on the shitty printers in the computer lab.

I take it from her though I don't want to.

I'm afraid to look.

I smooth out the wrinkles, battling against my churning stomach and the frantic thudding in my chest.

I see my mother, older but instantly recognizable, holding the hand of a small girl with blond pigtails.

"I think you have a sister," Cat says.

I look at that image, my mother holding the hand of the girl the same age that I was when she left.

The little girl looks up at her, happy and trusting.

I tear the picture in half, ripping mother and daughter apart.

Cat stares at me, stunned.

I rip those pieces into smaller pieces, and I throw them on the floor.

It does nothing to stifle my rage.

That paper might as well be tinder. My fury flames up ten times higher.

Cat is open-mouthed, already backing away from me.

"You had no right," I hiss, the anger rising and rising.

"But I—"

"You had no right!" I howl, snatching up the closest thing at hand, which happens to be my speaker, and smashing it against the wall. Cat jolts at the impact. The music abruptly cuts out, leaving a deathly silence between us.

"Dean…" Cat whispers. Her eyes are filling with tears.

"I don't want to know where she is! I fucking hate her!"

Cat flinches away from me, her hands held up in front of her in helpless defense. It's less than useless. We both know I could tear her apart as easily as that paper.

"I didn't know—"

"You don't know anything about me!" I shout. "You don't fucking know me at all. You thought I would like that? Are you fucking stupid?"

Now the tears are running down her face, both sides.

They don't placate me.

They only make me angrier because now I feel guilty as well as enraged.

How dare she do this to me? How dare she make me feel this way?

I knew this would happen. I knew Cat was too good to be true.

I knew she'd lie to me, sneak around behind my back, and stab me in the place that hurts the most. It was only a matter of time.

"I'm sorry—" she starts.

"Yeah, you're fucking sorry," I hiss. "You're pathetic and sorry."

She's fully crying now, sobs shaking her shoulders.

And I hate myself far more than I hate her, but I can't seem to stop.

"*You're nothing to me,*" I spit.

She's shrinking down, huddling away from me like a little kid scared of a monster.

I am a fucking monster. I know that. It was stupid to pretend any different.

Why did I think I could be happy?

I don't deserve that.

I expect Cat to break down entirely.

Really, I'm the one who doesn't know her. Because she surprises me yet again.

She straightens up, still shaking, pulling her shoulders back. She faces me with swollen eyes and trembling lips.

"This is over," she says. "I don't want to see you anymore. You're broken, and I can't fix you."

Her words hit me, straight and swift like arrow shafts.

All in an instant, the world flips and reverses.

I thought I meant what I said while I was saying it.

Now I see it for what it was: rage pointed in the wrong direction.

Whereas, with horrid clarity, I see that Cat is not speaking in anger at all.

Every word is true, and she means every bit of it.

I finally went too far. She's done with me.

"Cat—" I say, reaching desperately to take her hand.

Too late.

She wrenches it away from me and flees down the steps.

CHAPTER 22
CAT

I RUN AWAY FROM DEAN, DOWN TO THE UNDERCROFT WHERE HE can't follow.

Then I remember that he broke into my room last year, so he absolutely can find me down here if he cares to do it.

But I doubt he will.

I lie face down on the bed, guilty and miserable.

I shouldn't have gone looking for his mother without talking to him first.

I wanted to surprise him. But I knew how emotionally fraught that whole situation is for Dean.

On the other hand...

It's better that I know how he actually feels about me.

He doesn't love me. He never did.

Why would he?

Dean has always been one of the smartest, the strongest, and the most disciplined people at this school. With all I've changed, I'm still barely average.

But god, it felt good to believe that he loved me.

I can't stop crying.

I'm soaking my pillow like a fucking baby, all tears and snot and embarrassing sobs.

I'm glad Rakel isn't here.

How did I fuck that up so bad?

I'm stupid, just like Dean said. I think I understand what's going on around me, and then I don't, not even a little bit.

I didn't see what was going on between Rocco and my sister until it was almost too late. I wasn't able to help Hedeon. I don't know what the hell is going on with Ms. Robin. I'm a shit Spy.

Maybe Lola's right about everything. If Dean thought I was an idiot all along, maybe Anna and Chay do too. Maybe Ares does, and Hedeon. Even Rakel might only be tolerating me.

I'm spiraling down a greased slide into a pit of slime.

All my darkest thoughts and worst fears are waiting for me at the bottom.

I'm worthless. No one loves me. No one ever will.

Except Zoe.

The thought comes to me—one tiny beacon of light in the blackness.

I still have my sister.

I could call her right now.

I snatch up my phone, already dialing before I remember there's no service down here.

Without bothering to grab so much as a sweatshirt, I run out of my room and back up the stairs to ground level. I hurry north to the wall, too impatient to find my usual secluded spot on the far corner of campus. Instead, I wedge myself between the leafless orange trees and call my sister.

The phone rings several times. My stomach clenches up, thinking she's not going to answer.

Then Zoe's cheerful voice trills, "There you are! I haven't talked to you in forever!"

I'm already crying again before I can even say hello. Poor Zoe has to wade through my gulps and sobs to try to figure out what the fuck is going on.

"Are you okay?" she cries. "Did somebody hurt you?"

"No," I say miserably. "I just… Dean and I broke up."

"Oh," Zoe says.

I can tell this isn't exactly a surprise to her, which only makes me cry harder.

"I'm sorry, *conejita*," Zoe says, "but maybe it's for the best."

"No, it isn't!" I cry.

"But, Cat—"

"You don't understand," I sob.

"Then explain it to me," Zoe says.

She's such a good sister. She always wants to be on my side.

"I *want* to understand," Zoe says. "Tell me how this whole thing happened."

She doesn't know what she's asking. Still, I'm going to tell her. I'm so tired of carrying this secret.

I take a long, shuddering breath.

"I killed Rocco Prince," I say.

The silence on the other end of the line is deep enough to drown an ocean.

"No," Zoe whispers.

"I did. And Dean saw me."

I can almost hear her mind whirring, putting together the pieces with astonishing speed.

She knows it's the truth. Only her image of her sweet baby sister prevented her from seeing it before.

"Why didn't you tell me?" Zoe murmurs.

"I didn't want you to worry. I wanted you to be free."

"I can't believe it, Cat. How did you—"

"I don't want to talk about that."

I'm still filled with a sick sense of dread every time I remember waiting on the wall for Rocco Prince to arrive. Knowing that he was stronger than me, faster than me, and maybe smarter too… Knowing that if one of us was about to die, it could just as easily be me.

"It worked, and that's all that matters. No one else knows."

"Thank god for that," Zoe breathes.

"Dean promised not to tell. In return for, ah, a few favors."

"What!" Zoe shrieks, outraged. "Did he—"

"No! I mean, not exactly. It's complicated."

Now she's fuming on the other end of the line, imagining the worst.

"We weren't friends at first, but then we were, and then it turned into something romantic."

I'm trying to explain to Zoe what I barely understand myself: the long progress of Dean's and my relationship from hatred to lust to love.

If it ever was love at all.

"He changed, and so did I. We connected in a way I've never felt before. And I thought we were…I thought it was something special. But now I fucked it up. Or he did. I don't know. I'm so confused."

Zoe sighs, trying to parse my rambling to find the truth.

"He really hurt me," I sob, remembering Dean's words cutting me deeper than any knife.

You thought I would like that? Are you fucking stupid?

You're nothing to me.

"If he hurt you, then he doesn't love you," Zoe says.

It's not what I want to hear. But the wrenching pain in my chest tells me that she might be right.

"When someone loves you, they'll do anything to keep you safe."

I want Zoe to be wrong. She's never wrong, though.

"What should I do?" I ask her.

"Stay away from him," Zoe says. "And make sure no one else finds out about…you know."

"He won't tell," I assure her.

As furious as Dean might have been, he'll keep my secret anyway. I still feel certain of that.

A dry branch creaks behind me.

I whirl around, thinking Dean came looking for me.

There's nothing there.

It was probably just a squirrel or one of the several cats that prowl the school grounds.

"And by the way, Cat," Zoe says.

"What?"

"Thank you for what you did. I hate what it must have cost you… but just know, I'm finally happy. Finally at peace. Because of you."

Her words put warmth in my chest where there had only been ice.

"It had to happen," I tell her. "It's exactly what you said—when someone loves you, they'd do anything to keep you safe."

I'm gripping the phone tight, wishing I could hug my sister just as hard.

"*Te amo, hermana,*" she says.

"*Te quiero,*" I reply.

CHAPTER 23
DEAN

AFTER CAT LEAVES THE BELL TOWER, I STAY UP THERE ALONE FOR hours, pacing back and forth in an agony of indecision.

I fucking hate what Cat did. I hate the image she put in my head of my mother and her new fucking family, her new child, the one that replaced me.

I hate knowing that she's living in Chicago, fully moved on without me.

Yet pathetically, I find myself scrabbling through the torn-up pieces of paper on the floor until I find the ones that show my mother's face.

I try to piece them together again.

It doesn't work. I destroyed them past recognition.

I want to go find Cat. But she doesn't want to see me right now.

Actually, she said she never wants to see me again.

Did she really mean that?

If she did, then I don't know what I'll do.

Something fucking drastic.

Close to midnight, I finally leave the bell tower. I wander around campus until I happen upon a party in the old stables on the northwest corner of campus. The festivities are nowhere near as well organized as when Miles Griffin used to run the show, but the music is loud, and Louis Faucheux is selling forties for $100 a pop.

I don't usually drink.

Tonight seems like the perfect time to start.

I down half the bottle while gambling away the rest of my cash on street dice with Bram, Valon, Motya, and Pasha.

"That's more like it!" Bram says, roaring with laughter as I roll an eleven, winning a hefty bet off Valon. "Nice to have the old Dean back."

I take another swig of my drink.

"Yeah, you like the old Dean?" I say blearily. "That makes one of us."

Pasha calls Bodashka and Vanya Antonov to join us. They're at least as drunk as I am, Bodashka's broad face flushed red and Vanya swaying a little as he saunters over.

Bodashka gives me a grudging greeting, and even Vanya nods in a manner that might be interpreted as friendly.

"I didn't think you drank," Vanya says to me.

"I don't."

"What's that, then?" He grins, jerking his chin toward my half-empty bottle.

"Anesthetic."

"Oh yeah, the new doctor gave you that?" He chuckles. "She's a hell of an improvement over the old one."

"Careful," I say.

"Don't worry." Vanya holds up his hands in mock surrender. "I have no intention of drawing the wrath of our boxing instructor. I learned my lesson the first day of class."

"Not your most brilliant moment, Dmitry," Bodashka snickers.

"It was certainly educational," I say, taking another swig.

Bodashka and Vanya look surprised that I'm not instantly infuriated by their comments.

The truth is I'm only half listening to them. The rest of my brain is wondering what Cat is doing right now. I had hoped she might drop into the party, but no luck yet.

"Well, whatever's in that bottle, I think it's good for you, Dmitry," Vanya says with the audacity to give me a friendly punch on the shoulder. "Chills you the fuck out. It's better to be friends than enemies, don't you think?"

I look at Vanya's smile, full of perfect white teeth but stopping dead at his cheeks. His dark eyes remain as flat and predatory as a shark's.

I bet Brutus looked like that when he smiled at Caesar.

"You need all the friends you can get, Dmitry," Bodashka says quietly. "Big things are coming back home. And your father isn't there to look out for your interests anymore."

"You want to pick your alliances very carefully," Vanya says, those shark eyes fixed on my face. "Kade Petrov is a poor choice."

I wish I weren't so drunk.

They're trying to tell me something.

"What do you mean?" I ask Bodashka, struggling to focus on his pale, bloodshot eyes.

"The high table isn't happy with the Petrovs. Ivan Petrov is barely in contact, and his brother is siphoning off money. If Ivan can't even keep his own house in order—"

"There's upheaval coming," Pasha says, his tone conspiratorial and eager. "If you pick the right side...all of St. Petersburg could be up for grabs."

I look at Bodashka and Vanya. Motya, Pasha, Bram, and Valon too. All my oldest friends and one enemy who wants to become allies. They stare back at me, expecting me to jump at the chance to pillage the territory of the Petrovs. It could be the making of all of us.

I think of Kade Petrov, laughing when I pop him in our boxing class. Struggling with all his might to win the Quartum Bellum even when it's clear that he lost, even when the waves washed over his head.

I just met that kid. Why should I care what happens to his family?

Why should I believe Dominik Petrov is a good man just because he refused to fuck some ballerina? Everyone else says he's turning on his own brother.

And yet…I trust the Petrovs more than I trust this group of schemers.

Or maybe I've just gone soft.

I stand up abruptly, scattering my remaining cash.

"It's foolish to divide the meat when the bear hasn't been shot," I say.

"We're not talking about the meat. We're talking about the hunt," Vanya hisses.

"Don't mistake absence for weakness. Ivan Petrov is a powerful man. One I don't want for an enemy."

"You're a coward," Vanya spits.

"And you're a traitor," I retort, staring him down. "I'd take Ivan as an enemy before I'd take you as a friend."

Bodashka, Vanya, and Pasha glare at me. Motya and Valon look torn. Only Bram gives me an affirming nod. He likes Kade Petrov.

"You better keep your mouth shut about this," Bodashka hisses.

I scoff in his face, leaving the dice and cash scattered on the stable floor.

It'll be a dark day when I take orders from Bodashka Kushnir.

Sunday morning, I wake up with a raging headache. This is why I never fucking drink—I hate paying the price the next morning.

I go looking for Cat anyway, determined to talk through our argument.

But I can't find her anywhere. She's not in the dining hall, the library, or her dorm room.

I know she's avoiding me intentionally. That sneaky little kitten can be quite elusive when she wants to be.

She won't be able to hide on Monday. She'll have to go to class, and I have her schedule memorized.

I corner her outside chemistry before first period.

"Cat," I say, grabbing her arm. "I need to talk to you."

She shakes me off, snapping, "Don't touch me!"

"Are you going to pretend you don't like when I touch you?" I growl, pinning her up against the rough stone wall.

"I'm not playing games with you anymore!" she cries, trying to get past me.

I'm not looking at her angry expression—I'm fixated on the shockingly bare expanse of collarbone where the ruby necklace usually sits.

"You took off my necklace?" I say, outraged.

"It's *my* necklace," Cat snaps, "and I'll throw it in the fucking toilet if I feel like it!"

"Don't you dare, you little—"

My words are cut off by a swift and accurate knee to the groin from my beloved.

I double over, groaning. Cat slips neatly past me.

"Leave me alone, Dean. I mean it!" she cries, darting into the classroom.

I lean against the wall, sweating and breathing hard until the throbbing pain in my balls dissipates.

"You should be more careful with something you might want to use again," I grumble toward the closed door of Cat's class.

Straightening up, I give my head a shake.

I should be angry with her. But I'm well aware of Cat's claustrophobia. There's a fine line between restraining her and trapping her.

Besides…I always enjoy a glimpse of Cat's ruthless side. Even when it's directed at me.

The bigger issue is how I'm going to make her talk to me.

I ponder this conundrum during boxing.

I pair up with Kade Petrov intentionally to annoy Vanya and Bodashka. Sure enough, they glower and mutter to each other as they watch us spar.

"I can never tell if they're mad at me or you," Kade says, sending a rapid combination my way.

"Both," I say, blocking each punch in turn. "And they're not mad. They're just…malevolent."

Kade laughs. "I'm glad I can always get a vocabulary lesson along with my boxing instruction."

"Maybe you should be an English teacher, 'cause you ain't never gonna be a boxer," I tease him, sending a combination back at him.

Kade slips the punches with promising speed.

"There you go!" I say. "Not too shabby."

He fires back at me, and I bat his fist aside.

"Not too great either," I snort.

I don't know why I'm laughing. I've got a hundred different problems plaguing me, and I'm still fucked in the head from seeing that picture of my mother. But Kade is so easygoing that it lightens my mood to spar with him, even on the worst days.

He refuses to quail under the obvious antagonism of the older students. And he never shirks from practicing with me, even when he can't land a single hit. His persistence is infectious.

Kade attacks again, even faster. This time, he manages to get a rapid jab inside my right glove, and it grazes my chin.

"Oh, you felt that one!" Kade chortles, bouncing on the balls of his feet.

"Not as much as you will," I growl.

After class, I help Snow pick up the discarded sparring pads.

He sprays them with sanitizer and wipes them down with a towel.

"Well," he grunts, throwing another pad on the pile of those that have been cleaned. "What is it?"

"What do you mean?"

"I know you're not helping me tidy up out of the goodness of your heart."

"I could be."

"You're not."

I pick up a sweaty towel and chuck it in the laundry bin, irritated by how easily he sees through me.

"I got in a fight with Cat the other night," I admit.

"What happened?"

"She found my mother. Living in Chicago, under her sister's name."

Snow is silent a minute, digesting this.

"Why did that occasion a fight?" he says at last.

"Cat tracked her down without even asking me. She shoved a picture in my face."

Snow cocks an eyebrow at me. "And that made you angry?"

"She had no right."

He makes a dismissive sound. "She has every right."

I wring the towel in my hands, glaring at Snow. It's just like him to take her side for no fucking reason.

"How do you figure that?" I demand.

"It's called intimacy, Dean. You let someone in your life, and they're in your life. She's not a doll you can put on a shelf until you want to play with her again. She's gonna have her own ideas of how to do things."

"It's my fucking mother! It's my choice if I want to find her or not."

"Cat didn't fly her to the island. It's still your choice if you want to see her, isn't it?"

My blood pressure is rising, thudding in my temples and behind my eyes. I don't know why the fuck I come to Snow for advice when he's just as infuriating as Cat. Maybe even more so.

"She had the balls to try to break up with me!" I say.

Snow chuckles, and I'd like to chuck this towel right in his face. "Sounds like she *did* break up with you."

I fling the towel into the hamper, biting back the torrent of angry words that wants to spill out of me. I regret how I spoke to Cat. I don't need to set another relationship on fire, even if Snow is seriously pissing me off.

"Well?" I demand.

"Well what?"

"What am I supposed to do?"

"Have you considered apologizing?"

"Why the fuck should I apologize? She's the one who should beg me for forgiveness."

Snow sighs, picking up the last of the pads and carrying them over to the storage cabinet.

"Dean," he says. "I don't think this is the first time you've blown up your own life. Have you ever tried fixing it instead?"

"What do you mean?"

"You want connection, don't you? Stop pushing away the people who will give it to you."

"I don't want to see my mother."

"Then don't. But Cat is right here."

I look down at the mats, my guts churning.

"I don't think she is. I really fucked up."

Snow closes the cabinet and locks it.

"No relationship is built without mistakes," he says.

I cast a quick look at his stony scowl. "You think she'll forgive me?"

"Maybe. If you learn how to say sorry and actually mean it."

"What does that look like?"

Snow folds his arms across his substantial chest. "Only you can figure that out."

I think about that while I gather up my duffel bag and prepare to leave.

Right as I reach the door, I pause and turn back.

"Snow," I say.

He turns around, waiting.

"With Sasha…how did you know you were really in love?"

Snow answers without hesitation. "I knew when I was willing to do anything for her. Give anything. Risk anything."

Then he heads back to his office, not waiting for my response.

CHAPTER 24
THE SPY

This school year has seemed the longest yet.

I'm so tired.

I never realized what a strain all the lying would be.

The rest of the students are energized by the warming weather. For me, it has the opposite effect. Another summer rolling around—another anniversary I don't want to mark. I never thought I'd be here three years later.

Ms. Robin still hasn't found what she's been searching for day and night for all this time.

"If we can't find it, maybe we should consider—"

"No," she snaps. "We proceed with the rest of the plan either way."

My stomach clenches. I don't like the rest of the plan. I've never liked it.

She lays her hand on my arm, looking in my eyes.

"I know this is hard for you. But it's the only way. She's coming here next year. She'll be alone and unprotected."

Kingmakers: the safest place on earth, invulnerable to attack.

Unless the enemy is already inside.

Ms. Robin squeezes my arm, her fingers frightfully strong.

"This is not a world made for the gentle and the just. You are a wolf and always have been."

I remove her hand from my arm and hold it between my own. "I'll do what has to be done."

She gives me a long, steady look. "I know you will."

For now, I have another task at hand. Much simpler than the task awaiting me come September.

I find Cat Romero plodding across campus with her arms full of books.

Cat always looks too small to carry whatever she's carrying. I have to resist the urge to offer to take the stack out of her hands.

"Hello, Cat," I say.

"Oh, hello," she replies miserably.

Her face looks thin and drawn, her shoulders slumped.

Probably something to do with Dean.

Too bad—I was almost starting to root for him.

He became my unwitting ally this year without ever knowing it.

"How are you doing?" I ask her.

"I'm fi—" she starts and then abruptly changes her mind. "Not good," she admits.

"Anything I can do to help?"

"No," she sighs. "Thank you, though."

"Are you sure? I could strangle Dean in his sleep."

Her lower lip trembles. "I'm afraid I'm a long way past when that would help me."

"How's Zoe doing, then?" I say, knowing that will cheer her up.

Sure enough, she gives me a wobbly smile.

"She's so happy," Cat says. "She sold another script. Can you believe it?"

Nothing pleases Cat more than something good happening for her sister.

"I was talking to Perry Saunders at the library," I mention oh-so casually. "She's a friend of yours, isn't she?"

"Mm-hmm." Cat nods, glancing across the open lawn. Probably looking for Dean.

"Have you ever visited her in Kyiv?"

"Oh, she doesn't live in Kyiv," Cat says distractedly. "Her mother doesn't like it there, so they live in Naples and her father flies back every couple of weeks. Her mother breeds horses."

"I'm surprised he's willing to live on his own," I chuckle. "Mafia men aren't exactly known for their housekeeping skills."

"He stays at the Four Seasons," Cat says, now scanning the students exiting the dining hall.

"Well, I won't keep you," I say, ready to part ways now that I've gotten what I needed. "Have fun in class."

"You too," Cat says vaguely.

It's to my benefit that she wasn't entirely paying attention—Cat Romero can be a little too curious for her own good. Ms. Robin already warned me about that.

She guessed almost immediately that Cat was the one who killed Rocco Prince. That was an unwelcome complication. Dr. Cross's lung infection was another.

With all the near misses we've had, I've almost become numb to the danger of our position.

There's only so many times you can face down death without wanting to open your arms to him out of sheer exhaustion.

CHAPTER 25
CAT

DEAN CORNERS ME AGAIN OUTSIDE THE DINING HALL. I TRIED TO come to dinner late to avoid him, but apparently he's been waiting out here for over an hour.

"Leave me alone," I say, trying to push past him.

"No," he says. "Not until you talk to me."

"I've got nothing to say to you."

"But *I* have something to say to *you*."

I turn to face him, fully annoyed.

"And it's what *you* want that matters, isn't it, Dean?"

"No," he says, somewhat abashed. "I mean, maybe..."

It's hard to look at him because the handsomeness of his face never fails to work its subversive magic on me, even when my stomach is still clenched up in knots and my heart is still aching from a weekend of bawling my eyes out.

Dean is bad for me. I've known that from the beginning.

Yet my body craves him like fresh oxygen. I'm already missing the taste of his mouth and the feel of his hands on my flesh.

"You hurt me, Dean," I tell him quietly. "You really hurt me."

"I know," he says. "And..." He swallows as if he's choking on something. "And I'm sorry," he says in a strangled tone.

I almost want to laugh.

It sounds like he's never apologized in his life.

He looks ridiculously relieved, as if he thought saying those words might kill him.

Unfortunately for him, no amount of apology is going to wipe his insults out of my brain.

"I don't care," I say coldly.

"Why not?" he demands.

"Because you told me you loved me, and then you said I meant nothing to you. So your words are meaningless."

Dean flinches, looking guilty.

"I know, Cat, but I was so angry—"

"You're always angry," I interrupt. "Always pouring out your rage on everyone around you. Well, it's not going to be me anymore."

"Cat, you can't be serious."

He's trying to take my hand, but I yank it away from him.

"I'm very serious. Don't make me hurt you again."

Dean laughs, knowing as well as I do that I only managed to knee him because he wasn't expecting it. I have no chance of actually injuring Dean. Only he has the power to hurt me.

And he did.

Too much and too well.

I push past him into the dining hall.

He accosts me again the next morning, apparently hoping that a good night's sleep will have improved my mood.

It hasn't.

I barely slept at all. I tossed and turned in an agony of indecision until Rakel snarled at me to hold still or she'd duct-tape me to the bed.

I miss Dean. I miss him badly.

But I can't stop remembering Lola's taunts and Dean's insults following directly afterward, proving the truth of her words.

Just because he likes fucking you doesn't mean he gives a shit about you.

He's using you because you'll do whatever he says.

And then, worst of all, echoing over and over in my brain:

You're nothing to me.

I never really believed that Dean could love me.

What fragile hope I had was shattered as he raged at me in the tower.

Zoe's right: love doesn't hurt like this. Love doesn't bring you to your knees with grief and misery.

"Cat, you're being ridiculous!" Dean cries, annoyed at my continued resistance. "You can't throw away everything we have over one fight."

"I didn't throw it away," I say coldly. "You did."

I can already see his temper rising, right now, when he's supposed to be begging for forgiveness.

"You're getting mad all over again, aren't you!" I cry. "I bet you want to shout at me, don't you?"

"Only because you're being—" Dean raises his hands like he's going to strangle me and then abruptly cuts himself off.

I laugh in his face.

"Being what?" I demand. "Tell me again how awful I am."

Dean takes several deep breaths, his lips pressed tightly together in a thin line.

It would be funny watching him try to control his temper if it didn't make me so sad at the same time.

"I'm sorry I insulted you, Cat," he says. "I didn't mean it. I was out of my mind."

"So was I," I say quietly. "But I'm sane again now."

I walk to my first class, having missed breakfast by talking to him.

CHAPTER 26
DEAN

I'M STARTING TO REALIZE THE DEPTH OF MY MISTAKE.

Cat is not forgiving me.

And I know the reason why.

I really fucking hurt her. I can see it in her eyes every time I force her to look at me. She's trying to be so cold, so aloof, but I hear the tremor in her voice, and I see her hands shaking.

I never realized how fragile our relationship was.

I flung it against the wall like that speaker, and it shattered into a hundred pieces. Now I'm trying to glue them back together, and it isn't fucking working. I don't know how to restore her trust.

I try giving her space for a couple of days, but when I approach her again outside the keep, she's as determined as ever.

"It's over, Dean," she tells me. "Our relationship was wrong from the start. Nothing built out of violence and lies and coercion could ever turn into something good."

"That's not true!" I cry. "It can be whatever we want it to be. It's our choice what it becomes. It doesn't matter how it started."

She shakes her head at me, her eyes sad and unbelieving.

It doesn't help that I can barely contain my frustration every time she shuts me down again. I'm trying to prove to Cat that I can be calm, controlled, reasonable, but it's driving me insane that she won't speak to me, that she won't give me another chance.

"I love you!" I say, seizing her hand. "And I know you love me too. Look at me and tell me you don't."

She refuses to look at me.

And refuses to answer.

The next time I see her, she's walking to class with Hedeon Gray.

It feels intentional, like she's trying to enrage me.

She knows I don't trust Hedeon. I don't trust any man around her. I'm the one who should be walking at her side. I'm the one she should be gazing up at, smiling in that way that feels like a hand reaching into my chest, squeezing my heart…

I cut across their path, making Hedeon pull up short.

"Thanks for keeping her company," I say to Hedeon. "I'll take it from here."

Hedeon throws a quick glance at Cat, which only infuriates me more.

"I don't think—" he starts.

"Yeah, don't think," I hiss. "Don't strain your brain. Just carry on your way."

Hedeon glares at me, fists clenched at his sides.

Hedeon's a decent fighter, and he's not afraid to face off against even Silas. But he knows if he goes toe-to-toe with me, I'll knock him flat.

Plus, I haven't slept in three days. I probably look none too stable at the moment.

Deciding it's not worth the hassle, Hedeon stalks off toward the keep.

Cat rounds on me, cheeks flaming and eyes snapping. God, she looks sexy when she's angry.

"What the fuck do you think you're doing?" she demands, stomping her foot in a way that's utterly adorable.

"I'm walking you to class."

"I don't want you to walk me to class. I don't want you anywhere near me."

"Yes, you do," I growl. "You miss me, and I miss you. Stop torturing us both."

"You have no right to scare off my friends or to harass me!" Cat cries. She's angry too. The air between us crackles with that tension that's so familiar to me—the kind that makes me want to seize her and kiss her until both our lips are bloody.

I'd do it if I weren't afraid it would break the last bonds between us.

Because Cat really is pissed, and I don't trust myself not to make this worse.

"You leave me no choice!" I say. "I can't just walk away from you. I need you, Cat. I love you."

"It's always what you want, what you need," she says, tears glinting in her eyes.

"Then tell me what you need! Tell me what to do, how to make it up to you! What will it take for you to forgive me?"

Cat looks up at me with a quizzical expression.

"Do you really mean that?" she says.

"Yes! Yes, I mean it."

"You want to prove to me that you're sorry?"

"Yes, I told you that a hundred times."

"Alright then," she says, folding her arms across her chest. "I want a month."

I stare at her, at her pale face and stubborn jaw.

"A month?"

"That's right. I gave *you* a month once. Now I want the same in return. A month of you obeying my every command."

I can't help the smile tugging the corner of my lips. "That doesn't sound so bad."

"Don't be so sure," Cat says sternly.

"And at the end of the month, we can start over again?"

"Maybe," she says, still frowning at me.

Maybe is better than no.

"What's the first order, boss?" I grin.

"You can carry my books," she says, dumping them into my arms. "Walking five feet behind me."

"No problem," I say. "This is my favorite view."

"And don't talk," Cat snaps over her shoulder.

I follow Cat to her next class, silent and obedient.

It's a good thing she can't see me, because my cock is already rock-hard from watching that cute little ass stomping away five steps ahead of me.

———————

Over the next week, Cat dredges up every bit of humiliation I put her through and heaps it back on my head.

She makes me dash around running errands for her until my head is spinning. She orders me to feed her grapes in the dining hall like I once did to her and even demands that I strip off my shirt and fan her with a folded pop quiz, like she's Cleopatra and I'm an Egyptian slave.

It's not the ideal time for me to look like a fucking idiot, since Vanya Antonov was already trying to siphon off as many of my friends as possible, and Bodashka, Pasha, and Valon have joined him in openly mocking me.

Cat has forbidden me from fighting any of them.

She says I'm not supposed to lose my temper whatsoever.

You might as well ask a shark not to swim.

I'm fucking drowning in all the aggression I have to stuff back down inside me every time Vanya throws another jeer in my direction.

The only silver lining is that Bram is still sitting next to me at Cat's table, seeming to find the whole thing amusing and even slightly admirable.

"Wish I had someone to do weird kinky shit with at lunch," he says, stuffing half a bacon sandwich in his mouth.

He glances across the table at Rakel.

"You look like you know how to get nasty," he mumbles around a mouthful of bread. "How about it?"

"What a tempting proposal," Rakel says acerbically. "Unfortunately I'm already dating Joss Burmingham."

"That spotty little Spy? I'm way hotter than him."

"But he's learned to chew, swallow, and then speak, so he's got that going for him."

Bram gulps down his bite. "How 'bout now?" He grins.

"Still no," Rakel sniffs.

Anna and Leo have maintained an admirable level of silence through all this, though I know Leo is dying to give me shit about the fact that I'm once again stripped down to my trousers, holding up Cat's water glass so she can take a sip, while barred from speaking to her.

Leo can barely lift his eyes from his plate, and I think Anna has kicked him under the table at least three times.

I have the strangest sense that Anna is rooting for me. She meets my eye across the table, giving me an encouraging smile.

Chay is less restrained. She keeps coming up with new ideas for Cat to torment me.

"You should make Dean wear knee socks and a skirt!" she says cheerfully.

"Chay," I say. "Please shut the hell up."

She ignores me.

"Oooh, make him stand up in our International Banking class and sing the Russian national anthem! I'll tell you if he does it."

"Professor Graves will expel me," I complain.

"Quiet!" Cat hisses at me, snapping her fingers for another sip of water.

I never realized she was such a little sadist.

It only makes me like her more.

I can't be certain, but I think she's thawing toward me, just a little. I don't think she believed I'd last one day of this treatment. It's going on seven, and I'm determined not to crack. I'll show her that I've learned to control myself. That I'm really fucking sorry. And that I'll do anything to make her happy.

That's what I realized after talking to Snow.

I *will* do anything for Cat. Sacrifice anything. Pay any price.

I'll grovel forever if that's what it takes to get her back.

I don't give a fuck if I look stupid in front of the whole school or if Vanya spreads the news of this to all of Moscow, undermining my position in the Bratva.

I want Cat more than I want anything—even to become *pakhan*.

I've never loved someone more than my own ambition.

It's terrifying.

Because I'm not in control of Cat. I can't make her love me.

All I can do is hope.

CHAPTER 27
CAT

I CAN'T BELIEVE DEAN HASN'T SNAPPED YET.

I only started this whole thing because I thought it would be the easiest way to get him to leave me alone. I thought I'd give him one order and his pride would intervene. I expected him to tell me to fuck off, and everything would go back to the way it used to be.

That's not what I wanted, but it seemed inevitable.

Instead, he keeps coming back for more.

Day after day, he lets me order him around. He listens to the jeers and catcalls from Vanya and Bodashka. I can see his hands shaking, his fists clenching. I know how badly he wants to rain down retribution on their heads.

But I told him not to do it. And he's actually obeying.

I'm not getting any pleasure out of this. I'm not dominant by nature. I don't enjoy being cruel.

Still, I feel driven to push him and push him.

Only then can I believe that he truly loves me.

I want to give in. It's torture sitting next to him, worse even than when I was his slave. He smells so fucking good, and he's so goddamned handsome. He's even developed enough of a sense of humor that he can laugh at himself when Leo throws some gentle teasing his way. A year ago, he would have flipped the lunch table over.

Maybe I should end this and tell him he's forgiven.

It's what I want to do.

But there's one cold kernel of fear inside me still.

I don't know what it will take to wash it away.

As a complicating issue, Lola is up to new tricks. Someone broke into my room, and I know it was her. She rifled through all my belongings—just mine, not Rakel's.

When I found the room in upheaval, I ran to my dresser, terrified that she'd stolen the ruby necklace. I almost cried with relief when I found it still tucked safely inside a clean pair of socks in the back of my drawer. Though I told Dean I was going to throw it away, I never could.

Only after I put everything back in its proper place did I discover my missing sketchbook.

The sketchbook contains nothing but drawings. I have no diary, no personal letters kept in my room.

Still, it felt like the worst kind of violation.

My drawings are highly personal. They're my outlet, my most private thoughts and feelings.

I only hope that stealing that book and burning it is the worst that Lola plans to do. It hurts to lose it, but I dread what other plans she might be concocting.

The next morning, Dean is waiting outside the undercroft to walk me to class.

He's not supposed to talk to me, but as soon as he sees my face, he asks, "What's wrong?"

His voice is so gentle and genuinely concerned that before I can think better of it, I tell him, "Lola broke into my room. She went through all my stuff and stole my sketchbook."

Dean frowns, considering.

"What do you think she's doing?"

I instantly feel a wash of relief that he doesn't dismiss the action as more of her harassment. He knows what Lola is like, and he knows she's building to something nasty.

"I really don't know," I say. "I don't know why she's so determined to turn this into a vendetta."

"Some people hate to see other people change," Dean says quietly. "It threatens them. They can only feel in control when their environment stays static."

"I don't want to be static," I say, looking into his face.

"Neither do I," Dean agrees.

It's the first calm conversation we've had together in a week.

I expect Dean to start pressing me to forgive him again, but instead he simply holds out his hand for my book bag so he can carry it for me.

"It's alright. I've got it," I say.

I sling the bag over my shoulder and offer him my hand instead.

My fingers slip inside his, warm and natural and comforting.

We walk to class hand in hand, over fresh grass with the first buds of purple clover coming up. The breeze from the fields outside the castle walls smells of spring.

Now that Dean is finally staying quiet, not pushing me for conversation, there's a hundred things I want to say to him.

He walks with his long strides carefully matching my pace. He's been right beside me this whole school year, one way or another.

We reach the keep. I'm supposed to go up to the third floor, and I know Dean has his boxing class over in the armory.

All of a sudden, I don't want to part, not even for an hour.

I clutch his hand, looking up into his face.

Dean smiles down at me.

"I'll be right out here waiting for you," he says.

But when I come out of the classroom after chemistry, Dean is nowhere to be seen.

CHAPTER 28
DEAN

As I'm walking from the keep to the armory, two hulking groundskeepers step out of the shadows of the grand hall and flank me, one on either side.

The Kingmakers staff are all ex-soldiers, ex-mercenaries, combat-trained and Mafia-initiated. Their daily tasks may involve menial activities such as tending to the greenhouses and building the infrastructure for the Quartum Bellum challenges, but at the end of the day, they're here for security purposes.

Like a stag encircled by wolves, I have the instinctive impulse to fight or run.

It takes all my discipline to face them calmly.

"Back up to the chancellor's office?" I say.

"Not this time," the one called Brenner says.

Closing in on me from both sides, they herd me in the opposite direction, to the northwest corner of campus.

I see our destination, dark and plain and isolated from every other structure around it: the prison tower.

My stomach clenches, and my legs go stiff.

Of all the places on campus you don't want to go, this is the most dreaded.

If you walk through those doors, something has gone very wrong.

This is where they brought Miles Griffin and Ozzy Duncan before Ozzy's scheduled execution.

I don't know exactly why they're "escorting" me here, but I can guess what the topic of conversation will be.

Brenner uses a key card to unlock the door—the only doors at Kingmakers that are electronically sealed, impervious to the students' lockpicking techniques.

The other groundskeeper shoves me through the doorway.

"Keep your fucking hands off me, or I'll break your arm," I snarl. "I can walk on my own, unlike you, who barely looks like you can blink and breathe at the same time."

The groundskeeper clenches his fist, taking a menacing step toward me. Brenner clears his throat, reminding him that, for the present at least, their orders are to transport and not attack me.

The prison tower has a squat and ugly shape, the interior damp and cold from the thick stone walls and lack of windows. I can hear water dripping somewhere in an irregular, maddening rhythm. The low ceiling of this bottom floor makes me feel cramped and claustrophobic. I could reach up and touch it without stretching.

"This way," Brenner says quietly.

He leads me through a weathered wooden door.

On the other side, as I knew he would, the chancellor waits.

And worse, much worse—this time, he's accompanied by Professor Penmark.

Lola Fischer stands off to the side, looking simultaneously eager and slightly nauseated. She shifts from foot to foot, fiddling with a lock of her long, wavy hair.

The room is empty of furniture—no tables or chairs, no rug on the floor. The walls are bare stone without any windows. Yet I notice the presence of several metal hooks and rings bolted to the walls and draped from the low ceiling. The shackles hang in the still air like a hangman's noose.

The door closes behind me, Brenner remaining in the room with us, the other groundskeeper staying outside.

I stand before my three accusers. Taking a slow breath to calm my heart, I tuck my hands in my trousers so no one will see them shaking.

"Dean Yenin," the chancellor says in his low, gravelly voice. "Do you know why you're here?"

This is the oldest trick in the world, used by every traffic cop in existence when they pull someone over.

You should never guess at your own misconduct.

"No," I say mildly. "I have no idea."

I refuse to look at Lola or Penmark either. I keep my gaze fixed steadily on the chancellor, his eyes glinting like sunken treasure in the wrinkled coral of his face.

"You've been accused of a very serious infraction," the chancellor says quietly. "Or more accurately, your inamorata has been accused. You have a right to face your informer."

He nods toward Lola.

I don't give her the satisfaction of a single glance. She's nothing to me. No matter how hard she tantrums for attention.

My only concern is discerning what Lola knows and what she's told the chancellor.

The chancellor waits, the silence thick and cold as fog.

I keep my mouth shut.

He who speaks first loses.

"Cat Romero killed Rocco Prince," the chancellor declares.

Oh, fuck.

I stand perfectly still, hands in pockets, face expressionless. He won't get so much as a flick of an eyelash out of me.

"Lola Fischer says you witnessed the murder," the chancellor says. "She says you've been using that information to blackmail Cat Romero for almost a year."

I stay silent, waiting to hear what else he knows. And, more importantly, what evidence they have.

"If you were not involved in Rocco's death, now is the time to speak," the chancellor tells me, his coal-black eyes boring into mine. "This is your only chance for clemency. Tell me everything you know, and you may be absolved."

He wants me to throw Cat under the bus. He brought me here first, without her. He's trying to get me to crack. Which means…he doesn't have enough evidence without my testimony. Whatever Lola told him or showed him, it's not quite enough.

That doesn't mean we're not in a fuck of a lot of trouble.

It only means I might have a chance to take the heat off Cat.

I take a deep breath, hoping I know what I'm doing.

"Yes," I say boldly.

The chancellor quirks one black eyebrow.

"Yes, what?" he demands.

"Yes, I know who killed Rocco Prince."

Professor Penmark leans forward with a hungry expression on his hollow face.

"Well?" the chancellor says impatiently. "Are you going to tell us?"

"No," I say.

This next silence is like the vibration after the ringing of a bell. A bell that can't be unrung.

"Dean," the chancellor says ominously. "Choose your next words very carefully. Are you telling me that you did indeed witness the murder, but you refuse to confirm if the perpetrator was Cat Romero?"

"That's right," I say. "I know. And I won't tell."

Professor Penmark lets slip a horrible smile of anticipation.

The chancellor clenches his jaw, disappointed but resolute.

"We'll see about that," he says.

Brenner strides forward and seizes one of my arms, Penmark the other. They force me down on my knees and raise my arms on either side of me in the shape of a pall.

Penmark pulls the chains down from the ceiling, closing the manacles around my wrists and wrenching them into position so the chains are taut and I can't move.

Lola stares at me, fixated. She looks like a child who flipped a switch and now stands in awe of what she's put into motion.

Strangely, I'm not afraid.

Whatever happens next, I know I won't break.

I'm the only thing left standing between Cat and certain destruction.

Once I'm fixed in place, the chancellor nods to Brenner.

"Go get her," he says.

CHAPTER 29
CAT

THE MOMENT I SEE THAT DEAN IS NOT WAITING FOR ME OUTSIDE chemistry class as promised, I know something's wrong. Dean wouldn't forget. He wouldn't be late.

So I'm not entirely surprised when a brawny groundskeeper seizes me by the arm and begins to drag me in the direction of the prison tower.

I suppose I wouldn't have been surprised either way. This is something I've dreaded every day since I chucked Rocco off that wall. Since I even started planning it.

I did my best to cover my tracks, but I always knew this particular skeleton in my closet was clawing at the door, desperate to get out.

I feel a numb, floating sensation as the groundskeeper pulls me across the endless expanse of lawn that separates the keep from that dark, lonely tower.

I should be terrified. But I'm not thinking about myself. The thing worrying me most is the knowledge that Dean failing to show up after class means they must have him too.

Sure enough, as the groundskeeper shoves me inside a small, dark room on the ground floor of the tower, I immediately spot Dean chained up in the center of the cramped space, on his knees with his arms up in the shape of a Y.

"Dean!" I cry, wrenching out of the groundskeeper's grasp and running over to him. I throw my arms around his shoulders as if I could shield him from harm.

Quickly, before anyone can yank me away, he whispers in my ear, "Don't admit to anything, Cat. Not one fucking thing!"

Now the full force of fear hits me, and my legs begin to shake. I feel very small in this tiny space and horribly confined. The rings and shackles on the walls aren't helping. Worst of all is the fact that I'm trapped in here with three of my least-favorite people: the chancellor, Professor Penmark, and Lola Fischer.

Lola looks torn between gleeful satisfaction and a strange, sick nervousness. I know she put this in motion. Now she's learning the difference between a plan and reality.

I learned the same thing the day I became a murderer. Nothing prepares you for blood on your hands.

"Cat Romero," the chancellor says without preamble. "Did you kill Rocco Prince?"

I look at Dean's face—pale and as determined as I've ever seen it. He gives one minute shake of his head.

"No," I say firmly.

"Can you tell me what you were doing the day he died?"

"It was the final challenge in the Quartum Bellum," I say carefully. "My team was already eliminated. At breakfast, I cut my arm accidentally. I went to the infirmary. Dr. Cross stitched the wound. We talked for a while. I helped him change the sheets on the bed. Then Dean arrived at the infirmary—his shoulder had been dislocated in the challenge. I helped Dr. Cross to reset it. Afterward, Dean and I walked back to the field together, and I sat with my roommate, Rakel, to watch the remainder of the event."

In the days after Rocco's death, I repeated this alibi to myself over and over so I'd be able to lie smoothly. But it's been several months since I rehearsed. I stumble over my sentences.

Apparently the chancellor already checked on my movements

that day. He counters at once. "I called Dr. Cross. He told me it's possible that he fell asleep for a time while you were in the infirmary."

It takes everything I have not to wince.

Dr. Cross didn't fall asleep—I drugged him.

I don't think he knows that, and I doubt he knows he was supposed to be my alibi. He probably answered the chancellor's questions blithely, not knowing that my life was in his hands.

"His head might have nodded for a moment," I say. "But he was never asleep."

The chancellor watches me closely, his eyes like two black scarab beetles, crawling over and biting my skin. I know he'll catch the slightest hint of a lie.

I use Professor Penmark's interrogation advice while the man himself stands only a few feet away from me, smiling in his horrible way: I try not to fidget too much or too little, to give too many or too few details. I will maintain my baseline behavior no matter what.

"Lola's lying!" Dean shouts abruptly. "She hates Cat. She's jealous of her! She's trying to get her in trouble."

"I heard her!" Lola cries. "I heard her admit what she did!"

Fuck. I knew I heard something moving behind me the day I called Zoe and spilled the whole history of me and Dean. God, that was so fucking stupid! How could I have been so careless?

"She's making it up! She doesn't have any proof!" Dean says.

"Then what about this?" Lola cries, yanking my sketchbook out of her backpack.

"Show it to me," the chancellor says.

Lola passes the sketchbook. The chancellor flips through the smudged pages, his eyes crawling over each and every drawing. He turns the book so Dean and I can see it.

"What is this?" he says. "And this?"

He shows me the drawing I made directly after I killed Rocco— the girl sitting on the edge of a dark well, looking down into the yawning emptiness. And then, several pages later, a picture of a male figure falling through dark scribbled space.

"Those are just sketches," I say quietly. "I draw all sorts of figures."

The chancellor continues to turn the pages.

He passes through my drawings of Chicago—the Centennial Wheel, the Bean, the statues in Mount Olive Cemetery, the city skyline along the lake. And then after that, a portrait of Dean standing on the deck of the ship, his shirt stripped off and his face ferocious as he looks back over his shoulder at me. Then Dean again, closer up, just his face from the angle I see when he looks down at me, a mocking smirk on his lips. Dean again, lying back against the pile of pillows in the bell tower, with a rare expression of gentleness that only occurs after we've exhausted ourselves together. Then another of Dean and another and another.

My face is flaming. I can hardly meet Dean's eyes.

I never told him that I draw him.

Actually, I hadn't realized how many times I'd done it.

When I finally dare to look at him, he's staring at the sketches, stunned.

"Those don't mean anything," I tell the chancellor. "It's just practice. I planned to go to art school…"

The chancellor turns the pages back to the figure of the man falling through empty space.

"This isn't Rocco Prince?"

"No," I lie. "It's just…a nightmare I had."

"She didn't kill Rocco!" Dean shouts.

"Then who did?" The chancellor rounds on him.

"I'm not going to tell you that," Dean says.

My mouth falls open in horror.

Why did Dean admit that he knows?

Dean shoots me a swift, repressive look, reminding me to keep my mouth shut.

"If you won't tell us what you know…" the chancellor says.

"Do what you have to do," Dean says. His jaw is stubbornly set, his pale hair hanging down over one eye.

The chancellor nods to Professor Penmark.

Penmark strips off his suit jacket, revealing a gray dress shirt with garters to hold up the sleeves. His bared forearms are lean and sinewy, his hands bony and dexterous as twin spiders.

Now at last I understand why Dean admitted a portion of guilt—so he'll be the one interrogated, not me.

"No!" I scream.

The groundskeeper grabs my arms and yanks me back.

Lola also takes a step backward, her hand flying up to her mouth. She's pale, but her eyes are brightly interested, fixed on Dean's kneeling figure.

Professor Penmark pulls a silver knife from his belt.

"Stop!" I cry.

He ignores me. With four quick slashes, he cuts off Dean's shirt, baring his torso to the cold. Dean's flesh glows white as chalk in the dim light. The Siberian tiger tattoo on his back seems to snarl with rage at being so rudely uncovered.

"Do you have something to say?" the chancellor asks me coldly.

"Don't say a fucking word!" Dean shouts at me.

I'm frozen in place, not because the groundskeeper is holding me tight with arms pinned behind my back but because I don't know what I should do. I can't bear to see Dean tortured by that fucking sadist Penmark. At the same time, Dean is begging me not to speak. We both know the drastic consequences that will follow if I admit the truth.

Penmark stoops and rummages in a black leather bag that looks very like the kind a doctor might carry. Only Penmark is nothing like Dr. Cross or Dr. Rybakov—he prefers harm over healing. He straightens, holding a cat-o'-nine-tails loosely in his left hand.

In an awful way, it reminds me of the whip Dean used on me

during our very first encounter in the bell tower. Dean had carefully crafted his whip with soft leather thongs that wouldn't actually cut or injure me.

Penmark's is made for maximum damage—the nine lashes cruelly knotted at the tips, then bound to an ivory handle.

"I'm sorry it had to come to this," the chancellor says.

Penmark stands behind Dean, raising the whip overhead.

His teeth glint as he grins.

He swings his arm down with vicious force. Instantly, nine gashes open up on Dean's back, splitting his tattoo.

"Nooo!" I shriek.

Dean lets out a strangled yell, jaw clenched and face sweating. His arms strain against the chains binding them in place as his whole body jerks under the impact. Blood runs down his back in thin, bright lines.

"Dean!" I cry. "I can't—"

He turns his head to look at me as best he can in his constrained position.

"*Don't*," he says, through gritted teeth.

Penmark swings the lash again. It bites into Dean's back, crossing over the former cuts, making Xs out of horizontal lines. I jolt and cry out as if it's me being hit.

"You can stop this any time," the chancellor tells me.

He knows I killed Rocco. But he doesn't have proof. He's trying to goad me into confessing by torturing Dean right in front of me.

Lola stands with her back against the far wall, biting on the edge of her thumbnail. She looks sick and yet captivated, like someone binging on too much cake.

The rage I feel in this moment would make me a murderer all over again. If not for the groundskeeper holding me back, I'd cut her fucking throat for this.

Penmark whips Dean again and again and again.

Dean's tattoo is obliterated, his back a hash of blood and raw flesh. His head lolls, jerking up with each strike.

Tears pour down my face. I struggle futilely against the groundskeeper's iron grip.

I have to stop this. I have to tell them the truth. I can't let them hurt Dean anymore.

As if he can read my mind, Dean turns his head once more and hisses at me, "*If you say one fucking word, I'll never forgive you.*"

My heart is ripping in half, torn between my need to help him and the knowledge that if I confess, we'll never be together. I'll be dead, and he'll despise me forever for my weakness.

Dean doesn't want me weak, guilty, and giving in.

He wants me strong. Ruthless. Doing whatever it takes to get what we want.

I look at Dean, and he looks back at me, his face whiter than death but fixed and resolute.

"I love you," I whisper.

Penmark raises the lash again.

He whips Dean with cruel fury, five more times.

"Stop," the chancellor says.

Disappointed and resentful, Penmark lowers his arm.

"Dean, you have been punished for your refusal to reveal what you know," the chancellor pronounces. "With no further evidence…I consider the matter closed."

He sweeps out of the room, disgusted with all of us.

Lola hurries after him, probably knowing that the second I'm released, I plan to claw her fucking face off.

Penmark follows at a more leisurely pace, throwing one last wistful glance at the ruin of Dean's back as if admiring his handiwork.

I want to kill him too. I'd already be making plans to do it if I could think of anyone but Dean.

The moment the groundskeeper releases me, I run to Dean.

I kneel in front of him, taking his face in my hands, bawling and kissing him and begging for him to tell me he's alright.

The groundskeeper unlocks the manacles. Dean slumps forward, falling into my arms.

I can't stop crying, and I can't stop holding him.

I can't believe he did that for me.

I don't know how I didn't see this sooner. Dean loves me. He loves me past anything I could have imagined.

If his anger is a furnace, then his love for me is the sun, burning bright enough to light the universe.

"Baby, are you okay?" I sob.

Dean nuzzles his face against my neck, still leaning heavily against me, his arms dead weight around my shoulders.

"How come you always smell so good?" he groans.

I let out a strangled laugh. "It must be to lure you."

I feel his fingers gripping loosely on my back, trying to pull me tighter against him.

"I'm so sorry," I sob. "I can't believe you did that."

He struggles to sit up a little, slipping his hand under my hair to hold me at the place where my head meets my neck. He presses his forehead against mine.

"Are we even now?" he says.

"Oh my god." I shake my head. "You're insane."

"I *am* insane," he growls. "I'm crazy for you, Cat. I always will be."

"It terrifies me how much I love you," I tell him, holding him as tight as I can without hurting him more.

The groundskeeper clears his throat.

I completely forgot he was still in the room with us.

"Are you going to help me take him to the infirmary?" I bark, furious at him and every other barbarous employee at this school.

"Yes," the groundskeeper says in an almost apologetic tone.

He was no rougher than he needed to be, holding me back

while Penmark had his fun. Actually, now that I'm really looking at him, his brown hair and close-cropped beard are vaguely familiar to me—he might have been friends with Miles once upon a time.

He stoops to take Dean's arm over his shoulder so he can help support his weight. I try to do the same on the other side, though I'm too short to be of much use.

"Thanks, Brenner," Dean groans. "Why'd they have to bring Penmark in for that? He's such an asshole."

"Agreed," Brenner grunts. "It's one thing to do a job, another to enjoy it."

We hobble off in the direction of the infirmary, moving slowly so we don't jolt Dean too much.

He's weak and reeling but not in terrible spirits.

"I don't know what they're making such a fuss about," he says. "Nobody liked Rocco anyway."

"I sure didn't," Brenner mutters. "After all, I'm the one that had to clean him up."

CHAPTER 30
DEAN

THAT FUCKING DICKHOLE PENMARK REALLY FUCKED UP MY BACK, and now I have to lie in the infirmary bored as hell.

I'm missing all my boxing training *and* the last event in the Quartum Bellum. I have to hear about it secondhand when Cat comes to visit me.

"It was a shooting challenge with stationary and moving targets."

"Did we win?"

"Of course." She grins.

"Fuckin' Leo." I shake my head. "He always wins. It's not even exciting anymore, just takes all the surprise out of it."

"It's so tedious being an eternal champion, isn't it?" Cat laughs.

As she tilts her head to smile at me, I see a glint of scarlet in the hollow of her throat. The necklace I gave her—restored to its rightful place.

My heart burns as bright as that stone.

"Was Claire Turgenev disappointed?" I ask her.

"It was actually really close. She's a fantastic captain too. I'm sure she was upset, but she shook Leo's hand, all classy and kind."

"Fuck being classy," I say. "I like to gloat."

"Maybe I will too," Cat laughs, "if I ever win anything."

Snow pops his head through the infirmary door.

"Hey," he says. "How are you feeling?"

"Great. Ready to be back in class."

"Good," he grunts. "I have a lot of mats that need cleaning. Towels that need washing…"

"You know I'm only helpful when I need advice."

He nods to Cat. "Will you break up with him again so he'll be useful?"

"Sorry," Cat laughs. "Can't do it."

"Ain't happening. Thanks for visiting, though."

"Oh, I'm not here to visit you. I'm here to see my wife," he says, striding across the room to wrap his arms around Sasha while she's trying to scrub an instrument tray at the metal sink.

"He's lying," Sasha calls back to us. "He's been asking about you every single day, Dean, even after he visits you."

She leans back against Snow's broad chest, humming cheerfully to herself as she works.

"Well…he's the best in my class." Snow shrugs.

"I never thought you'd admit that," I say. "You know, you're not a bad coach either. I wish you'd be here next year."

I say it lightly, but my stomach clenches up all the same. Losing Snow feels like losing a lot more than a coach.

"We've got to get back to the kids," Snow says. "Even if they're not kids anymore, we still like to see them."

He lets go of Sasha to turn back toward me.

"I've got a good gym in New York, Dean. You could come train with me. Zane is there. You'll never find a better sparring partner."

"If he hits like you, I doubt anyone wants to be his sparring partner," I say.

Zane Rybakov's hammer fist aside, it's a tempting offer. Unfortunately, I owe Danyl Kuznetsov two years' service.

"I'll think about it," I tell Snow.

"I'd better go," Cat tells me, gathering up her book bag. "I've already missed an alarming number of classes."

She squeezes my shoulder and kisses me on the cheek.

"You can give me a proper kiss," I growl. "They don't care."

Cat blushes but kisses me right.

"Young love." Sasha smiles. "It keeps the world running."

"You're still young," Snow tells her, "and beautiful as ever."

He kisses her even harder.

I leave the infirmary the last week of school.

I tell Cat to meet me in the bell tower one last time.

But first, I have an errand to run.

This particular errand is something I should have done a month ago and saved myself a lot of trouble. Better late than never.

I find Lola Fischer swanning down the hallway on the ground floor of the keep, accompanied by her perpetual shadow Dixie Davis.

I'd have no problem taking on the both of them, but I'm saved the trouble when Lola ducks into the nearest bathroom.

"I'll meet you in class!" she calls over her shoulder to Dixie.

I wait for Dixie to amble off an appropriate distance down the hallway, then I follow Lola into the ladies' room.

Lola, of course, is no fucking lady.

She's a conniving little bitch too stupid to take the hint the first time around. This time, she'll get the message.

I wait for her to finish pissing, then pounce on her the second she emerges from the stall.

I'm still not back to a hundred percent mobility, my back stiff with freshly healing scars, but I'm still plenty strong enough to seize Lola and fling her against the wall.

Lola screeches, her blue eyes wide with shock and terror.

"Yeah, I'm out of the infirmary," I growl. "So you probably should have kept your posse closer. Or better yet—you should have fucking listened when I told you to stay away from Cat."

"Nothing happened!" she squeals, trying to squirm away from me. "They didn't do anything to her!"

I grab her by the throat and slam her against the wall again, bouncing her head off the tiles.

"Oh yeah, it was a Sunday picnic," I snarl. "Other than Penmark's back massage."

"I didn't know they'd do that!" Lola cries.

"It doesn't matter," I say. "You tried to fuck over my girl, and now you're gonna pay the price."

Lola's blue eyes narrow. She sneers, "You can't do anything to me. Don't forget the rule of recompense. You harm one hair on my head, and you'll get the same thing done to you."

"Funny you should say that," I tell her. "That's exactly what I had in mind."

Lola stares at me, not understanding.

Until I pull the clippers from my pocket.

"No!" she shrieks, trying to twist out of my grip.

I flick the switch, the clippers making an aggressive buzzing sound like a swarm of angry hornets.

"Hold still. Or this will get a whole lot messier."

"No! You can't!"

"Why not? What are they gonna do, shave my head too? Saves me going to the barber."

I swipe the clippers right across her scalp, leaving a long bald patch down the middle of her head. A sheet of wavy caramel hair tumbles to the ground.

Now Lola is fully blubbering, all her toughness melted away like ice cream in the Mississippi sunshine.

I shave her bald, every fucking bit of that hair cut off and tossed on the grimy bathroom floor.

I hold the last lock up in front of her eyes.

"You say one word to Cat, you so much as fucking look at her, and I'll be back for your finger. You saw the whipping I took for her—I would gladly lose a pinkie to see you lose one of yours."

Lola stares at me in horror, her big blue eyes rather disturbing without the accompanying mane of hair. She looks like a baby doll shorn by a callous toddler.

"Your hair will grow back," I say softly. "But your finger won't."

With that, I drop the last few strands on the floor and leave the bathroom, Lola's whimpers trailing after me.

For once, Cat beats me up to the bell tower.

She's waiting for me, a dozen candles lit all around, the pillows neatly stacked. She's dressed simply in a T-shirt, sneakers, and skirt, her hair pulled up in a loose ponytail, the spattered freckles on her cheeks already darkening from the spring sunshine.

She's never looked more beautiful.

She seems strangely nervous, maybe because the last time we were up here, she tried to do something kind for me and I shouted at her.

"It's good to be back," I say.

"I'm not...expecting anything," she tells me awkwardly. "If your back isn't healed yet—"

"Don't worry about my back," I growl. "It would take a lot more than that to get me to keep my hands off you."

She flushes, that mischievous smile tugging at her lips.

Still, there's an invisible barrier between us, something we both have to navigate. I'm not in control of her, and she's not in control of me. We both stand here free and unencumbered, wondering what that looks like for both of us.

"I never thanked you," Cat says. "For what you did for me."

"I did what had to be done," I tell her. "Just like you would."

"I shouldn't have made those sketches."

"Cat, those drawings are what put the heart in me for everything that came after. The ones you drew of me…I saw them, and I thought you must love me. Then I knew I could endure anything."

Cat stares at me, eyes wide.

"Didn't you already know that I love you?"

I swallow hard, embarrassed.

"I just…I fucked up so bad…"

"Dean. You really don't know how I feel?" she says, tears gathering in her eyes.

I clench my fists, not knowing how to tell her this thing that I can hardly admit even to myself.

"I don't think…anyone could really love me."

Cat stares at me, part tearful and part angry.

Then she runs at me, beating on my chest with both hands.

"Why can't you see that I love you? I fucking love you! I don't care what you do to me. I don't care what you say to me. I don't care if you lie or scream or try to run away. I don't care if you're filthy or soaked in bleach or set on fucking fire! Why can't you understand I love you? Without limit or reason."

I look at her furious face, those brilliant dark eyes, and finally after all this time, the key turns in my heart.

I believe her.

I fucking believe her.

She loves me.

She loves me the way I love her.

I seize her and kiss her, her arms around my neck, her legs around my waist. I taste the sweetness of her mouth and the salt of the tears running down her face. I bite her lips. I breathe in her breath.

"Cat," I say. "You don't know what a monster I can be, but I'll be your monster. Everything I do will be for you. To protect you. To help you. To love you every day of my life. I'll burn this whole fucking world down for you if that's what you want."

She presses her forehead against mine.

"I know exactly who you are, Dean. And that's who I love."

CHAPTER 31
CAT

DEAN KISSES ME LIKE MY LIPS ARE THE ONLY THING KEEPING HIM alive.

He slams me against the crumbling tower wall and gropes my body with both hands. Bits of mortar and stone rain down on our heads, covering us in soot and dust, but we don't give a fuck. We barely even notice it.

I had planned to be careful of his injuries. Now I can't think of anything but how badly I need him.

It doesn't matter. Nothing can dampen Dean's fire for me, not heartbreak or time apart or even a whipping.

He's tearing my clothes off, and I'm ripping at his, desperate to put my hands all over him, to smell his sweat and his skin, to lick him and bite him and suck every place I can reach.

I tear off his dress shirt, buttons ricocheting off the huge bronze bell. Dean shoves my skirt up around my waist, shredding my panties with his fingers and yanking them aside.

I can't stop kissing him. I thrust my tongue all the way in his mouth, wanting to taste every bit of him, obsessed with the fullness of his lips and the way his tongue feels against mine.

My hands are in his hair, gripping tight right at the scalp.

His hands are wrapped around my waist, lowering me down on his raging hard cock.

He thrusts into me in one motion, his cock tearing into me like we've never fucked before. His cock is a battering ram, his hands invading armies. I surrender to him, every bit of me, while still biting and clawing at him as if I want to fight.

We fall to the ground, dangerously close to the hole in the center of the floor, through which the rope to ring the bell once descended. Now the bell lies silent on its side, likewise straining the limits of the uneven, weakened floor. Dean's and my combined weight crumbles the edge even more, knocking several more stones down into empty space. We have to roll away to avoid tumbling down ourselves.

Dean fucks me hard against the stone floor, scraping my back on the rough ground.

I roll over on top of him, mounting his cock, digging my nails into his chest as I ride him hard and fast.

I can't get enough of him. It feels like years since we did this. It feels like I might have died if we were apart any longer.

We've knocked over several of the candles. I smell smoke and singed fabric—one of the pillows most likely. I don't give a fuck. I'm not stopping, not even slowing down, not for anything.

Dean flips me over and enters me from behind, his hips slamming into my ass. He grunts as he drives into me, a primal, animalistic sound. He's a beast, and I love it.

My left hand drops through a hole in the floor as another stone falls away.

This whole tower is going to collapse.

I must truly have lost my mind because in this moment, I don't care. I don't care if the whole thing crumbles around us, as long as I'm locked together with Dean, his arms around me, his cock inside me.

Dean picks me up again, scooping me up in his arms like I weigh nothing at all. He's so phenomenally strong that he can fuck me at any angle, any position. He takes over my body, and all I can do is gaze in wonder at the slabs of muscle on his chest, the straining tendons running up and down his arms like cords.

The floor shifts and cracks under our feet. I hear more stones falling down.

That noise is distant compared to the pounding of my heart and my relentless hunger for Dean.

With each stroke up and down on his cock, I feel my climax building. We've come too far now—I'm hurtling headlong into this raging pleasure. Nothing can pull me back now.

Dean's hand clenches around the back of my neck, his other hand gripping my ass as he fucks me harder and harder. He slams me against the side of the bell, driving into me with all his might. Our impact against the bronze makes a dense, echoing clang. The whole bell shakes, sending a deep vibration across the floor. Dean lets out a roar at the same frequency, his cock twitching inside me. I start to come too, biting down hard on his shoulder.

I'm made of pleasure—every nerve, every cell.

The whole floor splits beneath us, the bell tipping down through the jagged hole.

Dean scoops me up in his arms and sprints for the stairs. The tower lists to the left, stones raining down like deadly hail. The stairs fall away under his feet. Dean is jumping as much as running, leaping over empty space.

The bell crashes down, bouncing off the walls with huge, hollow booms. It slams to a halt with a noise like an explosion, right as we burst through the door at the base of the tower, a landslide of rock and grit tumbling after us.

We stand panting on the grass, naked as the day we were born and covered head to toe in gray dust.

The bell tower is still standing, but just barely. It now tilts to the side worse than ever, with several more holes in the walls and no steps to climb up to the top.

Shouts come from the windows of the Accountants' tower, the

students roused by the crashing and clanging of the bell falling down. Lights snap on in the infirmary—probably Sasha and Snow rising from their bed in their private quarters.

Laughing madly, Dean and I sprint for the stables before anyone can see us. We hide inside, among the piles of old furniture and files, until we find a box of ancient jerseys.

My jersey covers me much better than Dean's—it hangs down to my knees, while his resembles something worn by Winnie-the-Pooh.

I can't stop laughing.

"Maybe wrap another one around your waist?" I snort.

He seizes me and kisses me again, our mouths tasting of sex and ash.

Dressed but not exactly decent, we each run for our respective dorms.

"What in the hell?" Rakel says when I try to sneak into our room unnoticed. "Have you been down in a coal mine?"

"I can't possibly explain," I tell her.

"Well, you missed a hell of an evening. Lola's been bawling in her room, and she won't come out."

"What happened?"

"Someone cut her hair off. She won't say who." Rakel gives me a suspicious look. "You didn't have anything to do with it, did you? Because I would hope you'd involve me in any revenge plots against Lola and Dixie."

"I didn't know a thing about it." I shake my head, mystified. "For once, I'm actually innocent."

Rakel snorts.

"I don't know what you were doing, but you're the furthest thing from innocent."

CHAPTER 32
DEAN

THE LAST WEEK OF SCHOOL IS THE HAPPIEST WEEK OF MY LIFE.

I spend every moment possible with Cat. We go for long walks all over the island—across the vineyards fragrant with ripening grapes, down through the shady river bottoms, and along the wild salt-swept beaches.

When the final marks are posted, I'm not in first place for my year. Anna Wilk took that honor, and Ares took second. I barely scraped third.

And yet…I don't care.

Who would I have told if I were first?

My father is dead. I can no longer impress or disappoint him.

And I no longer care what Danyl Kuznetsov or Abram Balakin think. In fact, when I consider the prospect of becoming Danyl's lieutenant, all I feel is anxiety at the possibility that he might share Bodashka and Vanya's ambitions of overthrowing Ivan Petrov and taking control of St. Petersburg. I want nothing to do with that.

The only person I want to impress now is Cat. She would much rather spend another lazy afternoon together than see me score a few points higher on my final exams.

I'm dreading a long summer without seeing her.

As we sit up on the cliffs overlooking Moon Beach, the breeze tossing Cat's curls around her face, I ask her, "Are you going to Los Angeles for the summer? To visit Zoe?"

"Actually..." Cat pulls up a blade of new green grass, twisting it between her fingers. "Miles and Zoe are coming back to Chicago for a few weeks. I was planning to meet them there. And I hoped you might come with me..."

"To Chicago," I say.

It's not really a question. I'm just voicing the words aloud, as if that will help me understand how I feel about that idea.

"Not to see your mom," Cat amends quickly. "But I thought... maybe...you might want to see some of the rest of your family."

She means my aunt Yelena, Leo's mother.

She was my father's twin. They were best friends growing up. The closest people in the world to each other.

I suppose Leo told her what happened. I wonder if she was upset.

"They're not my family," I tell Cat. "I've never even met them."

Cat looks me in the eye, laying her hand on top of mine on the warm grass.

"They could be," she says. "If that's what you wanted."

I turn my hand over so I can grip her fingers tight.

As always happens when I consider the ugly, bloody history of my forebearers, my stomach churns, and my face gets hot. Usually a wave of anger and resentment washes over me.

But today, I feel something different. A little bit like fear and a little bit like longing.

"I don't think any of them would want to see *me*," I say quietly.

Cat reaches up to touch my cheek, her hand softer than any pillow.

"Do you want to be with me always?" she says.

"Yes," I tell her.

"Then you're going to be tied to the Griffins and the Gallos twice over. We'll all be connected to each other. We'll all be family."

I take her hand off my cheek and bring it to my lips, kissing it gently.

"I'll do whatever it takes to be with you, Cat. I'll do whatever it takes to make you happy. If you want me to come to Chicago with you…then that's what I'll do."

The morning we're due to leave Kingmakers, I visit Snow one last time.

He's in the gym, straightening the mats and putting away any errant pieces of equipment, even though there's no more classes and no students dedicated enough to train on the last day of school.

Not even me.

When he sees me standing in the doorway, he straightens up, smiling without any surprise.

"Did you change your mind about coming to New York?" he says.

"No," I reply. "But if the offer still stands in a few years…"

"It will always stand," he says quietly.

"Thank you." I pause, wanting to say this right. "Thank you for everything, Snow. You helped me when I didn't want it or ask for it. When I wasn't grateful or even deserving."

"You were deserving," Snow says, his eyes as clear and piercing as ever. "I saw that from the start."

I cross the mats and embrace him one last time.

I hope I can give that sort of hug to someone someday.

"Cat asked me to come to Chicago with her," I tell him. "Over the summer."

"What did you say?"

"What do you think I said?"

Snow smiles slowly. "I think you agreed."

"You were right." I nod. "I'd do anything for her."

Snow rests his hand on my shoulder.

"You're a man now. And that's what a man does."

Cat is waiting for me just outside the gym. She bounces on her toes, her eyes bright and excited.

"There's an hour left before the wagons leave," she says. "Want to walk around campus one last time?"

"That sounds ominous," I tease her. "You're not planning to take me up on the wall, are you?"

She smacks my arm.

"Don't joke about that!" she hisses at me. "Don't ever say it out loud. That's how I—".

"*Shhh*," I say, clamping my hand over her mouth to irritate her all the more. "You're gonna spill all our secrets *again*!"

Cat is ready to kill me for real, but I can't help it. I've always loved the way she looks when she's furious—eyes glittering, cheeks flaming, body shaking.

"Alright, I'm sorry," I say, releasing her. "Look, there's nobody around."

Cat tosses her dark curls. "You better not plan on harassing me all the way home. It's a long flight to Chicago."

"Two long flights," I say. "And a boat ride. But don't worry. I'll be pampering you the whole way. Rubbing your shoulders and letting you sleep on my lap…"

"Really?" Cat perks up at once, already willing to forgive me for teasing her. "That would be so nice, actually. I can stretch all the way out on two seats…"

We're walking down the annex of the armory together, down the double row of photographs bearing all the winning captains of Quartum Bellums past, stretching back before the dawn of photography when the portraits were painted or sketched.

"There's Adrik Petrov," I say to Cat, pointing to the three photographs of the grinning Adrik, his black hair wild and windswept, his expression ferociously triumphant. "He's Kade's older brother."

In the third photograph, the defeated captain standing behind him looks battered and miserable, barely able to stand upright. That must have been an awful challenge.

"Oh, I've heard of him," Cat says, pausing to stretch up on tiptoe so she can see the pictures better. "You met him in Moscow?"

"Just briefly," I say. "I liked him, though."

"He doesn't look very nice," Cat says doubtfully.

"You don't like nice," I growl, slipping my arm around her waist.

Cat leans her body back against mine, arching her back with pleasure.

I stoop to kiss the side of her neck.

She turns all the way round to kiss me long and slow. The sun filters down through the high windows, turning the edge of her face gold. Her mouth is as warm as the sunshine.

When we break apart, I feel lightheaded.

Cat leads me farther down the hallway, her fingers linked through mine.

"There's no other captains that won three years," she says, examining the photographs. "Barely any that even won twice."

"Mm," I say, still distracted by the kiss.

"I haven't seen any girls that did," Cat says, those keen dark eyes combing the walls.

"There's fewer girls that attend the school. Probably barely any in the olden days."

"I'm not looking at the olden days," Cat laughs. "We're only twenty years back. Oh, here! There's one…"

She runs a few steps down, looking eagerly up at the photograph of a black-haired girl with bright blue eyes. Her mouth is open in gleeful laughter after her first win.

"And look! She was only a sophomore," Cat says, highly

impressed. "Then next year…" She follows down to the next photograph, where the same girl stands in the place of honor, right in front. This time, she isn't laughing. In fact, she hardly looks triumphant at all. Maybe it's because the losing captain is so bitterly angry that she doesn't like him standing right behind her.

"It's funny, though," Cat says, walking down a few more steps. "She wasn't captain her senior year."

"Maybe she didn't win."

"No, look. She's not in any of the pictures, even in the background."

I scan the photos, seeing that Cat is right.

"That is odd," I admit.

Usually, a winning captain is voted back every year, unless they fuck up. If the girl won in her sophomore and junior years, you'd expect that the senior class would be desperate to have her lead them again.

"Maybe she didn't come back to Kingmakers at all," I say slowly.

Miles and Zoe dropped out. The girl might have gotten married.

"Maybe she didn't," Cat replies in a strangely distant voice. Her eyes look unfocused and dreamy.

"What?" I say.

Ignoring me, Cat dashes back to the first photograph of the black-haired girl. Then she returns to the second. She goes back and forth several times, examining the winning captain closely.

"What is it?" I ask Cat again. I come to stand beside her, trying to see what she's seeing.

"Do you think she looks…skinnier in the first picture?" Cat asks.

I squint closely, looking at the girl's slim, athletic frame.

"I don't know," I say. "She's a year older in the second picture. But…I guess…"

There is a slight difference in her figure, or at least I think there might be. It's difficult to tell in her loose uniform. And she's so much more serious in the second picture. But still, she might be a little bit fuller.

"What does it matter?" I ask Cat. "What does it mean?"

"This will sound crazy," she says softly. "But I think that's Hedeon's mother."

We fly from Dubrovnik to Chicago, with a short layover in Berlin where we part ways with Chay Wagner.

Anna and Leo sit directly across the aisle from Cat and me.

Leo leans over to talk to us so often that one of the flight attendants hits him with the drink cart on purpose, just to remind him to stay out of the way.

I can tell he's trying to make me feel comfortable, and I have to admit, when I'm not doing my best to despise Leo, his warmth is irresistible. He almost makes me believe there won't be any awkwardness at all in finally meeting the people I was taught to hate and despise all my life.

Ignoring the glares of the flight attendant, Leo leans his rangy frame across the aisle once more to say to me, "You like movies? There's this outdoor theater we can go to. They show all these eighties slasher flicks late at night down by the lake. It's nice and creepy with the trees all around and the water…"

"You hate horror movies!" Anna says to Leo. "You almost leap out of your chair with every single jump scare."

"That's just my highly tuned reflexes," Leo says and grins. "If there is a murderer behind us in a hockey mask, you're gonna be glad I'm not lying back in my seat half-asleep."

"I'll go!" Cat says gamely. "As long as there's popcorn."

She glances at me to see if I'm amenable.

"In Moscow, we eat sunflower seeds at the movies," I tell her.

"We'll sneak those in too," Leo says.

I pause a moment, wanting to ask Leo something before we land.

"Leo…" I say.

"Yeah?"

"Did you tell your mother what happened? At Christmas?"

"Yes." Leo nods, his smile fading.

"Was she…how did she take it?"

"She was devastated," Leo says simply. "She always hoped that she and Adrian would reconcile eventually. She wrote to him every year on their birthday. I don't think he ever wrote back."

I nod slowly.

I never saw those letters, but I'm sure Leo's telling the truth.

"My father could be very cold. His capacity for love was… limited. And conditional."

"Well," Leo says quietly. "I can only imagine the pain he suffered."

I can see on Leo's face that there's regret on both sides. I was raised with anger; he was raised with sorrow. The difference between his mother and my father.

We pass over the Great Lakes as the plane begins to descend. The vast, shining bodies of water each look as large as an inland sea. Around the edge of Lake Michigan, the gleaming spires of downtown Chicago jut up into the sky, opulent and golden-hued in the late-afternoon sunshine.

My heart rises up in my throat.

I'm finally returning to the city where I was born.

I never thought I'd make this journey alone.

But I'm not really alone. Cat slips her hand in mine.

Across the aisle, my cousin smiles at me.

"You're gonna love it," he says.

We disembark the plane and retrieve our luggage from the conveyer belt. Then walk past the security gates.

I see Leo's parents waiting for us—his father as tall, tan, and athletic as his son, his hair graying but still thick and wavy. Sebastian

Gallo wears a pair of stylish eyeglasses and a neatly pressed polo shirt tucked into slacks.

Next to him, a tall blond woman pushes a space-age pram. I look at her face, and I see…something painfully familiar to me. The high cheekbones, the stubborn jaw, the full lips and eyes of that unusual shade that I've only seen twice in my life: on my father's face and my own.

She is Adrian Yenin's twin in every way.

Except that the moment she sees me, her eyes fill with tears. She opens her arms and wraps them around me, pulling me tight against her in a hug.

"Dean," she says. "I've wanted to meet you for so long."

I can feel my body stiffening. My own eyes are burning, my heart beating too fast. I know her husband is watching.

But also…there's something familiar and comforting in Aunt Yelena's clean, sweet scent and in the shade of the silver-blond hair that falls across my shoulder.

So I push away my usual response to fear and confusion. Instead, I take a deep breath, and I hug her back.

When she lets go of me at last, I face Sebastian Gallo, and I look him in the eye.

This is the man who mutilated my father and strangled my grandfather. He's also the man who loved Yelena Yenina enough to marry the daughter of his worst enemy.

I hold out my hand to him to shake.

Sebastian grips my hand in his warm grasp and pulls me into an embrace, hugging me just as hard as his wife.

"Welcome home," he says.

EPILOGUE
CAT

CHICAGO

Dean and I had only intended to visit Chicago for a couple of weeks, but we end up staying almost the entire summer.

We stay at Leo's parents' elegant mansion in the downtown core. The six of us—Anna, Leo, Miles, Zoe, Dean, and me—explore every part of the city and the surrounding countryside. Sometimes Miles's little brother, Caleb, tags along, incensed at being left out when he himself will be attending Kingmakers in the fall.

I thought Dean might be irritated by Caleb, since Caleb is brash and loud and desperate to prove himself. But Dean responds to him with surprising patience, even consenting to meet Caleb on his favorite basketball court, despite Dean barely having played before.

It reminds me of Dean's strange protectiveness of Kade Petrov.

I always thought Dean was a bully. But in actuality…he's got a soft spot for the underdog.

Soon Dean, Caleb, Leo, and Miles are all playing basketball together on the outdoor courts almost every morning. With his typical determination and total disregard for his own physical safety, Dean is picking it up much faster than anyone expected.

When Dean teams up with Leo, the best player of the bunch, they're fairly evenly matched with the Griffin brothers.

"Dean's gonna be better than you soon," Leo teases Miles.

"I'm not exactly practicing on the regular," Miles scowls. "I'm running a business, not fucking around taking three months off like the rest of you."

"Oh, you're working right now?" Leo says, pretending to look around the court. "That definitely explains the score."

All four boys are sweating under the sweltering summer sun. Dean and Leo join Miles and Caleb in stripping off their tops, though it's supposed to be shirts against skins.

When Miles sees Dean's back, he grimaces.

"Jesus, Dean," he says. "There's easier ways to get a tattoo removed."

Dean lets out a huff of air that's something like a laugh. "Well, that's Penmark for you. He didn't respect my safe word."

He tips me a wink.

I shake my head at Dean, surprised at his willingness to find the dark humor in anything.

That was one of the most painful and impactful experiences of my life—the agony of watching the man I love be tortured—but also the moment that I finally understood how much Dean loves me.

The boys asked Zoe and me if we wanted to play, but Zoe said it was too hot, and I was in the mood to sketch. Zoe is stretched out on the park bench reading a novel. I'm filling some of the last pages in my sketchbook with yet another drawing of Dean—this time, sweating and laughing as he manages to sink a shot over Caleb's head.

Caleb scowls but acknowledges that it was a pretty good shot.

"I had a good coach," Dean says, punching Caleb lightly on the shoulder.

Once the boys have thoroughly exhausted themselves, we all pile back into Caleb's Escalade and drive back to the Gallo mansion for breakfast.

Since it's Saturday, Sebastian Gallo has a half-dozen pancakes sizzling away on the countertop skillet. Yelena is making fresh-squeezed orange juice, filling the kitchen with a fresh citrus scent that reminds me of Kingmakers.

Leo scoops baby Natasha up out of her high chair to stop her from fussing. Unlike Leo, Natasha inherited her mother's fair hair and violet-blue eyes. Her curls are wild and puffy as dandelion fluff, and her little eyebrows point upward in the middle in a way that makes her look perpetually quizzical.

Leo sits his baby sister on his forearm and pats her back until she stops squawking. Then he gently rubs his nose against hers and blows little puffs of air in her face until she giggles and tries to grab his cheeks with her chubby hands.

Dean watches all this with a strange expression on his face—part curious and part pained.

If my research was right…Dean has a little sister too.

"Go ahead and sit down," Sebastian tells us. "The first batch of pancakes is ready."

We arrange ourselves around the farmhouse table, Leo depositing Natasha back in her high chair so Sebastian can drop a pancake on her tray.

Yelena sets a glass of juice down in front of each of us. As she gives Leo his glass, she ruffles his hair affectionately. Then she rests her hand lightly on Dean's shoulder and squeezes it in turn.

Dean and Yelena have been spending a lot of time together. She's been telling him all about her and Adrian's childhood in Russia—their summer holidays on the Black Sea and ski trips to Krasnaya Polyana. She tells him about distant cousins he never met and talks about his grandmother that Adrian Yenin never mentioned.

I've likewise been catching up with Zoe. I told her most everything that happened this year at school, other than a few things between Dean and me that are too private to share.

"So you really love him?" she asked me. "And he makes you happy?"

"Extremely happy. Sort of sickeningly happy, actually."

"Perfect," Zoe laughed. "That's all I care about." She wrapped her arm around me to pull me close and kissed me on the temple.

With only a few weeks left before September, Dean knocks on the door of the Gallos' lovely guest room on the top floor in which I've been staying.

"Hey," he says, poking his head inside. "Do you want to come somewhere with me?"

"Of course," I say, setting down the book I was reading.

It's a gray Sunday morning—one of the only inclement days we've suffered over the summer.

As I follow Dean down two flights of stairs, I see that he has Leo's car keys in his hand.

"Is Leo coming with us?" I ask.

"No." Dean shakes his head. "Just you and me."

Dean looks especially pale under the gloomy sky as we stride across the driveway to the waiting car. Almost as soon as he fits the key into the ignition, raindrops begin to spatter against the windshield.

"Where are we going?" I ask him.

"Gillson Park," he replies.

We drive north of the city, up through Lakeview and Lincolnwood. As we pass into Evanston, I know where we're going. But I stay quiet, feeling the tension in Dean's fingers as he grips my hand harder and harder.

Gillson Park is located right on the rim of the lake, with a sandy beach on one side and a wildflower garden on the other. Dean parks the car, his hands paper-white where they grip the wheel. I can almost hear his heart hammering.

"Did you talk to her?" I ask him.

"Yes," he says. "Last night on the phone."

"She's meeting us here?"

He nods.

We cross the parking lot hand in hand, making our way toward the garden. As the rain drums down, the park empties out until we're some of the only people left walking the paths.

It's easy to find the lone woman sitting on a park bench, dressed in nurse's scrubs and a light jacket. She holds a blue umbrella open overhead.

As we approach, she looks up. Slowly, she lowers the umbrella and stands, uncovered, in the rain.

Rose Copeland is smaller than I expected—only a few inches taller than me. She's beautiful—I knew that from her photograph. But unlike Yelena, long, unhappy years have worn themselves into her face. She's one of the saddest-looking women I've ever seen.

The rain beating down on her head darkens her hair from honey-blond to light brown. She can't tear her eyes off Dean's face.

Dean walks up to her, rigid and blanched.

I don't know what he's feeling in this moment. I don't know how he'll react.

Mother and son look at each other for a long time.

Then, finally, Dean manages to say, "I missed you."

Rose's face crumples. She collapses against Dean, sobbing against his chest. Dean puts his arms around her, stroking her back gently, not unlike how Leo comforts his baby sister.

We all sit down on the bench together, sharing the umbrella overhead.

I can't help crying, but I try to do it quietly so I don't draw attention away from Dean and his mother.

Dean puts his arm around me anyway, holding his mother on one side and me on the other.

"I could never...explain to you..." his mother sobs.

"It's alright, Mom," Dean says quietly. "I know why you left."

She looks up into his face, her pale blue eyes as translucent as glass under their film of tears. "You do?" she says.

"Yes," Dean says. "Because of her."

He nods toward a willow tree a dozen yards away. In the protected shelter beneath the low-hanging branches, a little blond girl sits on a picnic blanket, headphones over her ears, reading a chapter book.

"That's Frances," Rose says.

"You were pregnant," I say, understanding at last.

Rose nods. "Adrian was...deteriorating. The pregnancy was accidental. When I realized it was a girl..." A shudder runs down her slim frame. "I know how the Bratva treat their girls."

Dean's lips tighten.

He might have dismissed that fear several months ago. But he's spent enough time talking with his aunt Yelena to understand what her life was like, growing up as the only daughter of a Bratva boss. Her experience was much different than her brother Adrian's.

"I thought Adrian would take care of you at least," she says quietly. "His heir."

"I saw him push you," Dean says, his face darkening.

She nods. "I hit my head. And that night, I had spotting...I thought I might lose the baby. When I didn't..." Her face contorts in misery, and she has to work to regain enough control to get her words out. "I didn't want to leave you, Dean. I knew he'd never let you go. I never meant to choose between you and Frances. I thought you'd each have one parent. It seemed like all I could do under the circumstances. But I've regretted it...every day since."

She breaks down again, the rain washing her tears away as quickly as they fall. I try to shift the umbrella to cover her better.

Dean holds her, his hands trembling from how tightly he's squeezing her.

"I don't want to be angry anymore," he says. "I don't want to be full of regret. And I don't want that for you either."

"I'll never stop being sorry," she sobs. "I missed you so much. It almost killed me. If I didn't have Frances…"

She looks across the stretch of field dotted with blue and yellow wildflowers. The little girl is still utterly absorbed in her book, her expression as serious as Dean's.

"Can I meet her?" Dean asks quietly.

"Yes," Rose says. "That's why I brought her."

"You weren't afraid to bring her here?" Dean asks. "You weren't afraid what I might be like now?"

Rose looks up into Dean's face, shaking her head.

"I know who you are, Dean. I know you would never hurt us."

With Rose's approval, Dean crosses the field and ducks under the low, reedy branches of the willow. He sits down on the blanket next to his little sister. Frances sets down her book and shifts her headphones from ears to shoulders. I can't hear what they're saying, but I can see the identical expressions of concentration on their faces.

Rose takes a tissue out of her purse and tries to clean her face.

"I'm sorry," she says. "I haven't even said hello."

"Oh, it's okay," I say. "I'm Cat, by the way."

"Dean told me about you," Rose says. "He said you were the one who found me."

I can feel myself blushing.

"Yes…uh…sorry about that," I say, realizing how drastically I breached the privacy of this woman who hid so well for so long.

"I'm grateful that you did," she says. "I didn't know that Adrian was gone."

She looks across the lawn to her daughter. I feel her relief that Frances is safe now, truly safe. And I understand what an impossible choice she had to make.

"You're right about Dean," I say. "He's a good man. The best man. No one loves harder than him."

"That's how he was as a boy," Rose says softly. "He felt things so intensely. I never knew if it would make him or destroy him."

Frances is showing Dean a particular passage in her book.

Dean's silver-blond hair falls down over his left eye, his expression intent. In the gray light, his skin glows pearlescent, and his body looks immense and powerful next to the slim girl. I've never seen him look more godlike. Yet he's gentle and careful as he turns the pages of the book.

Rose and I sit side by side, loving him with all our might.

ABOUT THE AUTHOR

Sophie Lark writes intelligent and powerful characters who are allowed to be flawed. She lives in southern California with her husband and three children.

The Love Lark Letter: geni.us/lark-letter
The Love Lark Reader Group: geni.us/love-larks
Website: sophielark.com
Instagram: @Sophie_Lark_Author
TikTok: @sophielarkauthor
Exclusive Content: patreon.com/sophielark
Complete Works: geni.us/lark-amazon
Book Playlists: geni.us/lark-spotify